DISCARD

MURDER IN THE
MANUSCRIPT
ROOM

ALSO BY CON LEHANE

Beware the Solitary Drinker

What Goes Around Comes Around

Death at the Old Hotel

Murder at the 42nd Street Library

MURDER IN THE
MANUSCRIPT
ROOM

A 42ND STREET LIBRARY MYSTERY

CON LEHANE

MINOTAUR BOOKS
A THOMAS DUNNE BOOK
NEW YORK

This is a work of fiction. All of the characters, organizations, and events portrayed in this novel are either products of the author's imagination or are used fictitiously.

A THOMAS DUNNE BOOK FOR MINOTAUR BOOKS.
An imprint of St. Martin's Publishing Group.

www.thomasdunnebooks.com
www.minotaurbooks.com

Designed by Omar Chapa

Library of Congress Cataloging-in-Publication Data

Names: Lehane, Cornelius, author.
Title: Murder in the manuscript room : a 42nd Street Library mystery /
    Con Lehane.
Description: First edition. | New York : Minotaur Books, 2017. |
    "A Thomas Dunne book."
Identifiers: LCCN 2017021222 | ISBN 9781250069993 (hardcover) |
    ISBN 9781466879898 (ebook)
Subjects: LCSH: Murder—Investigation—Fiction. | Libraries—Fiction. |
    GSAFD: Mystery fiction.
Classification: LCC PS3612.E354 M88 2017 | DDC 813/.6—dc23
LC record available at https://lccn.loc.gov/2017021222

Our books may be purchased in bulk for promotional, educational, or business use. Please contact your local bookseller or the Macmillan Corporate and Premium Sales Department at 1-800-221-7945, extension 5442, or by email at MacmillanSpecialMarkets@macmillan.com.

First Edition: November 2017

10   9   8   7   6   5   4   3   2   1

To Carlos R. Spaulding

Acknowledgments

Once more, thanks to my agent, Alice Martell, my editor, Marcia Markland, and her cheerful, patient, and extraordinarily helpful assistant, Amanda "Nettie" Finn. Thanks, too, to the production team at Macmillan, who have designed and produced stunning books and book jackets for both of my 42nd Street Library books. Shailyn Tavella, Hector DeJean, and the rest of the folks in the publicity department at Minotaur Books have been unfailingly responsive and helpful no matter how frequent or far-fetched my requests for promotional support. Special thanks to the library marketing team at Macmillan, Talia Sherer and Anne Spieth, who introduced my hero, librarian Ray Ambler, to thousands of real librarians across the country.

Speaking of real librarians, retired research librarian Thomas Mann read the book in its early stages and once more saved me from embarrassing myself. Any future embarrassment is on me. Maryglenn McCombs, a Nashville-based book publicist, has provided advice and encouragement, as well as promotional opportunities for me for years. Thanks once more to Roan Chapin, a great early reader, whose insightful comments made the book better than it might otherwise have been.

To the independent mystery bookstores that support me and writers like me by hand selling our books and hosting author visits goes my eternal gratitude. Likewise, my gratitude to the nation's libraries that are responsible for probably half, if not more, of my overall sales, as they are for many mystery writers. In addition, librarians are among the staunchest defenders of our rights as Americans to read and write what we wish. Without libraries, writers, readers, and communities in general would be very much poorer indeed. Finally, special thanks to the New York Public Library's Humanities and Social Sciences Library, the Stephen A. Schwarzman Building, the magnificent edifice at the corner of 42nd Street and Fifth Avenue that provides a fictional home for my stories.

The city of New York
Has erected this building
To be maintained forever
As a free library
For the use of the people

—NEW YORK CITY, APRIL 1983

MURDER IN THE MANUSCRIPT ROOM

Richard Wright locked the door of the union office behind him. The office was in a loft building on 37th Street between Seventh and Eighth Avenues in the Garment District. Preoccupied, he felt, more than saw, the rough texture of the wooden flooring, the industrial-sized, no-frills elevator. The rattle and tapping of sewing machines from seven in the morning until three thirty in the afternoon from the stitching shop three floors below was silenced now.

Not long before, his job had been backing a truck into the loading dock next to the building's doorway. He thought it important when he was elected president of the local that the office be in the area where the members work. This way, they could feel the union belonged to them, and, if they wanted to, come in and look around, keep an eye on things. Not like the way it had been.

A car waited for him in in the loading dock. He thought it pompous and unnecessary that he be treated like some kind of royalty. That was the old way. He'd promised transparency and access to the members who elected him. After the second attempt on his life since the election, the executive board demanded he have a driver and quasi-bodyguard. The kid they picked was useless, scared of his own shadow, sullen, high on coke when he wasn't stoned on weed, but he was a member, so Wright wouldn't blow the whistle and get him fired. If the kid didn't straighten out and was sent back to driving truck he would get himself fired anyway. Too many of the truckers were driving high, another problem the union needed to work on—a drug program, getting guys clean and back to work, rather than firing them, losing them to the street.

The kid didn't turn around when Wright opened the back door; listening to music on his Walkman, he was in his usual fog. Wright was heading out to meet with a group of truckers at a nonunion textile jobbing house in Brooklyn. It was after rush hour so the trip didn't take as long as it might. The meet was at a warehouse on the waterfront in Red Hook. The drivers interested in the union were scared, as they should be. A few workers by themselves were no match for the gangster overlords of the trucking companies.

It was already dark, the streets deserted, most of the docks and warehouses in Red Hook long abandoned since the arrival of containerized shipping in the seventies. Wright was a courageous man but not a fool. The drivers chose the meeting place, not a place he would have chosen. They wanted to meet on the down low, and he understood this. His driver was armed and he carried a weapon himself, though, a pacifist at heart, he'd hesitate to use it.

"Where you going?" Wright asked, as the car turned into an alley. No answer, and the car speeded up. He reached into his pocket for his gun, a relic from his days in the South, a present from the Deacons for Defense in Mississippi. It was too late. The car skidded to stop. The door beside him opened. He saw the midsection of a well-dressed man—white shirt, blue tie with a pattern in gold, the front panel and arm of a dark blue suit jacket. At the end of the man's arm was a snub-nosed revolver that spat fire and bullets a half-dozen times.

Chapter 1

The day had gone badly for Raymond Ambler, a bitterly cold, gray, January day not long after New Year's, the wind like a knife, slicing into the cavern cut by 42nd Street between the skyscrapers on either side. The wind stung his face and whipped under his trench coat as he walked the couple of blocks to the library from Grand Central, where he'd gotten off the subway from the courthouse downtown. Banks of piled-up snow, stained and filthy as only snow on a city street can get, hanging on from the storm the day after Christmas, lined the curb, the gutters at each street corner a half-foot deep in slush and muddy water.

Fuming after four hours of haranguing by a trio of five-hundred-dollar-an-hour attorneys against him and his representative, an Orthodox Jewish family lawyer from Borough Park, the ink on her Brooklyn Law School diploma barely dry. The custody battle was over a grandson he never knew he had until they'd come together under tragic circumstances when the boy was eight.

He'd had to take the morning off from work, so his coworker and friend, Adele Morgan, was helping as best she could assemble an exhibit Ambler was curating at the 42nd Street Library. The exhibit, celebrating the library's collection of American mystery novels, had taken two years of planning. *A Century-and-a-Half of Murder and Mystery in New York City* was scheduled to open in a few weeks. The preparation was behind schedule because of the Christmas blizzard and now more delays because of family court dates, meetings with attorneys, and mediation sessions. His grandson Johnny's grandmother, a wealthy socialite, was trying to undermine Ambler's relationship with the boy so she could alter the terms of the custody agreement. So far, because Johnny wanted to live with Ambler, she'd been unsuccessful. But she was relentless.

As he climbed the steps between the two marble lions standing guard in front of the library, he saw a man in front of him at the top of the steps and recognized the broad shoulders, the bulky shape, the close-cropped gray hair. He hadn't seen Mike Cosgrove, a NYPD homicide detective, since Mike had persuaded a young—everyone was young these days—Manhattan assistant district attorney not to bring murder charges against him over a year ago.

Despite the frigid weather, groups of tourists, bound up in colorful and fashionable down jackets and coats, many of them young, slim, dark-haired, and Asian, took photos on the library steps, or passed one another in a steady, if disheveled, parade up and down the steps. He caught up with Mike inside the cavernous, ornate foyer, Astor Hall. When Cosgrove turned around, Ambler realized someone was with him.

"Ray. I was just coming to see you. . . ." Cosgrove put his hand on the shoulder of the man beside him. "Paul Higgins." He reached for Ambler's shoulder with his other hand. "Paul, this is the man you want, Ray Ambler." Seeming pleased with himself, he stood between them with a hand on each man's shoulder like a referee between two welterweights.

Ambler shook the man's hand and met his gaze. It was steady and probing, at the same time ingratiating, eager; you'd have to say genuine. A thatch of red hair rusting to gray, a scar on his forehead, his nose broken more than once, shoulders slightly stooped, he moved stiffly, as if in chronic pain from long-ago injuries, a guy you might think of as an old warhorse, or a former athlete, football more than tennis.

"Paul," the man said, "Paul Higgins," pumping Ambler's arm vigorously. "I've been anxious to meet you."

"Oh?" Ambler took a mental step back from Higgins's enthusiasm.

"Paul's a writer," Cosgrove said.

"You probably haven't heard of me." Higgins said, "I'm kind of an amateur." The admission didn't dampen his enthusiasm.

Given a minute to sort through the zillion book titles and authors in his memory, Ambler did recognize the name. A retired cop, maybe FBI, Higgins had written a couple of all-American-vigilante-hero versus evil-to-the-core criminal thrillers that made an initial splash and quickly faded. He was being modest, not as obscure as he implied, not far off on the "amateur" appraisal.

"Of course," Ambler said. "*Dark Night of Terror*, right?"

"*Night of Black Terror*," Higgins said. "I'm amazed you know of it." He knew better, it seemed, than to ask if he'd read it.

The point of meeting Ambler, Higgins got to quickly enough, was he wanted to donate his papers to the New York Public Library's crime fiction collection. Because he had some concerns, Cosgrove suggested he meet Ambler.

Ambler wasn't interested—he didn't think Higgins as a writer had much in the way of lasting value—until something Cosgrove said rang a bell.

"Paul worked NYPD intelligence for over thirty years, Ray. He's got stuff no one would believe."

"Oh?" said Ambler.

                What struck him was a coincidence. A week before, his son John had called him from the upstate prison where he was serving time. A lifer there told John he was a friend of his father and wanted to talk to him. The prisoner, Devon Thomas, in fact had been Ambler's friend—a very good friend—from sixth grade until Devon dropped out of high school at sixteen to run with the Black Peoples Party, the last time Ambler had seen him, except in a *Daily News* photo wearing handcuffs.

On his monthly visit to his son the previous Saturday, he looked up his friend. Devon told him he was in prison for a murder he didn't commit.

"My kid brother did the murder." His hard stare faltered. "Trey was a snitch. I took the rap because I knew someone would kill him in here."

"And now?"

"He died a couple of weeks ago."

A skeptical person might doubt Devon's story—that he'd spent his adult life in prison for a crime he didn't commit out of loyalty to his brother. Ambler believed him. He'd met Devon in sixth grade at a new school for Ambler. The first day, he was surrounded in a hallway by a half-dozen would-be hoodlums taunting him for some imagined or fabricated slight, when he felt an arm around his shoulder. It was Devon, who amiably brushed aside the thugs and walked him into the classroom.

Ambler knew some of the history behind Devon's arrest and conviction because it was major news in the tabloids at the time. In the early eighties, a group of truck drivers took on a corrupt union in the garment trucking industry. One of the leaders of the insurgents, Richard Wright, was murdered shortly after he was elected president of the local union in a government monitored election. Devon Thomas killed him, the newspapers said, in a feud between rival gangs over drug territory.

"No way I'd kill him," Devon said. "I loved him like a father. Trey was a rat, a snitch. I didn't know. Never thought it. Never suspected, until he got scared and told me. Told me his handler told him to off Richard.

"When he told me, I wanted to kill Trey myself. You became a snitch because you were paid or you did it to keep yourself out of prison. His handler from the NYPD told Trey he'd get off. Then, something went wrong and the handler told Trey he'd have to plead to manslaughter. They'd get him out in three years.

"Trey told me he whacked Richard and was going up for it. I couldn't let him do it. I took the rap. I thought I'd get the same deal they told Trey, manslaughter, a three-year bid. Hah! I got life."

Devon's hair, still kinky, had turned gray, tight curls now, where years before it was a giant Afro; his eyes were clear, still hard, still something friendly in them, too, a flash of kindness behind the hard; his skin darker than Ambler remembered, his features as much European as African, a slender nose, thin lips. He'd developed a prison body, muscular, athletic. As he talked, he'd reach out now and again, putting his hand on Ambler's forearm to make sure he had his attention, to reinforce the connection. He did this now.

"Trey got the AIDS. I got compassion leave to visit him in the hospice. He was out of his head a lot. Right before he died, he told me he didn't kill Richard. They killed him."

"Who's they?"

Devon shook his head. "I don't know. I got some ideas. I been going back over what happened back then. I'm using the prison library. But it's slow. I thought you might see what you can find in that library of yours about what happened back then. I read about you. That's what you do, right? You find out what really happened when someone was killed."

"Not exactly. You can tell the truth now, right? Your brother's dead. You didn't commit the murder."

Devon's eyes locked on Ambler's. "Who'd believe me?"

Ambler nodded.

"I know you, Ray. We were bros." Devon laughed. It began as a kind of giggle, catching on like an uncertain motor until it became a chuckle, and then a full-out laugh. The sound of it rolled back the years to the endless summers he and Devon, baseball gloves and bats over their shoulders, rambled through Flatbush seeking out pick-up games in school yards and vacant lots, the nights they played stickball under the streetlights between the parked cars on East 19th Street off Beverley Road.

It was a long shot that Higgins knew anything about the murder Devon was in prison for. Still, it was worth asking. "Tell me about the collection," Ambler said. "What's in the papers? Is it about your undercover work?"

"I kept a lot of things." Higgins's tight-lipped expression made clear he'd play his cards close to the vest. "Newspaper clippings, photos, tapes of conversations, transcripts, interviews I did with assets I handled, copies of reports I filed—"

"Why would you do that, keep your own files?"

"At first, it was for protection, to have my own record in case something came up." He sized up Ambler. "Later, I saw it as material for stories I might write." As he said this, he dropped his gaze, looking at the marble floor as he spoke, suddenly shy. "I have this idea that what I have here is history no one knows about, and won't know about unless they find it here."

Ambler paid closer attention.

"The thing is I'm not going to get anyone in trouble. I can't do that. Some of what went on, people wouldn't understand; maybe they will later, years from now. Those weren't church picnics we infiltrated."

Ambler raised his eyebrows. "I imagine you infiltrated those, too."

Cosgrove chuckled. Higgins glanced sharply at Ambler. Menacing without making an effort at it, he was a hard, tough guy who didn't need to prove it.

"You might restrict parts of the collection until the statute of limitations runs out or—"

"There's no statute of limitations on murder." Higgins's tone was matter-of-fact.

Ambler snuck a glance at Cosgrove, who seemed to take the revelation in stride. Higgins's wide-eyed expression was a burlesque of a boy trying to look angelic.

Ambler nodded in the direction of the stairway. "Let's go up to my office."

Halfway up the massive staircase, they ran into Adele Morgan and her friend Leila Stone, a research assistant in Manuscripts and Archives Division, on the way down. Adele stopped to say hello to Mike Cosgrove. Leila stopped for a second, glanced at them, and hurried on, so Adele, with an exasperated shrug, followed. The three men watched the two women descend the stairs.

"Looks like we scared them off," Cosgrove said.

Ambler led Cosgrove and Higgins to the small reading room on the second floor that housed the library's crime fiction collection. Bookcases lined the walls on one level; a narrow stairway like a fire escape led to a mezzanine level with wrought iron railings and more bookcase-lined walls.

Higgins took in his surroundings with a kind of awe, as if he might take off his hat, if he wore one, and tiptoe to his seat; his reverence for the collection softened Ambler's attitude toward him. They sat at an oak library table in the middle of the room.

"Where is everyone?" Cosgrove asked, a good-natured needle.

Ambler rose to the bait. "Today's quiet. Lately, it's been busy." He caught Mike's little grin and felt foolish for being defensive, yet how could he not be with so much of the library, especially what might be thought an underused collection, on the chopping block?

"All of this is crime fiction?" Higgins waved his arm to take in the bookshelves.

Amber smiled in spite of himself. "Where are your files now?"

Higgins lowered his eyebrows. "Somewhere safe."

Ambler told him the library didn't like to restrict access to collections. "We like to think we're here so people can find things, not build collections people can't get at."

"Some of my notes and reports on my undercover work, real-life operations my books are based on, I'd have to know for sure no one would see them. Or I'd have to get rid of them."

If the collection was valuable, Ambler told him, the library could restrict a limited part of it for a period of time. He'd have to look into it and get permission. They talked for a while longer, with Higgins describing what was in the collection and telling Ambler about some of his undercover work.

After a while, when Higgins seemed to have gotten comfortable talking about the past, Ambler asked, "Do you remember in the mid-eighties a truckers union leader, Richard Wright, was murdered?"

Higgins knitted his brow and then shook his head.

Ambler told Higgins and Cosgrove the story Devon had told him.

"Sounds like bullshit to me," Higgins said. "His brother's dead. Why not hang the murder on him?"

"Maybe you're right. But it could have happened the way he said, couldn't it? You used bad guys to set up other bad guys. Nothing ever got out of hand? Suppose he's telling the truth—"

"He's not." The change in Higgins's expression was remarkable, as if someone yanked a cable tightening everything in his face. He turned to Cosgrove. "What's with this guy? You said we could trust him."

"I trust him," Cosgrove said mildly.

Higgins turned sullen. "What's in my papers might help if someone wants to write my biography someday, if a scholar wants to analyze my books, if someone studying crime fiction wants to know the history behind the books. That's why I'm donating the papers. Nothin' in there's gonna help some gangbanger who thinks he got a raw deal. All them fucking lowlifes think everything they did is someone else's fault." He drilled Ambler with a rock-hard stare. "I gotta think about this." Higgins then turned an accusatory glare on Cosgrove.

Ambler watched them leave. It was unlikely Higgins would drop a collection of incriminating documents into his arms. If he did donate his papers, he'd most likely purge the collection of anything incriminating, preserving documents that reflected his unique view of the history of his times. "History is written by the victors."

Chapter 2

The main exhibition room on the first floor was closed to the public while the library staff assembled the exhibit Ambler was curating. He'd chosen a dozen crime-fiction writers who either lived in the city or whose stories were set in the city, beginning with Edgar Allan Poe.

He found the Edgar Allan Poe Cottage records in the Manuscripts and Archives Division's holdings. The other holdings included a facsimile of "The Murders in the Rue Morgue," as well as a lock of Poe's hair, an original calling card of E. A. Poe, and a few original letters to Poe, including one written by Washington Irving. There were also prints from the library's collection, including one entitled *Mary Rogers, The Cigar Girl, Murdered at Hoboken, July 25, 1841*, the real-life murder case that inspired Poe's "The Mystery of Marie Rogêt."

Late that afternoon, Adele closed a display case containing book covers from the library's Dime Novel collection and looked up at Ambler. "Sorry about what happened on the stairs. I hope Detective Cosgrove didn't think I was avoiding him."

"No. It was Leila avoiding us. She needs to practice if she hopes to do well in the Miss Congeniality contest."

"She's really not so bad, Raymond. She's abrupt. That's her manner. I don't know why you're so hard on her."

Ambler rolled his eyes.

Adele began shuffling through Ambler's notes. "Georges Simenon? He's a stretch. Paris? The Riviera?"

"Two books set in New York. He lived here for a time."

"And he's one of your favorite writers. I'll let it go. Dashiell Hammett? San Francisco." She put her hands on her hips.

"*The Thin Man,* New York."

"Vera Caspary? I never heard of her."

"*Laura.* You've heard of *Laura,* right?"

"I saw the movie."

"She wrote the book here. She was a Communist and a bohemian."

"My kind of girl," said Adele. "Chester Himes?"

"The Gravedigger Jones and Coffin Ed Johnson books are set in Harlem—an imaginary Harlem, but isn't everything in fiction imaginary?"

She winked. Her habit was to wink at odd moments, sometimes after a wisecrack, sometimes to make a point. He wondered if she knew how cute she was when she did it. She laughed, too, after the wink, and her face lit up. He felt it, too, her happiness in the moment. Often, she was engrossed in her work or deep in her thoughts. At those times, she was pretty, but remote, lost in herself in a way that seemed to exclude anyone else, including him. At those times, he felt sad for her; she seemed so alone. She had some darkness in her, deep unhappiness. He didn't know what it was or what caused it. That part of her she kept to herself. So when she laughed like she did now and her brown eyes danced, he grew happy right along with her. He had some dark places himself that, without knowing she did, she yanked him out of when she was cheerful.

Talking about books, doing his work, absorbed Ambler, too. Engrossed in preparing finding aids for the collections, browsing in auction catalogs, digging through piles of long-ago correspondence or hand-written spiral notebooks of once-famous mystery writers, he could spend an entire afternoon without noticing the time passing, never looking at a clock, bent over his work long enough for his bones and joints to practically freeze in place.

A Century-and-a-Half of Murder and Mystery in New York City would come together, despite the difficulties. He'd been able to put the custody battle out of his mind for a few hours and spent part of the afternoon with Adele. It was a good day. Later, when he'd look back, he'd remember this afternoon among manuscripts, diaries, letters, and notebooks as a last moment of serenity—a prelude to the turmoil and tragedy to come.

Chapter 3

When the library closed at 6:00, Ambler walked with Adele to the Library Tavern on Madison Avenue where they often stopped for a beer after work. On the walk over, he told her about the custody mediation session that morning.

She walked close to him, her hip every few steps bumping his, close enough so that every few steps he caught a wisp of a scent like roses from her hair. She wore black slacks of a loose, thin material that drifted against her slim legs, a long, pale green cardigan sweater over a loose-fitting white blouse, her hair tied in a ponytail. Most of the time she was casual and relaxed in dress and manner but striking all the same.

"Those lawyers arguing over Johnny like a pack of wild dogs fighting over a carcass, they only care about winning and making money, not him—and his grandmother doesn't even show up. What kind of grandmother is that?" Her reaction was because she was protective of him and especially of Johnny. He smiled.

After they'd seated themselves at the bar and said hello to

McNulty the bartender, who set them up with their mugs of beer, Ambler told her about Paul Higgins.

Only the slightest hesitation in McNulty's movements tipped off Ambler that the bartender was listening. Ambler caught this because of something McNulty told him one night. "Like the book," he'd said then. "The guy sweeping up, sometimes the cab driver, the bartender, the secretary—when there used to be secretaries—people talking, especially about something intense, they forget you're there. They don't notice you, especially bartenders, unless we want to be noticed, the 'invisible man.'"

"You can listen," Ambler said.

McNulty raised his eyebrows, not allowing he'd been caught. Ambler had known him a long time. It was as if McNulty worked at the library. He knew everything that went on there, especially anything to do with Ambler's crime fiction collection.

"This one might interest you. The FBI spied on your father, right?"

"They probably still do," McNulty said. "They spied on me. They might be spying on you. Lots of dangerous stuff in libraries—books, ideas, stuff like that."

"McNulty, you're paranoid," Adele said.

"Like Yossarian was paranoid." McNulty wasn't a big guy; his gruffness made him seem big. The gruffness was an illusion, too. He'd been a bartender a long time and looked it, a paunch a bit more formidable than middle-aged spread, wrinkles around his eyes and mouth, a kind of florid complexion, and a keenness in the expression in his eyes that suggested you wouldn't put much over on him.

Adele turned to Ambler. "So what happened?" She put one hand on her hip and pressed the index finger of her other hand against her lip, an unconscious pose she struck when she was thinking. He looked into her eyes, feeling more than thinking he was happy she was beside him.

He told her about Paul Higgins's proposal.

"So you think his books aren't so good but what's in his papers might be interesting, if not incriminating, but you scared him off."

"Yes."

"You think you'll find anything?" asked McNulty, who'd hovered nearby. "A lawyer I know did a Freedom of Information request for my files from the FBI. I got about fifty pages; most of them had black lines drawn through them, blotting out anything that would give away who the stool pigeons were."

"The what!?" Adele laughed. "You sound like James Cagney."

"I doubt—" Ambler paused because Adele was gathering herself to leave. He looked at her questioningly.

"I'm meeting Leila for dinner."

"Why didn't you tell her you didn't want her to go?" McNulty said.

"What're you talking about?" Ambler took a drink of his beer.

"You should see your face. You don't play poker, right? If you do, stop. You'll go broke."

Ambler grimaced.

"If you were a man of conviction, you'd run after her."

Ambler knew what McNulty was doing, and he'd still fall for it. "What? What?"

McNulty's eyes sprang open. "What's the poor woman got to do? After what you've been through together? Her taking care of that kid like he's her own. Her taking care of you, too—" McNulty shook his head. "She'll find another guy. She'll find another guy whenever she wants." He glanced behind him and then drew a draught of beer into a coffee cup and took a drink. "Maybe she's the one needs her head examined. Who's this Leila you don't like so much?"

Ambler started to say one thing and changed his mind. "I wouldn't say I don't like her. It's that there's something blank about her. She's guarded, too careful. Almost always, librarians have interests: art history; Jane Austen; the lives of ants; opera; the costumes French royalty wore. For me, it's crime; for someone else, it's homing pigeons on rooftops in the Bronx or collecting tea sets. I don't say librarians have to be interested in things; they just are. She isn't. It would be as if someone came to work behind the bar who didn't bet on horses or argue about the Yankees or yell at the servers. It would be weird, right?"

"Such things happen." McNulty said. "You told Adele about that undercover cop who wants to donate his papers. That's who you find behind the bar who don't belong: management plants. Snitches."

Because the FBI had spied on his Communist father for a half century, McNulty had an abiding hatred of informers and made sure everyone who stayed at the bar long enough for more than one drink knew it.

"Hey, sorry I'm late."

Leila looked up from the folded *New York Times*. She had a pencil and had been working on the crossword puzzle. Lost in thought when she glanced up, her expression unguarded, she seemed fearful—fear and irritation. She didn't like being taken by surprise. "No problem." She forced a feeble smile and folded the paper again, placing it in a cloth bag at her feet. "Working late?"

"I stopped to have a beer with Raymond."

A flash of irritation crossed Leila's face. Her expression always severe, irritated if not angry, fit her sharp features, thin lips, the muddy, lifeless, brown eyes. She wasn't attractive, didn't try to be; her hair a dull color somewhere between blonde and brown, neither long nor short, her clothes shapeless, she dressed like someone with no imagination would expect a librarian to dress.

Leila didn't like Raymond. She never said why and Adele didn't ask. Raymond hadn't warmed to Leila either, not when she began working in Manuscripts and Archives a couple of months ago, not after she and Adele became friends. Leila wasn't outgoing, certainly not flirty; but that wouldn't bother Raymond. You wouldn't mistake him for a charmer either, nor was he easily beguiled by flirty women. Whatever it was they didn't like about each other, the air crackled with it when they were in the same room.

She wasn't sure why she'd become friends with Leila. Taking the new kid under her wing had been her lot in life since elementary school. Growing up, she'd been reasonably popular and hadn't worried when she wasn't. Pretty enough to have a boyfriend of sorts—if not a Prince Charming—most of the time through high school and college; when she didn't, she had her poetry and her books, and volunteer work with younger kids, which she began in third grade. Now she had her work in the library, her poetry still her secret passion, a boyfriend-of-sorts in Raymond—if he'd ever get his ass in gear—and Johnny, his grandson, who filled her life in ways no one ever had before.

Leila's cell phone rang. She took it from her purse, looked at the number. "I've got to take this." She walked toward the restaurant door. When she returned, her face was frozen into the kind of numb stare you might expect when someone received terrible news. Adele feared the call had been to tell her someone died.

"No," said Leila. "It's not that. It's personal, a not-so-good memory. Not something I want to talk about."

They each ordered a salad and an appetizer. Adele drank a glass of Pinot Grigio, Leila a Diet Coke. For most of the meal,

Adele answered questions, though she tried to turn the conversation around.

"You're from Dallas?" Adele asked.

"A small town farther south. I went to college in Dallas and stayed for a few years afterward."

"Doing what?"

"Not much. Dead-end jobs, sales, telephone solicitation, stuff like that."

"Then you went to library school? Is that why you came to New York?"

"Something like that. A friend wanted to move here, so I came along." She sipped from her Coke. Her eyes narrowed and she lowered her voice. "I want to ask you something. It's about that reader who's using the Islamic manuscript collection."

"What about him?"

"What's he working on?"

Adele shrugged. "I don't have the slightest idea. The manuscripts are in Arabic." She was surprised by another look of irritation that crossed Leila's face, as if she, Adele, was an underling who'd screwed something up.

"Not translations?"

"Arabic."

Leila's expression didn't change.

Adele smiled mischievously. "He is kind of good looking and mysterious." She really wasn't one for girl talk. It came out when she talked with Leila—so much in need of a friend yet so hard to connect with.

"You seriously don't know what he's working on?"

"He's a doctoral student at Columbia. He speaks English. You can ask him. He's translating something; I guess for his dissertation."

"Is there a record of the documents he's using—what he calls up?"

"The call slips are there."

"Can you give me a list of books he's taken out?"

"No. You know we don't do that."

"Okay. Okay." She bent to her salad and ate in silence. Leila was difficult to figure out. She pouted, as if Adele failed her in some way.

By the end of dinner, Leila's mood improved; a look of vague worry replaced the irritation. She told Adele about a Korean nail salon near the library that did leg massages. It sounded creepy but Adele feigned interest, agreeing half-heartedly she'd give it a try. Leila decided they'd go on Saturday; she'd make appointments for both of them. Adele really wasn't interested, yet it was touching Leila tried so hard to be friends. When Leila's phone rang again as they walked toward Fifth Avenue, she let it ring. When it rang again, she did look, withdrawing into herself, putting up a shield, as she lifted the phone to her ear. "Yes? What?" She walked away, her back to Adele.

Adele took a step or two in her direction. She wasn't exactly trying to listen, but she wasn't averse to overhearing. What she heard were snippets, words disjointedly floating on the wind between long pauses and garbled sounds. "You're not supposed to know . . . pretend . . . don't . . . I won't . . . don't . . . my assignment."

That night, after being chastised by McNulty, as Ambler put the key into the outside door lock of his building, he felt that something was wrong, something off. He'd lived in the city long enough for it to be second nature to be aware of what was around him on the street at night. He hadn't noticed anything unusual, or what he'd noticed didn't register as unusual, until he felt uneasy as he opened the door. As soon as he felt the uneasiness, he remembered a battered, white, Chevy van parked in front of a fire hydrant near Third Avenue, realizing now it shouldn't have been there, the motor shut off, no lights, apparently no one inside.

Before he could turn, he felt someone beside him. Sinking into a crouch, he prepared to turn. A voice stopped him. "Stay cool. It's Paul Higgins, Mike Cosgrove's—"

"I know who you are." Ambler kept his tai-chi crouch, turning slowly.

Higgins wore a windbreaker with the collar up and a Yankee cap with the brim pulled low on his forehead. More than once, he glanced over his shoulder checking the street and sidewalk in both directions. He gestured with his hand, which was in his jacket pocket. "I need you take a ride with me." He nodded in the direction Ambler had come from—toward the white van.

Ambler hesitated. He met Higgins's gaze. "Why would I do that?"

Higgins half smiled and glanced at the pocket of his jacket. "Why are you doing this?"

"I don't have time to explain." It was easy to believe him because he kept glancing over his shoulder. Though he was on edge, he was cocky. His body tense, he was on alert; but the expression in his eyes stayed calm; he seemed slightly amused. "At the risk of sounding trite, if you do what I tell you, you won't get hurt."

Ambler shrugged and walked in front of Higgins to the van. Thoughts, possibilities ran through his mind: What if he ran? Would Higgins shoot? Would he miss? Why was he doing this? He had no reason to do what he was doing. Ambler considered explaining this to him. But of course that would be useless.

Higgins opened the door on the passenger side and gestured for Ambler to get in. He had a moment while Higgins walked around to the driver's side. But he'd already dismissed the idea of making a break for it, and he didn't have any confidence that he could win a wrestling match over a gun with Higgins, so he watched him walk past the front of the van. Higgins kept an eye on Ambler, as well as the street and sidewalks around him, not jittery, quite at ease actually. He climbed into the driver's seat, put a small pistol in his lap, and turned the ignition. With much creaking and groaning the truck pulled away from the curb, Higgins dividing his attention between the side mirrors, the street in front of him, and Ambler. He took Third Avenue uptown, went east on 42nd to First Avenue, north again to 57th Street, where he turned left and headed cross town, shifting his gaze between the mirrors, the traffic in front of him, and Ambler. When he reached Ninth Avenue, he headed downtown. At one intersection, Ambler looked out the side window, judging the time the truck was stopped at a traffic light and the distance from his seat to the street below.

"Don't unbuckle your seatbelt," Higgins said calmly.

Ambler took a deep breath and watched his captor.

After a moment, Higgins said, "As you might guess, I'm making sure no one's following me. . . . Probably a waste of time. They could have a GPS stuck to the bottom of the truck or follow signals from my cell phone."

Ambler noticed the dozen or so file boxes in the back of the van and began to put together a version of what might be taking place in Higgins's, and now his, world.

Higgins saw him looking at the boxes. "I'll explain. For the moment, I need to concentrate." Despite paying so much attention to what was behind, he moved through the city traffic with ease, switching lanes, speeding up, slowing down, keeping abreast of the cabs, making the timed lights.

"Am I your prisoner?"

Higgins gave him a sidelong glance that he couldn't decipher.

"Are those the papers you told me about?"

Higgins glanced at the boxes. "I told someone I shouldn't have I was donating them to the library."

"You're giving us the collection?"

"I talked with Mike." He glanced at Ambler. "Mike and I were in Nam. People like us, our generation, we're dying off." Higgins talked on, weaving through traffic, turning corners, inching through waves of pedestrians crossing the street, heading uptown, crosstown, downtown again. What he took a long time to say, what Ambler understood him to say, was that he'd come to believe that history—if not the present—deserved the truth. "Everything's there. I'm asking that until I'm dead, or enough almost dead for it not to make a difference, you won't let anyone get at certain parts of it. That's what you told me. That's part of the deal, right?"

"It might have been before you abducted me."

The van was a bare-boned contraption, standard shift, a gear box in the middle of the floor between them, an unadorned dashboard, levers to roll the windows up and down, sturdy seats that handled bumps and potholes like a wooden bench.

"You'll be okay."

"Restrict part of the collection? It can be part of a deal, unless your spy-on-your-fellow-citizens friends get a court order. There's a lot of that going around."

Higgins shook his head. "They wouldn't. It'd be opening a can of worms."

"Aren't we trying to lose whoever's following us because they want those documents?"

Higgins shook his head. "Nothing official. This chase is someone's freelance project."

"Who?"

Higgins turned to Ambler. "If I told you, I'd have to kill you." Ambler froze. Higgins laughed. "Trust me, you don't want to know. Is there somewhere we can drop this stuff tonight?"

"Tonight? I don't know." On one of their passes across 42nd Street, Ambler noticed the library lit up like New Year's Eve, as it was often in the evening for one society function or another. As long as all the systems were running, security and maintenance were on hand. The guards might let them drop off some files. It was worth a try. He told Higgins his thinking.

"With luck, security is a retired cop." Higgins said.

They were both right. A library police supervisor, retired from New York's finest, was at the 40th Street service entrance shooting the bull with the guard on duty. After some ex-cop reminiscing with Higgins, he gestured to the guard to open the garage door and Higgins backed the van up to the loading dock. The guard called maintenance to help deliver the boxes to the crime fiction reading room on the second floor.

Higgins left after that, not offering Ambler a ride home, which Ambler didn't want anyway. It may have crossed his mind that he might not see Higgins again, but if the thought was there, it never became fully formed.

Chapter 4

Wednesday morning, Harry Larkin, Ambler's boss, the director of Archives and Manuscripts, sat with his fingers tented under his chin and listened without interrupting, though his eyes lit up every so often with what Ambler assumed were unasked questions. Harry was a former priest, an ex-Jesuit, and sometimes seemed to revert to his former role of confessor and spiritual adviser.

"You were taken at gunpoint and chased through the city streets by a rogue secret agent of some sort?" Harry's cherubic face and granny glasses gave the impression he was bemused, which probably wasn't the case.

"Not quite that dramatic, Harry. I wasn't really threatened, and we might have been tailed; that's all."

"It's an unusual method of making a donation." Harry lowered his head to peer at Ambler over the top of his granny glasses. "He'll include a stipend for maintaining the collection?"

"So he says."

"What about a deed of gift?"

"Under the circumstances, we didn't get to it. I'll ask him to come in and sign it."

"We need to go through channels, Ray. One can't drop off a collection in the middle of the night. It might have been stolen."

"He's donating the collection, not selling it."

"You'll need the deed of gift if we decide to accept. You know I don't like restrictions on collections. And I'd like to meet this gentleman."

"What was that about?" Adele caught up with Ambler as he left Harry's office and followed him to the reading room.

He told her.

"You rode around Manhattan in a van with a renegade cop who kidnapped you from your apartment. Are you crazy?"

"Sometimes, I think I am. I didn't have much choice."

"There's something wrong here." She closed the door to the reading room behind her and turned her no-nonsense expression on Ambler. "A person can't hold you at gunpoint. That's illegal. It's wrong. You should have called the police. His donated collection be damned." Adele's bluntness might be at odds with her gentleness, yet the opposites came together in an appealing way in her. She was being protective of him again.

"I don't think the gun was for me; I think it was for whoever was following him."

"Even so, he's a bully." She noticed the stack of file boxes beneath the metal stairs that led to the room's tiny mezzanine and shifted her attention. "Is that the collection?"

"Harry didn't want to do anything with it until we have the deed of gift."

"Are you going to go through it?" Adele's eyes lit up with

something between naughtiness and evil, like the little girl playmate who goaded you into doing something you'd get in trouble for.

                        "I might take a look." He tried to shift his attention to some files on his desk.

Adele didn't let him get away. She had an eerie way of knowing when he left something out, an extra level of sensitivity where he was concerned, so that he felt sometimes she knew what he was thinking. "What would you look for?" She wrinkled her brow. "What did you tell me was in the files? You told me something . . ."

"My friend Devon, in prison—"

"Right. I remember. You think this Higgins person put your friend in jail for a murder he didn't commit."

"That's a big leap. I don't think that. I don't know what's in the file until I look."

"You do, too, think that, or you wouldn't go to all this trouble." Mischief sparkled in her eyes again. "You could look in the restricted box and seal it up again." Her smile was impish. She knew he wouldn't. For some reason, Higgins believed that, too.

"Nope. For all I know, the box is booby-trapped. I wouldn't put it past Higgins."

"You wouldn't open the box anyway."

"How do you know?"

"You're too upstanding." She half smiled and at the same time seemed sad. Her eyes met his and held.

"You make me sound like a Goody Two-shoes."

"You are." She smiled.

When she looked at him like that, with caring that seemed like admiration, he felt like a fraud. She didn't know him as well as she thought. He couldn't come close to being someone she should admire.

Chapter 5

The Arab seated at the table in the Manuscripts and Archives reading room had dark hair and darker eyes, a rugged, lined face, a wrinkled brow. Though still a young man, he had the gravitas of someone older. He spent hours at a time bent over the ornate ancient Islamic tomes he called up from the bowels of the library. Because of what Leila said at dinner the night before, Adele watched him with heightened interest. He glowed with seriousness and intensity. Nothing about him should scare you but something about him was chilling. You had a sense he wouldn't be afraid of anything. Not surprising Leila wanted to know about him. He was intriguing, mysterious—and handsome.

Adele was sitting behind the information desk lost in thought watching him when he looked up from his work and his eyes met hers. Nothing angry, nothing threatening, yet he was intimidating. He stood up and walked toward her. She watched him, mesmerized.

"Were you looking through my notes?" he asked in the level,

accented, precise tone of someone for whom English isn't a first language.

"Of course not." Her voice rose, her tone shrill. She hated that, yet she'd been unjustly accused.

His expression didn't change. "The other woman, dark hair, serious, at the desk this morning before I went for lunch. You were here when I returned. Someone else was here besides you both?"

"Leila? No one else. No one looked at your notes. I would have seen them."

His eyes opened wider, eyebrows raised, challenging. "I know."

He did know. Maybe she'd known, too, as soon as he asked. She hated being a bureaucrat, stonewalling. "I'll speak with the librarian who was here this morning. Perhaps she saw something. I'm sure there's an explanation." Her ears rang with the false earnestness in her voice.

Was that a smile twitching at the corner of his mouth? "Your fellow-worker, she's interested in ancient Arabic? Perhaps we can speak with her?"

This wasn't a good idea. To stall for time, Adele introduced herself. "And you are?" She held out her hand.

He hesitated and put his hand to his chest. She paused, irritated. The gesture seemed hostile, pulling his hand back, but his expression was tolerant, sympathetic. She drew back her hand. "Gobi Tabrizi." He bowed slightly.

"I can't leave the desk until my replacement arrives. I'll find Leila then." Sincerity returned to her voice. "I hope nothing is missing."

He raised his head, his eyes opening wider. "Disturbed. Not missing."

She felt a moment of dismay, dread. "I'm so sorry. Leila

wouldn't—" She couldn't finish the sentence. Flustered, she bent to her computer. The reader went back to his work.

Silence settled into the reading room. Adele, reluctant to meet his gaze again, kept her head down for nearly an hour. When one of the junior archivists arrived, she went to look for Leila, not sure how well this would work out. What in hell was wrong with Leila anyway? Halfway through the main reading room, she felt the Arab reader behind her. She started to walk faster, but the idea of outrunning him was foolish so she waited for him in the catalog room.

"I'm not sure your coming with me is a good idea."

He folded his fingers together in front of his chest. That slight smile was back, in his eyes and one corner of his mouth. "Shall I speak with her myself?"

Adele couldn't find an answer. She'd thought she was in charge of who saw whom; now it seemed he was. They found Leila in her cubicle in the labyrinth of workspaces behind the main reference desk. Her face when she glanced up might have been carved from ice.

"Leila, Mr. Tabrizi's research seems to have been 'tampered' with." She thought better of the word. "Disturbed, that is. Do you know what might have happened?" With her cooing voice and syrupy tone, she felt like a snake oil salesman.

Leila locked her icy stare onto the Arab reader and shook her head. "I have no idea."

"His documents are written in Arabic. I'm sure there's an explanation." Of course, she wasn't sure at all there was.

"Are you suggesting I did something with his research?"

Adele didn't know if Leila was addressing her or the man she was looking at.

"Do you suggest the documents were not disturbed?" The man's voice was controlled.

Leila's demeanor grew frostier if that were possible. "You and she," she gestured with her head toward Adele without taking her eyes off Tabrizi, "think I did something with your research. I told you I didn't."

"I didn't accuse you Leila." Adele felt her voice shake. "I asked what you knew about—"

The expression in Leila's eyes was as impenetrable as marble. "You're squirming, Adele. A reader makes an accusation. You turn on your colleague."

"I didn't hear an accusation." The smile on Gobi Tabrizi's lips was wider than it had been—but no longer in his eyes.

Leila's expression changed, ice to fire. Rage burned in her cheeks, flared her nostrils, smoldered in her eyes.

"I'm sure there's an explanation." Adele said again. Common ground seemed of no interest to Leila or Gobi Tabrizi.

"I hope you find it." Leila turned to her computer.

"I'm sorry, Mr. Tabrizi." Adele looked into his dark eyes, still tolerant, sympathetic. "Can we go back and look through the documents you were using, perhaps—"

"Of course." He turned to leave.

When he did, Leila looked at Adele and shook her head. Her expression now almost friendly, she rolled her eyes.

"One of them is lying," Adele said. She was having a beer with Raymond at the Library Tavern after work.

Ambler nodded.

"Harry was upset at me more than at Leila when I told him what happened." She watched McNulty making drinks at the service bar. He held the cocktail shaker near the side of his head parallel to his ear, shaking it vigorously. "Harry acts like she's someone else's responsibility."

Ambler thought Harry might be right, but kept it to himself. He'd asked him about Leila when questions she'd asked about one of the researchers bothered him. Harry didn't want to talk about her. She didn't like to talk about herself either. You weren't inclined to ask her anything because she had a forbidding quality that told you to keep your distance. He considered telling Adele then what he suspected, as he considered telling her now. He didn't then or now because telling her would turn his suspicion into an accusation.

"He's Muslim," Ambler said when Adele told him he wouldn't shake hands with her. "I think it's not proper for a man to touch a woman."

"Oh my God!" Adele said in a tone resembling a wail. "I feel so dumb." She shot a sidelong glance at Ambler. "Don't look smug." She took a sip from her beer mug. "We don't know she did anything. No one saw her. She said she didn't. And what's the big deal if she looked at the documents he's working on?"

"Why would she? And why would she deny doing it?"

"I don't know." Adele leaned back in her chair. "So, Mr. Smarty Pants, how will you prove Leila did anything? No witnesses. No evidence. What do you do?"

"Sometimes you don't know," Ambler said.

Chapter 6

The snow began falling as Ambler walked across 42nd Street late Thursday afternoon, tiny flurrying flakes from a leaden sky. He'd spent most of the day scrolling through newspaper databases looking for articles on the murder Devon Thomas was imprisoned for. He found a series of stories on state senate hearings and a subsequent investigation that led to a labor department supervised election in which the man who was later murdered, Richard Wright, was elected union president. He'd find more in the *Amsterdam News* archives at the Schomburg Center library in Harlem if he could find the time to get up there.

At Grand Central, he took the train uptown to pick up Johnny at the Flanders School on the Upper East Side, the tony private school his grandmother paid for and insisted he go to. Johnny spent most weekday nights with Ambler, Wednesday night and every other weekend at his grandmother's palatial apartment on Central Park West. By the time Ambler climbed the subway steps at 77th Street, the snow was falling heavily, not covering the sidewalk yet, but a thin layer of slush made it slick and slippery. From a block away through the swirling snow he saw Johnny sitting on the school's stoop with a couple of friends. He kept darting his tongue out trying to catch snowflakes.

When Johnny caught sight of him, a slight smile tugged at his mouth, a flash of something in his eyes. He was too old to jump up and run to his granddad, though not old enough not to feel the urge, on the cusp of that city-kid, much-too-early, preteen sophistication.

"Hi ya, pal," Ambler said, holding back his urge to grab the kid and hug him. So much had changed since the boy came into his life. After years of his being alone, Johnny came along, bringing this amazing joy. Yet restraint was in order when Johnny was with his friends; he might embarrass him. Actually, he could easily smother him, his attachment was so great, his fear of losing him so desperate. Those first days, after Johnny's mother's death, when the boy started school again, he'd had tears in his eyes each morning when he left him in front of the Catholic school in Hell's Kitchen.

Johnny jumped up, pushed and shoved with his friends, until they began scraping snow off the low wall in front of the school, putting together clumps of a watery substance barely resembling snowballs that disintegrated in their hands before they could throw them. Watching the increasing intensity of the wind-driven snow, feeling the chill that came with the descending darkness, Ambler guessed there would be plenty of ammunition by morning.

"Where's Adele?" Johnny asked as they began walking.

"Home, I guess. I don't know."

"She's not coming over?"

"Not tonight."

"Why not?"

Ambler hesitated. Where was he going with this? Johnny loved Adele. How could he not? She adored him and pampered him. Not so long ago she was ready to kidnap him and go into hiding rather than lose him. Johnny was too young to understand what went on between Ambler and Adele. He didn't understand it himself. They weren't married. They weren't "dating" in any recognizable sense of the term, yet she helped raise his grandchild, more important to Johnny in many ways than he was.

Johnny interrupted his reverie. "Why isn't she coming over? Can we go to her apartment?"

"We haven't been invited."

Johnny halted as Ambler headed for the subway entrance. The snow fell heavily, straight down now, large, fluttering flakes. "Can we walk instead of taking the train?"

Ambler looked at his shoes, at Johnny's sneakers, at the snow beginning to stick to the sidewalk, at Johnny. He was a kid. It was snowing.

"Is it going to snow a lot?" Johnny asked as they walked.

"It might."

"Will there be school tomorrow?"

"Probably."

"That's not fair."

Ambler was about to tell him life was unfair, but the kid already knew that better than most, didn't he?

"Can we walk to Adele's apartment? It's closer. We'll tell her we're stranded in the storm and need her to put us up until it blows over." Johnny looked up at him, blinking rapidly to keep the snowflakes out of his eyes.

"You should have a hat."

"You don't have one." Johnny made his sneakers into snowplows and plowed his way down Madison Avenue.

He didn't know why he hadn't invited Adele over. The day following the big storm after Christmas they'd gone sledding in Central Park. Everything the three of them did together was fun.

Lately, she'd grown impatient with him; he got on her nerves. She spoke sharply sometimes, irritated about little things—basketball on TV, not clearing the table, Johnny's bedtime. It was more than those things, he knew. She wanted Johnny. A twist of fate, a quirk in the law, made him Johnny's guardian.

He could fix things. She could move in with them. They'd have to get a bigger apartment, not so easy anymore. He could marry her. She might well marry him, but he wouldn't know if it was for him or for Johnny. Either way, how would marrying him be good for her? She was much younger than he was. Johnny would grow up, and she'd be stuck with an old boring man.

"I could drop you at your grandmother's. That's closer. You could watch the woods fill up with snow."

"The park, you mean? Nah." He brightened. "If we don't have school tomorrow, I don't have to do my homework. We could go out for Chinese and see a movie." He watched his sneakers snowplowing the sidewalk.

Ambler laughed. "Who said you won't have school?"

"Look at the snow." Johnny waved his arms about. "It's a blizzard."

"If you do your homework as soon as we get home, we'll go out for Chinese and you can stay up and watch the Knick game."

"Okay." Johnny twirled in a small circle and hopped onto a low wall alongside a church they were walking past, causing Ambler who'd gotten a few steps ahead to stop and turn around. When he did, he noticed a man a half block behind them, hunched into a trench coat, turn to look into a store window. The movement caught his attention.

Surely, the hundreds, if not thousands, of detective novels running around in his head helped create intrigue where none existed, yet the time he'd spent in the van with Paul Higgins, dodging city traffic, trying to shake a real or imaginary shadow, had made him wary.

He put his arm around Johnny's shoulders and tried to move him a bit faster, though there was little sense in that. It was a symbolic action to protect the boy, who'd already had far too much violence in his life. He needed to be more mindful of the effect things he did might have on the boy. He wasn't only responsible for himself anymore.

"Would you like to stop and say hello to McNulty?"

"Uncle McNulty? I sure would. Visit him at the bar?"

"I think it would be Uncle Brian, if that's what you want to call him."

"I like Uncle McNulty."

The early evening tipplers were already gathered at the Library Tavern, a clean, well-lighted place glowing through the gathering darkness and thickening snow. McNulty was busy, the bar two or three deep, two waitresses running. Ambler sat Johnny in a booth and went to the bar.

"I'll have a guy take a look," McNulty said when Ambler told him about the man he saw. "Usually, it's when the wife puts a tail on the husband I'm charged with ferreting out the gumshoe." He turned toward the service bar and hollered. "Stella! Watch the bar a minute." A young, pretty, dark-haired woman pranced up beside McNulty like he'd asked her to dance. Her name tag read quite plainly Anne.

"You're a riot, McNulty," she said. "What a cute little boy." She smiled at Ambler.

"I'll take care of the boy; you take care of the bar." He turned to Ambler. "You and Johnny sit at that booth near the waitress station until I tell you, while my guy takes a look outside." He eyed Ambler. "He could take care of the follower, too, if there is one."

"No. Not that."

McNulty went behind the bar. In a minute or so, he joined

them at the table, bearing a beer for Ambler and a massive concoction of crushed fruit, and juices, surrounding a clump of ice
cream, for Johnny.

"He hasn't eaten dinner." Ambler watched with dismay as
Johnny's eyes widened.

"A before-dinner cocktail, what's wrong with that?" McNulty
set down the drinks.

A half hour later, the walk home from the Library Tavern
was uneventful, though the snow had intensified; it lay thick on
the slippery sidewalks and blew sideways at their backs. McNulty's emissary hadn't seen anyone lurking in a doorway. If someone was following them in the snow, he'd be standing around
in wet shoes for most of the night.

Something buzzed loudly in the middle of
Adele's dream. She was late for a presentation in the library.
Not only was she late, she'd forgotten about it and wasn't prepared. When she arrived, the conference room was half-filled
with young people, like a college classroom, everyone talking
and the buzzer ringing incessantly. She hoped it was a fire
alarm. She tried to get everyone's attention, so they could all
leave and she wouldn't need to do the presentation. No one
listened. The buzzer kept buzzing; then darkness and the familiar
feel of the bedsheets against her, and still the buzzing. It was
the door, the downstairs door. Her first thought was panic.
Something was wrong—Johnny!—followed by a sly thought. It
might be Raymond. The way he looked at her earlier today, a
kind of longing. She wrapped a robe around her, padded to the
door, and pushed the intercom button.

"Who is it?"

"It's Leila, Adele. You have to let me in. Sorry. But please
buzz this door open. I'm in trouble."

Adele buzzed her in.

A couple of minutes later, a disheveled, snow-dusted, wild-eyed Leila bolted out of the elevator. Adele barely got the door all the way open as she charged through it. Taking her cue from Leila, she slammed and locked it—using all three locks—though she didn't see anyone in the elevator or the hallway.

"Is someone following you?"

Leila shook the snow off her hair and coat. "No. . . . No. . . . I had a bad experience, a fright." She kept shaking off snow. "It's snowing." She arced her hands, a flamboyant gesture, at snow puddling on the floor around her. "Obviously." She gave Adele an exasperated look. "Someone showed up in my life. He wasn't supposed to know where I was." She met Adele's worried gaze. "My ex-husband."

Adele went for a bottle of Irish whiskey McNulty the bartender had given her. You never know when you might have to pour someone a drink, he'd told her. Sure enough, Leila needed a drink to calm her nerves. She splashed some whiskey into a glass. "Drink this." She handed the glass to Leila.

"I needed to get out of my apartment. He didn't follow me. I made sure." Leila sipped the whiskey.

"Call the police."

Leila shook her head. "I can't."

"Of course you can." The poor woman was shaking.

"You don't understand. It wouldn't do any good." Leila's tone was weary, world-weary.

"What's to understand? You can't—" The look on Leila's face stopped her.

"Sit down." Leila's tone was gruff but trying for tender, as if she impatiently spoke to a child. "The police can't help with the man I'm talking about. I was young and stupid. I got involved with a man, married him. I was too naïve to be afraid of him.

He threatened to kill me. I got away . . . started a new life. He wasn't supposed to find me. But he did."

"How did he find you? Where? When?"

Leila stared into her glass. "It doesn't matter. I talked with someone who can get to him, can stop him. It'll be okay . . . if I make it through tonight." She laughed uneasily. "I didn't know anywhere else to go." Her smile was apologetic, a foreign expression for her. "I'm not explaining. One day I will." She reached for Adele's hand, leaning forward on the couch, grasping Adele's hand with both of hers, holding it against her knees. "It's been a long time since I've had a friend." Leila looked at her glass. "I needed that. Could I have another? It would put me to sleep." She patted the couch, a question in her eyes.

"Of course you can stay. There's the bottle. Pour yourself what you want. I'll get you a blanket and a pillow."

"Finished," Johnny proclaimed after about fifteen minutes on his homework, barely enough time to find the page he was on in history or the problems assigned for math. "Is it still snowing? Can we go out to eat? Walk in the snow?"

Ambler tried for a stern look but didn't have the heart for it. The kid was squirming with excitement. He hesitated a moment thinking about the man in the trench coat, yet once he'd gotten back to his apartment he no longer worried about him. Who would follow him? Someone after Paul Higgins's papers? They were in the library. What would following him tell anyone?

They went to the Szechuan restaurant on Second Avenue, though Ambler would have preferred one of the Curry Hill Indian places. The snow fell heavily as they walked to the restaurant and was driving and blowing sideways as they walked home. A hush fell over the city, the snow inches deep on the sidewalk and clogging the streets, though on Second Avenue, the cabs and trucks and cars were packed together so tightly, it didn't seem possible for snowflakes to make their way to the ground.

"Can I call Adele?" Johnny asked when they were back inside.

Ambler nodded and turned on the Knick game. A few minutes later, Johnny handed him the phone.

"I can't hear you," Ambler said.

Adele's frustration came through making her whisper a hoarse croak. "Leila's here. I don't want her to hear me. You'll have to listen harder."

Ambler smiled; only Adele or a child would come up with a request like that. She told him Leila's ex-husband was stalking her, so she was hiding out at her apartment. That wasn't good. He didn't want to alarm Adele, but Leila put her in danger by going to her. "It's a tough situation. It's hers though, not yours. Tell her to get help. What did she tell you about him?"

"She said she made a mistake marrying him. He threatened to kill her." She paused. "She said she could get someone, a third party, to stop him."

"Not the police?"

"She wouldn't let me call the police."

"That's not up to her. He might be a danger to you, too."

"He doesn't know she's here."

"Maybe," said Ambler. "If he shows up, don't open the door, and call the police, no matter what Leila says."

"I know that." She could put a pout into words. "I thought you might know something that would help."

"There are battered women centers and crisis hotlines."

"I'm not going to put her out in the snow. You're no help."

Chapter 7

The next morning dawned clear and cold, the sun bright, the city blanketed with snow. For the most part, the sidewalks had been cleared, so the walk to the subway to take moping Johnny to school wasn't as bad as Ambler expected. Adele called early to tell him she'd survived the night, and that Leila left for an appointment with someone who might rein in her ex-husband.

"Can we have lunch?" Ambler asked.

Leila and I were planning to have lunch. I'll ask her about you coming with us."

"I meant you, not her."

"No. It would be good. She might take advice from you. I'll call her."

A few minutes later, Adele called back to tell him Leila was going to do errands during lunch so wouldn't be coming after all.

Adele arrived at O'Casey's shortly after noon with Gobi Tabrizi in tow. Ambler, who'd hoped to have Adele to himself, wasn't pleased to see him. But he liked the man's manner, formal, reserved, but engaging. Dark hair, dark eyes, rugged face, dark coloring, a kind of easy grace and tolerance that comes from having seen things in life you'd rather not have seen. He and Adele seemed to have gotten to know one another; they were like pals, smiling, almost playful. And they looked good together, Tabrizi handsome, she pretty, about the same age. That recognition brought with it a sinking feeling. Ambler had a difficult time holding on to his smile.

Adele and Gobi sat next to one another, across from him, which made it difficult not to think of them as a couple. Tabrizi talked easily enough about his studies and his research at the library on the origins and evolution of Islamic law, Sharia. At the same time, he treaded lightly on anything political, emphasizing that his interest was scholarly. A Syrian, he said he'd been in the states for two years. He told them he was a Sunni Muslim but had little interest in going into detail on that, what he'd done before coming to the United States, or why he left Syria. Ambler wondered, but didn't ask, if his bangers and mash lunch was offensive to the Muslim scholar.

The way Adele looked at Tabrizi as he spoke about himself, with a kind of possessiveness, reminded him of how she looked at Johnny and, actually, how she sometimes looked at him. Near the end of lunch, Tabrizi asked about Leila Stone.

Ambler started to say something, but decided to let Adele answer. She told him Leila kept to herself and was hard to get to know.

"I thought you two would hit it off," Adele said after they'd divided up the check. "You're a lot alike." She looked from one to the other. Neither he nor Tabrizi said anything; probably Tabrizi had no more idea of how they were alike than he did.

On the walk back to the library, the sidewalks narrowed by snowbanks, Adele walked beside him, her body through her bulky coat brushing against him every few steps. He fought back an impulse to put his arm around her.

"I missed seeing Johnny last night." Her regretful tone said more than the words.

"I'm sorry. I should have asked you to come over." Their pace slowed. "You don't have to wait to be asked, you know."

"Yes I do. You're very independent." She picked up her pace and caught up with her new friend. Ambler trudged behind, the sidewalk too narrow for the three of them abreast.

He left Adele and Gobi Tabrizi in Astor Hall and took the staircase on the opposite side of the lobby from the one they took. Outside the crime fiction reading room, trying to dislodge from his mind's eye the picture of Gobi and Adele walking together, he almost bumped into Leila before he noticed her. She seemed rattled. He wanted to say something but didn't want to bring up her ex-husband unless she brought it up.

"Everything okay? Adele said you'd be out doing errands. You should have had lunch with us."

"I was delayed. I'm off to do them now.' She looked at him curiously. "That's nice of you to think about me for lunch." Her smile surprised him.

He hoped she'd bring up her troubles with her ex-husband. But she didn't, and his sense of decorum didn't allow him to mention something so private. As he watched her walk away, he wondered what it would take to figure her out.

When Ambler came back from the microform reading room on the first floor late that afternoon, he found Gobi Tabrizi waiting for him.

"In the restaurant, I thought you were about to say something about Miss Stone."

"Miss Stone? Leila?"

"Yes."

"Adele knows Leila better than I do."

"Miss Morgan told me something about you, that you . . ." He searched for the right words, "that you are an advocate for freedom of speech."

They walked into the crime fiction reading room together. "Librarians are free speech advocates. It goes with the job. It's what we do." He gestured at the walls of books surrounding them.

Gobi bowed, a kind of acknowledgment and mark of respect. "Miss Morgan said when you were a college student you created an exposé of spying on the part of your government." He waited for confirmation.

"She exaggerates. Do you think you're being spied on by my government?"

Tabrizi looked at the chair in front of the desk and then sat down. He chose his words carefully. He didn't have to be so careful but he didn't know that. "I don't mean to make you uncomfortable."

"I don't know if you're being spied on."

"But you think perhaps. You suspect—"

"Suspicion isn't enough."

Irritation flushed Tabrizi's face, darkened his eyes. "I believe you understand more than you let on. You have your reasons for—"

"Mistrusting Leila? . . . We'd like to think, in the library, we practice what we preach. If I knew someone interfered with your research, I'd do something about it."

"And you think?"

"I don't know." Ambler said.

Tabrizi stood. "Mr. Ambler—"

"Call me Ray."

"Mr. Ambler, I try to understand you are reluctant to accuse your coworker. Yet one is responsible to act when one knows something is wrong, even when it requires courage. You are in the unfortunate position of seeing a wrong others don't see."

Their eyes met. Some understanding passed between them. What Ambler saw in the other man's eyes was not so much an accusation, though it felt like one, but a requirement, not an entreaty, but a demand, like he might sometimes see in the eyes of a panhandler when he accidentally made eye contact on the street and quickly looked away.

Chapter 8

"What's going on?" Ambler stopped alongside Benny Barone, one of the younger librarians he'd become friends with, who waited with a cluster of other library employees near the 42nd Street entrance. NYPD police cruisers lined the curb. Others, lights flashing, were strung out along the curb on Fifth Avenue. Because it was Saturday, the normal workday crowds weren't rushing along the sidewalks. Instead, clumps of tourists had gathered, gawking and talking. Since most of them were foreign tourists, it sounded like the Tower of Babel.

Benny grabbed his arm. "The police are inside with dogs. Maybe they're searching for a bomb."

"They're cadaver dogs."

Ambler turned to see who'd spoken. A young man with long brown hair sticking out from under a watch cap and a wispy goatee, dressed more for the Alps than 42nd Street, smiled, an open, friendly expression you don't often see on the sidewalks of New York.

"I remember dogs like them from Iraq. One's a black lab."

He smiled again. "They're looking for bodies." His smile evaporated into a sad, troubled expression. "Gotta go." He heaved his backpack higher on his shoulder and headed toward the subway entrance.

Not long afterward, someone unlocked the door to the library, bracing it so it remained open. Police came out, a few at a time, including two uniformed cops with dogs on leashes, one a German shepherd, the other a black lab. Slowly, one by one, the flashing lights died out and cruisers slid into the morning traffic, some making U-turns with chirping sirens on 42nd Street. Conspicuous among the remaining police presence was the bulky white NYPD crime scene van—and conspicuous among the remaining officers of the law, wearing a blue NYPD windbreaker, was Mike Cosgrove.

He did a double take on Ambler and Benny and walked over. "What're you two doing here?"

"We work here. You don't . . . or at least we hope you don't." Ambler said.

"Someone called 911, said we'd find a body in the 42nd Street Library, didn't say where, how long it'd been there, who it was. It's a big building, lots of places to hide a body." Cosgrove darted a significant glance at Ambler. "We found her stuffed into a book shelf in your office."

Ambler wasn't sure if this was a joke. Cosgrove's expression didn't change. But then it wouldn't.

"The crime fiction reading room? A body? It wasn't there—" Of course it wasn't there when he left. What the hell was he thinking?

"A body among the murder mystery books. What do you think of that?" Cosgrove's expression was doleful. "You'd think I'd run into you two in a murder case maybe once in a lifetime and that only if I had bad karma."

"Who's the victim?"

He put his hands into the pockets on either side of his trench coat, pulling out a notebook from his left side. "You'd know her as Leila Stone."

"Leila? Dead? . . ." It took a moment for this to sink in. And then something else. "What do you mean we'd know her as?"

Cosgrove's face was gray, bags under his eyes. He seemed to sag under the weight of his trench coat. "Leila Stone. She's dead. How well did you know her?"

"Not so well."

"Well enough for her body to be in your office."

"I have no idea why."

The detective turned to face the door. A tall thin man in an expensive-looking black overcoat came out. He was talking to a higher-up uniformed officer, gold shield on his hat, while he held a cell phone down from his ear. Before the uniform finished speaking, he put the phone back to his ear.

The man in uniform gestured to Cosgrove, so he walked over to the two men, who took turns talking at him. Cosgrove listened, shoulders hunched. After a bit, he grew animated, his arms stretched out above his shoulders, a stance of exasperation you might have when your dog broke loose from its leash and ran down the street. He turned from the two men, coming back toward Ambler, his jaw jutted out, eyes blazing. Ambler thought better of stopping him as he walked past.

The morning was mild so most of the library staff milled around Bryant Park drinking coffee while they waited for the doors to open. Readers and tourists congregated on the steps of the Fifth Avenue entrance. When the library did open, Ambler couldn't get to his office because the crime scene technicians had it taped off. He went to look for Adele in the Manuscripts and Archives reading room and found it closed off also. Looking through the small window in the door, he saw Gobi Tabrizi sitting at a table ringed by three men, two of them bulky, in ill-fitting sports jackets, detectives straight from central casting; the third was the same tall, thin man he seen talking to one of Cosgrove's bosses when the police came out of the library. He'd taken off his expensive overcoat and wore what looked like a custom-tailored suit. Because he seemed out of place, Ambler wondered who he was.

Mike Cosgrove stood in ornate Astor Hall near the library's main entrance, not knowing what to do next. Once again there'd been a murder in the library that had something to do with Ray Ambler. Ray said he didn't know the victim very well—the same thing, if he remembered right, Ray said about the last murder victim, and look how that turned out. He wouldn't put Ray on his list of suspects—if he ever got a chance to make such a list—yet his pal had to know more about this than he'd said so far if the body was dumped in his office.

From the beginning, he knew this case was different. First, the brass show up and then intelligence, and right behind intelligence, Brad Campbell Security, in the person of Brad Campbell himself. Already, they were making decisions, keeping their own counsel, stepping all over his case—if it was his case. For them, Ray was a suspect since the victim's body was in his office.

They already knew he and Ray were friends, so he'd have to explain that. Then he'd be hard-pressed to explain why he sometimes talked things over with Ray during a homicide investigation. How long had he known Ray? Ten years maybe. How many cases had Ray stuck his nose in? A half dozen, probably more. Since that first one, where Ray saw something was wrong from a photo he saw in a newspaper, they'd sometimes locked horns but often saw the same things in a case, things no one else saw. He liked to think he'd led Ray into becoming something of an amateur detective, while Ray introduced him to the wide world of crime fiction.

Usually, when there's a murder, the uniforms seal the scene to keep it from getting contaminated. They identify witnesses, note any peculiarities. They call CSI. They call homicide. Everyone knows what to do. No one gets in anyone else's way. This one should have been fairly easy, at least orderly, with a kind of closed society of suspects in the library. So what happens is he's told not to do anything. Hang tight. They'll let him know when to get started. Sure, take some time to contaminate the scene and let the witnesses scatter and the trail grow cold; then, he can get started.

He could go get a cup of coffee, go back to the precinct and catch up on paper work, let this one go and catch the next one. Or he could hang around, see what develops. He decided to stop by Ray's office, despite the headache it might cause him later.

"I swear to God." He closed the door behind him. "It's not like I haven't investigated a couple of hundred murders in my time. They've turned this fucking department into a funny farm. You don't know who's running things."

Ray looked up from his computer. Cosgrove caught himself; he was talking to a civilian. He looked at the chair Ray gestured toward. "I don't want to sit," he said, shoving the chair sideways and then sitting in it. "A homicide investigation should be run by homicide. You'd think that wouldn't you?" He glared at Ambler.

Ambler shrugged.

"This department—"

"I saw your comrades in arms talking to a reader in Manuscripts and Archives. What's that about?"

Cosgrove shook his head. "Can't tell you." Actually, he couldn't tell him. He didn't know.

"Who are they?"

Cosgrove rolled his eyes, spread his arms, turned his hands palms up. "I'm not in charge." He stood, shoving the chair he'd been sitting in backward. "That's what I've been telling you."

"What are you telling me?"

"Maybe you can tell me something. Who's the guy they're questioning?"

"A reader, he's doing research in our Islamic manuscripts collection."

"That might explain it."

"Explain what?"

"Why the Intelligence Division jumped all over this. Why I'm sitting here with my thumb up my ass instead of investigating a homicide."

The afternoon felt even stranger after Cosgrove left. Ambler couldn't shake the creepy feeling someone was watching him, as if Leila's body—or her ghost—haunted the reading room. It was guilt. He hadn't given her a chance, didn't get to know her, judged her harshly and too soon. He should have done better by her. Now she was dead. He remembered her smile of the day before when he asked her about lunch. It wasn't that he didn't like her. It was he didn't trust her. That didn't mean he wished her dead. Her death wasn't his fault. He didn't have anything to do with it. So why was her body in his reading room? Deep in thought, he didn't hear Adele come in, so he jumped when she spoke to him.

"Why didn't you call?" Her voice was strained, cracked, her eyes red, cheeks tear-stained. He came around the desk and stood close to her. She came into his arms and pressed her face to his chest. Her sobbing was rhythmic against him.

"I'm sorry," he said.

"How horrible to die like that. The terror of knowing it was coming had to be even worse. It's my fault—" She pushed herself back from him, lifted her face, red and blotched.

"It's not your fault. How could it be?"

"I didn't call the police. I should have called."

He brushed at her hair. The action seemed to bother rather than comfort her, so he pulled his hand back. "It might not be what you think. She probably had a restraining order against her ex-husband anyway. Have you spoken to the police?"

"I tried. A uniformed officer wrote down my name and said they'd contact me. I told him I wanted to talk to Mike Cosgrove. The guy nodded and said they'd get back to me. They wouldn't let me into the reading room where a bunch of them ganged up on poor Gobi. They were hollering at him; I heard them. Browbeating him! I'm surprised they didn't shoot him. I'm sure they think he's a terrorist."

Later, after the library closed, as Ambler waited at the Library Tavern for Adele, he told McNulty about the murder.

"The library is cursed."

"You don't believe in curses. You're a Communist."

"I'm half Irish. My mother. That half believes in curses."

"What would make the library cursed? Who would curse it?"

"The ghosts from those murderous happenings a couple of years ago. And now, the ghost of the poor girl found in your office."

"On a bookshelf."

"There you go."

"Her murder doesn't have anything to do with me."

McNulty's response, if there was to be one, was interrupted by the arrival of Adele, with Gobi Tabrizi in tow.

"So good to see you." Tabrizi shook Ambler's hand vigorously, his expression an unguarded entreaty. "Ginger ale, please," he told McNulty. The bartender nodded, his face registering his concern. You could see he thought the man needed a drink.

Ambler hesitated to bring up the police interrogation. He

didn't have to. Tabrizi opened the spigot and out poured the story.

"They took my research materials. They questioned me about everything I did in the United States, going back to the day I arrived. Every place I've visited. Every person I know. They told me not to leave the city."

"You need a lawyer," Ambler said.

"He hasn't done anything," Adele said. "As soon as the idiot police come to their senses, they'll realize Leila's ex-husband killed her."

With Adele grieving for her friend and Tabrizi a nervous wreck, the conversation was disjointed.

"In Syria," Tabrizi said, "the police would come and your friends would disappear. Just like that. A car pulls up. Assad's police grab your friend, put him in the car." He paused. "Once you've seen friends disappear, you believe it can happen any minute to you, too." He looked helplessly at Ambler. "But not here."

McNulty had a lawyer friend who came from similar a subversive background to McNulty's and was known for his work on politically charged civil liberties cases. Given that Tabrizi was under suspicion and a Muslim, Ambler asked McNulty if he would call him.

Instead, McNulty gave Gobi the phone number and told him to tell the lawyer he was sent by McNulty.

Ambler walked Adele home that evening after Gobi left them. He didn't have much to say to her but thought she shouldn't be alone. As they walked, she talked about Leila but didn't seem to require that he do anything other than listen.

"She had a difficult life," Adele said. "She didn't talk about herself, but you could see she wanted to. She had this expression in her eyes, a kind of yearning, as if she were missing something in her life and had given up on finding it, except every now and then a glimmer of hope got through. She told me she'd thought since she was a little girl she'd be a mother, not to one child but be the mother to a bunch of kids like the pioneer families. That life never happened for her. She was young enough to hope it might still, if her life hadn't been snuffed out like that."

Adele's capacity for sympathy was large. Yet, she might be talking about herself, her own dashed dreams. Maybe she, too, dreamed of a large brood of kids. Adele would be a wonderful mother. She was already to Johnny. Dashed dreams were in some way the lot of almost everyone, dreams for yourself, dreams for your children.

"Leila must have a family," he said. "I suppose the police can find her relatives. Where was she from?"

"Texas, she told me, but I don't know where. She didn't talk about her family, only her goddamn ex-husband who killed her."

The ex-husband was a good possibility, but it wasn't for certain. Not a good idea to tell this to Adele in the state she was in. Rational thought only took you so far. You needed to be irrational sometimes to handle what life threw at you.

"I wish Mike would call me back," he said.

As if wishes came true, his phone rang. But it wasn't Mike; it was Johnny calling from his grandmother's.

"What happened at the library?" The boy's voice was strained and accusatory. "Someone was killed at the library. Weren't they? Who got murdered? . . . Where's Adele?" His voice shook.

"A woman who worked at the library was killed, Johnny. Adele's fine. She's right here with me." He should have called the boy and told him. He should have known a murder that close would bring back terrible memories of what happened to his mother. He could hear Johnny's rapid and uneven breathing over the phone. He was between tears and panic. His grandmother would be no help. Empathy and caring weren't her strong points. Her emotional connection to Johnny was like what one would have with a goldfish.

"I'm walking with Adele. Do you want to talk to her?"

He did and they talked for a couple of blocks. Ambler didn't get the gist of the conversation. Adele's tone was soothing and reassuring and she listened for long stretches. When she asked Johnny after a while if he wanted to talk with Ambler again, he evidently said no. She said, "Goodnight. I love you, so does your grumpy granddad."

As they walked up Ninth Avenue, Ambler suggested they have dinner.

"You're trying to comfort me, I know." She grasped his arm. "I appreciate it. But I'd like to be alone and remember Leila. I can't explain it. It's not anything about you. Do you understand? I'll think about Leila. I might find a church and light a candle. I'll be okay."

He found himself alone walking down Ninth Avenue with no idea where he wanted to go. It was cold but not freezing; he was dressed warmly enough, and walking, even if not briskly, kept him warm. Leila's death was on his mind. Johnny and Adele were on his mind. He wasn't as good at thinking about himself as he was at thinking about things outside himself. It was easier to think about who would have reason to kill Leila and why the murderer stuffed her body into his bookshelf. Someone was bound to find it. It would have been him if someone hadn't tipped the police that they'd find a body in the library. A sick joke? It made no sense. He tried calling Cosgrove again.

This time, the detective answered. "Where are you?"

Ambler looked around. "Ninth Avenue. I just crossed Eighteenth Street."

"What are you doing?"

"Walking."

"Wait on the corner of Fourteenth, northwest corner. I'll pick you up."

"So what's going on?" he asked when he got into Cosgrove's car a few minutes later.

"Everything's going to hell. Troubles ahead. Troubles behind. There's a joint on Eleventh Avenue where I can park without getting tagged. Let's get a drink."

"I haven't eaten."

"The hamburgers are pretty good."

They sat at a vinyl booth across from a worn and battle-scarred bar whose old-fashioned stools had a chrome base and red vinyl seats. The hamburger was thick, juicy, and good. The tap beer was crisp and fresh.

Mike had missed Ambler's calls because he'd gone home in the middle of the day due to a family situation, an altercation in an ongoing battle between his wife and daughter. "Denise slapped her mother, so Sarah called the cops. I'm a cop. The asshole. Why's she got to call the cops? She was drunk so when they got there she acted stupid. They wanted to lock her up. One of the guys knew me—actually, a young guy, he knew my partner, so they called me."

Cosgrove drank a shot of Irish whiskey before starting on his beer and burger. "I go out to Queens in the middle of my shift feeling like a fucking fool, both women bawling, cursing like truck drivers. I want to slug my wife."

He shrugged, his expression sheepish, and took a drink of his beer. "You know I don't mean that, right? I been through these things on the job a hundred times. The best thing is separate the combatants. Locking someone up is no good. But Sarah pissed off one guy, and he doesn't want to leave it alone. Finally, I get Denise out of there, but Jesus!"

It was easy to sympathize with Mike. Ambler had his own

train wrecks in life, with an alcoholic ex-wife and a son in jail for murder. He liked Mike's daughter Denise, had taken her in when she ran away couple of years before. She was Johnny's favorite babysitter, the few times he'd needed her. A pretty girl, full of life, she didn't realize her mother was jealous of her youth and prettiness. It wasn't his job to criticize her mother, so he didn't.

"Good to get that off my chest." Cosgrove looked down at the remains of his hamburger and a few leftover French fries and then up at Ambler. "You have one hell of a home life when a homicide investigation is a relief."

Ambler told him Leila had showed up at Adele's apartment in the middle of the night two days before she was killed to hide from her ex-husband. "She told someone at the scene. Strange no one's checking into that."

"Lots of things about this one are strange." Cosgrove's expression was a snarl. "We're sorting out how we do the investigation." His eyes widened. "Ever hear of that?"

"It's a homicide."

Cosgrove signaled for the check. "Not just homicide."

"National security?"

Cosgrove's eyes sprang open. "Why would you think that?" He waved his hand to ward Ambler off. "Don't answer. Think what you want. The walls have ears."

"It's national security because someone discovered an Arab in the building?"

"More complicated. Not one of your detective novels."

"I can figure that out, too."

Cosgrove locked his gaze on Ambler. "How about you sit this one out, take a short vacation? You stick your nose in I'll end up walking a beat in Staten Island."

"Someone dumped Leila's body in my office. I didn't—"

"Look, Ray. I'm in a tough spot here. Usually, I don't have

the brass looking over my shoulder; I have some say-so in what happens. In this one, I don't. Everything I do is being scrutinized. You're a suspect. The brass find I'm talking to you pretty soon I'm a suspect, too."

"You don't want to tell me why everything is so hush-hush?"

"No."

"You want me to tell you?"

Cosgrove let loose his penetrating cop stare.

"Leila Stone was an operative working undercover. If this gets out, becomes public, NYPD or another agency is embarrassed."

"That's speculation based on what?"

"Call it a working hypothesis. My guess is Leila was a confidential informant for NYPD."

Cosgrove's jaw muscles began to work, his eyes opened wider, moving as if something behind them was trying to escape. You forgot sometimes that Cosgrove was a powerful man. Ambler knew his friend's rage wasn't directed at him. But he didn't want to get in its way either.

"You don't want to fuck with these national security people, Ray. They're an army onto themselves. Resources you can't imagine. And you're in their sights."

"There's got to be more than a body dumped in my reading room to—"

"Not dumped." Cosgrove stood.

"Oh?" said Ambler. He stood, too. "I'll get the check."

"Next time." Cosgrove took the check and some cash to the bartender.

Chapter 9

Ambler was climbing the broad marble stairs in the rotunda of the library the next morning when an out-of-breath Adele ran up behind him.

She grabbed his arm. "There are men! They snatched Gobi off the street." She yanked at his arm. "You've got to come!"

He ran back down the stairs with Adele following him. She caught up near the bottom of the steps that led to the sidewalk on Fifth Avenue. "Right there," she shouted. "A black SUV with a black car behind it and a black car in front of it. A bunch of men jumped out of the cars. Two men grabbed him, another one frisked him; they handcuffed him and pushed him into the back of the SUV."

Crowds brushed by, pedestrians walking quickly that hour of the morning on their way to work, scraggly lines of tourists climbing the stairs. He and Adele stood looking down Fifth Avenue, as if they might catch a glimpse of the receding SUV.

"They grabbed him and were gone like that! She snapped her fingers. "It's a good thing I saw what happened or we wouldn't even know he'd been arrested."

Ambler continued to watch the traffic flow down Fifth Avenue. "That's what you'd think, the police. Who else would snatch a man off the street in broad daylight?"

She turned on him a look of dread. "What do you mean?" Her voice rose. "What are you saying?"

"No police cruiser? Did you see badges?"

Adele shook her head. "Who else would it be?"

"The Syrian police?"

As they walked back up the steps into the library, Adele again grabbed his arm. "I know why I thought the police. I recognized one of the men, a tall, thin man, chiseled face, brown hair. He stayed in the second car with the window rolled down, smoking a cigarette, watching everything. I saw him yesterday. He was in charge of the men questioning Gobi."

When he got to his office, Ambler called Cosgrove, who listened, didn't comment on what happened to Gobi, and said he'd see what he could find out. Still rattled, Ambler called McNulty to get his lawyer-friend's number but got his answering service. It was easier to find a vampire in daylight than to find McNulty in the morning. He left a message and then sat at his desk staring into space.

A half hour later, he snapped out of his trance, pulled up his notes, and went back to work on the catalog that would accompany the *Century-and-a-Half of Murder and Mystery in New York City* exhibit. But he kept drifting off into his thoughts. He couldn't stop thinking about why Leila's body was found in the crime fiction reading room. He gave up trying to work and went down the hall to his boss Harry Larkin's office. McNulty's lawyer friend had represented Harry when he'd been a person-of-interest in a murder case a couple of years back, so he might remember the lawyer's name or have his phone number. He found him in his office and told him one of the library's readers, Gobi Tabrizi, had been snatched off the street and hauled away.

"The man the police questioned yesterday? They must have learned something damaging about him."

"I'm going to get him a lawyer."

"You assume he's innocent?"

"Don't we all, 'until proven guilty?'" He asked about the lawyer.

"Levinson," Harry said. "I don't remember the first name."

Ambler rolled his eyes. "Do you know how many lawyers named Levinson there are in New York?"

Harry shuffled around in his desk drawer looking for Levinson's business card that he was sure he had somewhere.

"I want to ask you about Leila Stone."

Harry shook his head. "I've been told not to talk about her."

"By whom."

"The police."

"The police can't tell you who you can talk to and what you can talk about."

Harry looked up from digging in his desk drawer, knitted eyebrows, pursed lips, wrinkled brow. "I don't want to run afoul of them."

"You won't. Was it Cosgrove?"

Harry shook his head. "I don't know who it was, someone very authoritative."

"Jesus, Harry, get a grip. Leila was part of some sort of surveillance network in the library, right?"

Harry's jaw dropped. He bent to the desk drawer and didn't look up until he found the lawyer's business card. He handed it to Ambler.

"I think we should have a drink later," Ambler said. "Library Tavern after work?"

Ambler called David Levinson from the phone in his office. The attorney himself answered.

"I thought I'd need to go through a whole rigmarole of secretaries and assistants to get to you," Ambler said.

"Would that were true. The Mystery Writers were right: Crime doesn't pay enough. What can I do for you?"

"Brian McNulty—"

"Shit. McNulty's the main reason I can't make any money. He preys on my conscience. Go ahead."

Ambler told him about Gobi's arrest.

"A legitimate concern," said the lawyer. "I'm in a taxi on my way to a trial I'm late for in Brooklyn. When we hang up, call back and give me all the particulars on my voice mail. If I need more, I'll call you. Is he legal?"

"I think he's here on a student visa."

"Call me tonight if you don't hear from me."

A few minutes later, Adele tapped on the door to the reading room and came in. Her face was drawn, circles under her eyes, her expression dull and dolorous, when almost always it was bright and full of life.

"Feeling any better?" he asked, though he knew she wasn't.

Adele shook her head. "I'm trying to find out what the arrangements are for Leila's funeral. No one knows." She collapsed onto a chair. "I feel totally defeated. Why bother? What difference does it make? Leila thought there were important things she was going to do in her life. In the end, they turned out to not be important at all. She won't do any of them because she's dead."

"I'm sorry," Ambler said.

"And the stupid police arrest Gobi, whisk him away like the Gestapo. He didn't kill Leila. Why would he? Why won't they listen to me about her ex-husband? He told her he'd kill her."

She stood and walked slowly around the small room absently looking at the books on the shelves. He followed a few steps behind. After a moment, she changed direction, turned and came back toward him still looking at the books on the shelves until she stopped in front of him and looked into his eyes; hers were misty. He opened his arms slightly and began to say something about sorrow and memories. The next thing he knew she was in his arms, pressed against him.

After what seemed a long time, she put her hands on his chest and gently pushed herself back from him. "What's going to happen to us, Raymond?" Her tone was flat, so he didn't know what the question meant. Did she mean life in general? Did she mean now that Leila was killed? Did she mean them romantically?

He didn't want to give the wrong answer, so he said, "I don't know," which would pretty much suffice no matter which question it was. "Why don't you come with me to pick up Johnny this afternoon? He's been asking to see you."

"While you've been avoiding me?"

"I haven't—"

"Don't." She held up her hand. "Forget I said that." She went back to browsing through the bookshelves. Something caught her eye. She went to the file boxes under the stairs and knelt.

Ambler followed her to the file boxes—the boxes containing Paul Higgins's papers—knowing as soon as he looked that something was different. The sealed box, the box with the restricted papers, was the top box. When he piled the boxes there, it was at the bottom of the stack.

"Has it been opened?" Adele asked.

The tape had been replaced carefully, the tear in the tape imperceptible unless you bent closely to see if it had been tampered with. The box had been opened.

Adele hauled the box over to the library table in the middle of the room.

"What are you doing?"

"I'm going to find out what's in here. It's already been opened."

"That doesn't mean you can open it, too."

Adele paused. "Are you serious?"

"I told Paul Higgins no one would see what was in those files. I gave my word."

"Someone already did. It's been opened. The seal is broken."

"You can't open it."

She turned on him. "You'll stop me?" Her face registered incredulity and anger. Before this moment, he couldn't have imagined her looking at him like this.

"I'm not going to physically stop you. I'm telling you it would be wrong."

Adele's eyes narrowed. She scrunched up her face, a look of disgust. "You're such a fucking Boy Scout. You . . . You—" She stomped out of the room.

Ambler called Mike Cosgrove to tell him about the opened file box and to ask him to let Higgins know. He spent the afternoon in the exhibition hall setting up displays for the upcoming crime fiction exhibit. When he returned to his desk, he saw that the lawyer David Levinson had called. He called back.

"Is it unusual for an arrest not to be recorded? Yes." Levinson said. "Is it legal? No. Does it happen? More often than you'd think. They arrest someone, move him from precinct to precinct; they don't book him, hoping he'll talk before an attorney can reach him."

Ambler described the arrest as Adele had described it to him, with more detail than in the message he'd left on the answering machine.

"This person in charge, brown hair, high forehead, thin face, smokes cigarettes?"

"Yes, and well dressed."

"The man you saw, I'd bet, is Bradley Campbell. He used to be in charge of the NYPD Intelligence Division, a gentleman police officer."

"What's a gentleman police officer?"

"Someone who grew up amongst silver spoons and crystal chandeliers, part of the aristocracy, the one percent, who, for reasons known only to him, became a cop. He retired a few years ago, set up a private security agency, does work for Wall Street and the banks, foreign princes and potentates."

"Gobi Tabrizi was snatched by a security agency?"

"Possible. Campbell works closely with the NYPD; sometimes you can't tell them apart."

"Isn't snatching someone off the street kidnapping?"

"You want to call the police on them?" Levinson's tone was cheery but his syntax clipped. "I'll let Campbell know I'm looking for Mr. Tabrizi. See what that stirs up."

Ambler arranged for Mike's daughter Denise to pick up Johnny at school and bring him home. He then went to find Harry for their after-work tête-à-tête. When they arrived at the Library Tavern, McNulty stopped in the middle of taking an order from a waitress to walk to the opposite end of the bar to greet Harry. "I was afraid you'd leave if I didn't greet you since I obviously grievously offended you the last time you were here however many months or years ago that was."

"What was that?" Harry asked as McNulty walked back to the service bar.

"He expects loyalty from his regulars," Ambler said. "You should stop in more regularly."

Harry wouldn't tell him if there was a surveillance program in the library. He did weaken on the who-told-him-to-keep-quiet part. It was Brad Campbell.

"What did he ask you about Gobi Tabrizi?"

"I'm not going to answer that. You may be out of your league on this one, Ray. It's not a simple murder case—"

"Murder isn't simple."

"This is different."

"Why? Because it involves a government informant?"

Harry shifted in his seat, his gaze darting about the bar, anywhere but at Ambler. Eventually, he settled down and asked Ambler how he knew Leila was a government plant. Ambler hadn't known for sure until Harry confirmed it.

"She was sent to me. The director's office sent a memo. Someone from HR brought her to my office."

"Weren't you curious?"

"I was. It was a blessing. We've sent a half-a-dozen or more requests to HR to fill positions. With the hiring freezes, you make the requests and forget about them. I thought she might be the niece of someone on the board, or connected to someone in the mayor's office, or something like that. I wasn't going to say we couldn't use her." He faced Ambler over the lip of his rocks glass. "There you have it, not much of a conspiracy."

Ambler told Harry about the restricted files that had been tampered with. "I told Mike Cosgrove. He'll want to look at them. I'm going to tell him the police need a court order to open the box."

Harry examined his scotch. This time McNulty who'd been watching him came over and watched the glass of scotch with him. "It's going to evaporate before you get to drink it if you don't pick up the pace."

"I'm not much of drinker," Harry said. He turned to Ambler. "I don't agree with you on this, Ray. We never actually accepted the files. We don't have a deed of gift. And we're talking about national security issues."

A direct descendant of Ignatius of Loyola, Harry could turn the simplest idea into a convoluted argument, justifying whatever he agreed or disagreed with.

"What national security?" said McNulty who'd hung around on his side of the bar to listen.

"Leila Stone's murder," Ambler said.

McNulty's eyebrows went up. "I'm surprised they didn't figure you for that one. Did they know she was keeping Adele away from you?"

"What's this?" Harry jerked upright.

Ambler's cheeks burned. "Nothing. I tagged Leila as an informant from the beginning. Adele befriended her. It caused some tension." He turned to the bartender. "Go away, McNulty."

The argument went back and forth, until an incensed Harry slugged down the rest of his scotch.

"Another?" inquired McNulty politely.

"Yes." Harry pushed his glass toward the bartender. "Please."

Ambler laughed. After a moment, so did Harry. "I feel like St. Augustine," he said. "The barbarians are at the gates."

In the end, Harry agreed to talk to the library's attorneys about access to Higgins's files, and Ambler went outside to phone Denise to see how she and Johnny were doing.

"He told me you said we could order pizza when he finished his homework."

"I did. I should be there in an hour. How are things for you at home?"

"Awful, as usual. Can you adopt me? I'll be Johnny's big sister and you won't have to pay me for babysitting."

Poor Denise. She was a good kid. He didn't know why her parents were so hard on her. "I'll think about it."

"Really?" There was hope in her voice before reality set in. "What I should do is have Johnny's rich grandmother adopt me."

"Hang in there a while longer, sweetie. Things will get better."

"That's what you always say," this with a pout in her voice. "Oh I forgot. I'm so sorry. I should have told you this first. I'm so dumb. Someone called. I think it was your son but I wasn't sure what to do, so I didn't accept the charges. He had to hang up."

Chapter 10

Ambler hurried home in case his son John might call again. When he got there, he put Denise in a cab to go home, despite her insistence she would be fine taking the subway. After the tussle over the cab, irritated by her obstinacy, he felt more sympathy for her parents. When he got back upstairs, Johnny came out of the bedroom he shared with Ambler and poked around his books and book bag on the dining room table, clearly wanting something but reluctant to bring it up.

After a few moments, he said. "My dad called. He's going to call back." Johnny wouldn't have been able to talk to his father. He would have had to accept the charges for the call, and he wouldn't know to do that. John would have hung up anyway; he wasn't ready to talk to his son. It was difficult for the poor kid. He wanted so much to know his father.

The phone rang and it was John calling back. Ambler asked Johnny to read in the bedroom while he was on the phone.

There were no pleasantries to exchange. "Devon's dead."

Ambler's heart sank. He couldn't speak, too many images and memories went through his mind. He said, "Devon," the only thing he could think of to say.

"Too bad. Good dude."

"What happened?"

"A fight in the yard. He was stabbed. Word is a longtime grudge going back to the streets. When something like this happens, word goes through this place like the flu. The word gets started; soon everyone knows. Almost always, what they know is wrong." He paused. "You know these calls are bugged, right?"

Ambler said he did.

"When you coming up? This week?"

"I could." John never asked about him visiting, so his asking now seemed to be about Devon's murder. "I don't suppose you want me to bring Johnny."

After a long pause, speaking slowly, John said, "I thought about that. I think about it every day. I don't want to see him yet. I've begun writing a letter—"

"That's great. He'll—"

"Don't tell him. I'm not sure I can do it. I don't want him to think it's coming, be waiting for it, and then I don't come through. Okay? Don't tell him yet."

When Johnny came out of the bedroom, he puttered around for a moment and then asked, "Who's Devon?"

It wasn't right the kid had to deal with violent death again, twice in the same week. He was still trying to understand his mother's death, her life and death difficult for anyone, let alone a child, her child, to comprehend.

"Devon was a friend of mine when I was your age. I hadn't seen him for a long time. He went to jail, possibly for something he didn't do."

"Like my dad?"

"Your dad went to jail for something he didn't mean to do. Neither man is bad. For each of them, something went terribly wrong."

He couldn't tell how Johnny was taking this. It was a lot to swallow, not the way life was supposed to happen. He decided to keep talking until Johnny was satisfied, rather than send him off to bed to work through it on his own. So they talked. Ambler told him about his father's youth, not a great tale itself. His father and mother separating, his father leaving him alone with an incompetent mother far too often. He didn't want to spare himself in talking about the past but he didn't want to scare Johnny either, start him thinking that Ambler would desert him, too.

If he had it to do over again, he would have kept John with him. Back then, almost thirty years ago, he thought kids naturally stayed with their mothers. He was also self-absorbed, too engrossed in his own work to pay enough attention to anyone else. John wasn't a troubled kid. He did okay in school, kept off the streets. Music was his refuge.

What he'd told Johnny from the beginning, when Johnny first learned who his father was—and where he was—was that his father had killed a man accidentally, not meaning to, in a fight the other man started. Ambler believed this is what happened, though the court had not believed John's story.

John was a musician, playing in the rock and roll equivalents of honky-tonks. He'd been a drinker, a pot smoker, living the nightlife, not a gangbanger or drug dealer, not in the criminal life. He killed a man he shared an apartment with in a fight fueled by alcohol and drugs—wrestling for a gun the other man pulled on him. That was John's story. Though the police, the prosecutor, and the judge didn't believe him, Ambler did. He was stunned when his son was found guilty of murder rather than involuntary manslaughter. The look of hate John directed at him when the judge announced the verdict had burned a hole through his heart.

The look was because the advice he'd given him at a moment of crisis was wrong. That night, he'd opened his door to a wild-eyed, terrified young man. John was bruised, bleeding from the corner of his mouth, blood dried on his forehead from a cut above his eyebrow. His shirt—a white dress shirt—was ripped down the front, the buttons popped. Ambler thought he'd been mugged. John said he'd been in a fight. He needed money to get away. When Ambler tried to calm him, the boy hissed. "You don't understand, you fucking asshole! I killed somebody."

Ambler went limp. The room spun; his brain worked like an echo chamber. John's voice came from far away. Fighting back his own rising panic, Ambler got the story of what happened. He considered helping him run away but realized long before John did that he didn't have anywhere to run to. Even if he'd wanted to help John run, he didn't have enough money for him to get very far. Liz had less. After sitting with the terrified boy until dawn, Ambler came to believe that the only thing John could do was turn himself in.

"It was self-defense," he told the boy, "involuntary man-slaughter. You have no record. It will be all right."

John argued; he insisted; he begged. In the end, he followed his father's advice.

The trial was a horror. The young man presented to the judge by the prosecutor was no one Ambler recognized. Witnesses spoke against him. The dead roommate's girlfriend testified that she and the man he killed were terrified of John. There was an arrest John hadn't told his father about. No matter, Ambler was devastated by the harsh sentence—eight to 25 years. John blamed him for the outcome. Every time their eyes met, even now, Ambler saw the accusation.

When he finished, Johnny was sleepy but for unfathomable reasons, as kids' reasons often are, wanted to know more about Ambler's ex-wife, Liz, not something Ambler wanted to get into.

"She's my grandmother, right?"

"Yes."

"Where is she? When will I see her?"

Ambler didn't know. One night she called. Not so drunk, she said she was ready to talk to Johnny. A minute later she changed her mind and hung up. That was the last he heard of her. She wasn't at the phone number she'd called from. As was her custom, she'd left no forwarding address.

The phone rang, so he sent Johnny off again. As soon as he heard Mike's voice, he knew something was wrong.

"Look, Ray. If it's going to be late like this, would you please call a car service for Denise? I'll give you one we use. I'm happy to pay for it. I don't want her taking the subway this late."

Ambler was flabbergasted. "I put her in a cab, Mike. Stood next to it until it pulled away from the curb." As he said this, he had a twinge of regret, thinking he should take the blame, take some pressure off Denise. On second thought, he was right to tell Mike. He wasn't going to let her take chances with her safety, though in truth taking the subway to Woodside wasn't dangerous. Cops like Mike, who dealt with the worst humanity had to offer, got a distorted view of the world, saw evil and danger everywhere, and tended to be overprotective of their kids.

Mike's sigh came through the phone like the wayward wind. "This kid, I swear."

Ambler told him about the call from John and that Devon was dead. "You might remember I asked Paul Higgins about Devon when we first met."

Cosgrove mumbled something.

"Well, I did ask about Devon."

"Okay."

"Have you talked to Higgins yet?"

"Not yet. This murder has something to do with Paul?"

"I don't know. Devon's brother Trey was a confidential informant—"

Cosgrove didn't wait to hear the rest. "How did the guy in prison die?"

"Stabbed, a fight in the yard."

"So? What are you getting at?"

"Leila Stone was doing undercover work in the library. She was murdered in the crime fiction reading room. That's where Paul Higgins's papers are."

"This has something to do with the prison murder?"

"It might. Higgins supervised informants. One of the file boxes that was sealed was opened."

There was a silence before Cosgrove spoke. "And resealed, right? Tough for her to reseal it when she's dead. So someone was with her. I'll go along with that. From there, you make connections I don't follow."

"I asked Paul Higgins if he knew of Devon Thomas. He denied knowing anything about him."

Cosgrove grumbled and cleared his throat a couple of times, something he did when he grew impatient. "I'm sorry for your loss, Ray. I mean that, whatever the circumstances. If Paul has some thoughts on this, I'll let you know. I'm not counting on it. . . . I thought you were staying out of this investigation."

"I am. Or I was. I'm asking. I'm not investigating."

"You are, too. Remember, I'm not running this show. Everyone's not as tolerant of busybodies as I am."

"Now I'm a busybody."

Cosgrove's tone softened. "You always were, but you're an engaging sort, so I let it go."

Ambler sat for a long time after he hung up, thinking about

Paul Higgins and police informers and the murder of Devon Thomas on the heels of the murder of Leila Stone.

The next morning when he got to work, Ambler found Adele at the library table in his reading room with a file box in front of her. His first thought was she'd opened Higgins's restricted files. A quick glance told him she hadn't. If she caught his moment of doubt, she didn't let on.

"What are you doing?" he asked calmly enough, as he hung his jacket on the coatrack.

"I'm browsing through some of the boxes that aren't restricted. I hope this doesn't violate anyone's rights." The words were biting, but something in her eyes seemed playful.

He walked behind her to look over her shoulder.

She bounced around in her chair, her expression eager, a welcome change. "It's boring. Boring reports about boring meetings." She held up a handful of report forms. "They identify the informants as CI-1 and CI-17, and so on."

"Confidential informant. I want to tell you something." He sat down beside her and told her about Devon's murder.

"I'm sorry, Raymond." She grasped his forearm, leaning closer to him. Her soulful eyes searched his face. "The other night after Leila's death, when you walked me home, I told you I wanted to be alone. As soon as you were gone, I wanted you to come back."

"You could've—"

She slightly increased the pressure on his arm. "I'm too stubborn. I was mad at you." Her voice warbled, a lilt to it; a current beneath the words reached out to him, or perhaps he reached out to the current. He stood. And she stood. They faced each other for a moment. He began to open his arms but paused, waiting for her to tell him in some way what to do next. After a moment, she turned and sat down again.

"John had something to tell me he didn't want to say over the phone, so I'm taking tomorrow off to visit him."

"I'm taking a couple of days off later in the week, too. I'm going to Texas to Leila's funeral."

Ambler was surprised Adele felt close enough to Leila to want to do that, and wished he'd told her his suspicions before. Now, he had to. He touched her hand, so she'd look up at him. "You're not going to like this, and you may not believe me, and you'll get mad all over again. But I can't let you go on without telling you." He told her that he was sure Leila was a police informant who'd infiltrated the library.

Her reaction was a blank stare. "She was spying on us? You don't know that for sure, do you?" She sounded childlike in her denial.

"Before Paul Higgins retired from the policed department, he worked with confidential informants. If I'm right that Leila was an informant that might explain why she was in this room when she was murdered. She knew Paul Higgins and wanted something from his files."

"There might be another reason."

"I can't think of one. Someone came here with her or followed her here and killed her. Since the restricted file box was tampered with, you'd have to believe the killer was looking for something in those files."

Adele stood to leave. "I don't believe you. You could be wrong. You're not a hundred percent certain." She turned to face him but couldn't meet his gaze.

When she was gone, Ambler began to put the papers and calendars and reports she'd been sifting through back into the file boxes she'd taken them out of, intending to straighten things up and get back to work on the upcoming crime-fiction exhibit. Instead, Higgins's files caught his attention.

The boxes contained newspaper clippings, transcripts of phone calls, notebooks, reports from informers written by Higgins, reports from Higgins himself, and trial transcripts he guessed were for cases Higgins had worked. There were also photos and cassette tapes that could be recordings of conversations taped by a CI wearing a wire.

He began cataloging the un-embargoed files. He might find something about Leila or about Devon. At the least, the files would tell him something about Paul Higgins. Because he was taking notes for the finding aid as he went along, the job went slowly. He read only enough to identify each document as a CI report or a police report. Still, it took time, so it was early afternoon when he thought to break for lunch. As he was putting on his jacket, Mike Cosgrove appeared in his doorway.

"I've come for that box of papers that was broken into," he said.

"Did you bring a release from Higgins?"

"No." He puffed up and became blustery the way he did when he wasn't sure of the ground he was on. "I can't find him."

"What's that mean?" Ambler moved over to stand between Cosgrove and the files.

Cosgrove sighed and sat down. "He's gone. Skipped."

"Skipped?" Ambler's cell phone rang, so he answered it.

"They've booked him." David Levinson said.

"For murder?"

"No. Providing material support to a terrorist organization, Section 2339B of Title 18. If you haven't guessed, The Patriot Act."

"Where is he?"

"The Metropolitan Correction Center in lower Manhattan."

Ambler asked the attorney to arrange a visit. When he hung up, he told Cosgrove what Levinson had told him. "Why didn't they charge him with murder?"

Cosgrove shook his head. "Why isn't homicide doing the investigation?"

"I need to tell Adele about Gobi. What do you mean Higgins skipped?"

"Bailed. . . . Flew the coop. . . . In the wind. I've had suspects leave like that, with the clothes on their back, sometimes the TV running, the lights on, doors unlocked, a half a sandwich on a plate, a piece of bread in the toaster. They're gone. Solid gone."

"That's Higgins?"

Cosgrove kept his gaze on Ambler but seemed to be thinking something through. After a minute, he said, "I shouldn't tell you this. . . . You know where he used to work, Intelligence? I was thinking he might be doing something for them. He's retired but they might use him anyway, for this. So I ask them. Do they tell me? They never heard of Paul, don't know what I'm talking about. Assholes."

Ambler backed up closer to the stack of file boxes under the steps. "Harry's talking to the library's lawyers about Higgins's collection."

Mike looked longingly at the file boxes. "I'll talk to him."

As he was leaving, Ambler asked, "Will you be able to work things out with the Intelligence Division?"

Cosgrove halted in the doorway and turned. He looked puzzled and in another way he looked hurt. "I'll tell you, Ray. I've banged heads plenty of times. Seen my share of lazy or incompetent cops. Nothing like this. These guys aren't the cops I've known. Cops want to catch bad guys. That's what we do, like beagles chase rabbits. I don't know what these guys want."

Ambler found Adele at her desk and told her about Gobi's arrest. "As soon as the lawyer can set it up, I'll go see him at the detention center."

Adele's expression was strange, as if she were apologizing to him for something he didn't know about. "Maybe I should go."

"Why should you go?" It was a reaction, not a response he thought about.

She frowned. "I think he trusts me. I feel like we understand one another."

"Oh." He dropped his gaze. "Maybe we should both go."

"Maybe." She dragged out the word so it took on a different meaning. "He might be more comfortable if it were just me."

Ambler looked into her wide-eyed appeal.

"I'll tell you what he says."

He couldn't think of what to say or, really, say what he thought. It would be too embarrassing.

It was nearly three o'clock when Ambler sat down at his desk to eat the curried chicken he'd picked up from the Pakistani food cart on 43rd Street more than an hour before. The dish was cold now and kind of jellied. Before he finished eating, he had a visitor—the tall man in the overcoat he'd seen the morning Leila's body was discovered, the man Adele saw when Gobi was interrogated and again when he was arrested.

Chapter 11

"Raymond Ambler? . . . Brad Campbell." He handed Ambler a business card with a Campbell Security logo, his name, and President beneath his name. Tall and slim and somewhat rigidly erect, he carried himself with confidence that might better be described as arrogance. "I'd like to ask you some questions about the woman who was murdered in your office."

Ambler thought through some things before he answered. He didn't like Campbell's arrogance. "I'd rather talk to the police."

Campbell lifted his eyebrows ever so slightly. "Why wouldn't you answer questions about a murder, no matter who asks them?"

"Did Leila Stone work for you?"

Campbell wasn't surprised by the question, or if he was, he didn't show it. "I know who you are, Mr. Ambler." He pulled out a chair from the library table in the middle of the room, sat down, and crossed his long legs. He was supple, like a cat stretching. "I also know you're acquainted with a man named Gobi Tabrizi."

Ambler took a moment to get his footing. "You didn't answer my question."

Campbell held Ambler's gaze, as relaxed and at ease as if he were enjoying a cocktail on a Newport veranda, which, Ambler guessed, he'd done more than once. Yet beneath the suave manner, betrayed by a sliver of cunning in his eyes, was an impenetrable hardness, a ferocity you might feel from a wild animal tamed for the moment. "What were your dealings with Ms. Stone? Why was she in your office after the library was closed?" He spit out the questions one on top of the other, holding Ambler's gaze as he did. "Was she with Mr. Tabrizi?" The questioning was a kind of hammering intended to intimidate him. Clearly, Campbell was an experienced browbeater.

Ambler took his time replying, holding Campbell's gaze. "You're not the police. You don't provide security to the library. What's your interest? What was Leila Stone to you?"

Campbell's lips compressed slightly, a barely perceptible tightening of his face muscles. "You may have played detective in the past, Mr. Ambler. You're not matching wits with your friend Detective Cosgrove this time." He seemed to relax for a moment. "I suppose I shouldn't be surprised you're uncooperative."

Ambler's eyebrows went up, somewhat theatrical maybe, but he really was surprised. "What does that mean? Are you accusing me of something?"

The timbre of Campbell's voice changed to something harsher. "You were part of a group that broke into an FBI office in 1972 and stole some documents."

So that's what it was. He didn't ask Campbell how he knew about this. He'd had access to Ambler's FBI file before he stopped by for the visit. "That's a bit of leap. I wasn't charged. The stolen files, whoever stole them, showed FBI agents involved in criminal activity. They didn't push the investigation because they didn't want anyone digging deeper and finding more. They took their revenge in other ways."

Campbell absorbed his answer, thought about it for a moment, and let it go. He'd brought it up, Ambler suspected, to let him know he'd made it his business to know about Ambler's past. Campbell cleared his throat. "Your department has materials that belonged to Paul Higgins." His gaze settled on Ambler and his desk, noting the file box Ambler had been working in.

"That collection isn't open to the public."

"I'm not the public."

"It's not open to anyone. Some of the collection is embargoed. You or the police will need a court order." He appraised the man in front of him. "Why are you interested in Paul Higgins?"

Campbell's expression brightened, a kind of anticipation, like a confident pitcher waiting as a heavy hitter approached the plate. "You have a cocky attitude for a man who might be considered an accessory. Why was the murdered woman in your office?"

"I don't know."

"Interesting." Campbell's expression hardened. "You were a punk college kid, you and the other war protestors. Better than slogging through rice paddies or dying facedown in the muck. Attitudes are different now. You're naïve if you think they're not. College kids won't make you a hero for enabling terrorists." He didn't raise his voice, his expression remained placid, yet the force behind his words was unmistakable. "Sometimes you make compromises, a little less liberty for a little more safety."

"Gobi Tabrizi's liberty for my safety?"

His eyebrows went up. "You think he shares our values? Muslim fanatics don't believe in the things we believe in." He glanced slowly around him at book-lined walls that surrounded them and then settled his gaze on Ambler. "They destroy libraries, you know. Don't believe in them. That's what they've done in other countries—burned libraries right down to the desert sand."

Ambler didn't know if Campbell was trying to provoke him or believed he was tied to Gobi and both of them complicit in Leila's murder. "Gobi Tabrizi doesn't strike me as a fanatic. He's a scholar. Do you know something I don't know?"

"Not anything I want to talk to you about." He stood. His voice resounded like a confident prosecutor making the closing argument. "As of now, you're an uncooperative witness. I wonder what Detective Cosgrove will think about that." He watched Ambler and let his words sink in. "We'll be in touch with your attorneys."

Chapter 12

Mike Cosgrove found Adele at her desk in the warren of cubicles behind the main reference desk on the third floor of the library.

"It's about time you got here," she said. "How could you take so long to ask about an obvious suspect?"

He looked at the faces from the other cubicles turned toward him and gritted his teeth. "You taking over for Ray? I get you to tell me how to do my job, too?"

"Leila came to my apartment two nights before she was murdered. She was terrified because her ex-husband—who'd threatened to kill her and whom she was hiding from—found her. And no one in the police department cares? What's wrong with you?"

Cosgrove nodded. "I'm here now. Please calm down. You knew Miss Stone well? Good friends?"

Adele's response was subdued. "I thought we were. I thought I knew her. Is it true she was in the library on some undercover assignment?"

"Who told you that?"

"Raymond. Is it true?"

The question irritated Cosgrove. "How would he know?"

"I'm asking you."

Cosgrove took a deep breath and tried to smile. "The way this works, ma'am, is I ask questions. You, if you would, provide answers. I'm trying to find out who killed Miss Stone, asking you to help. Did you know this ex-husband? Do you know his name?"

Her face went blank. "No. She didn't say his name. You're the detective. Can't you find out?"

Cosgrove swallowed a couple of times and nodded even more times. "That's what I'm trying to do. How about what he looks like? Anything about him?"

"No. I never saw him. She didn't describe him."

He tried to sound patient. "Can you tell me anything about him?"

"She was afraid of him."

"I got that."

He was frustrated, not mad at Adele. He liked her. She was a scrapper. And if the Stone woman's ex-husband was in the picture, he was a suspect, a no-brainer, and he would have been on it long before this if it were up to him. The Intelligence Division didn't investigate homicide. So they might not be up on some things. But you didn't have to know much to make an estranged husband a suspect in an ex-wife's murder. They discounted the ex-husband because the Stone murder took place in the library, and why would he kill her in the library. Okay. But you still talk to him.

His assignment today, from Intelligence by way of his chief, wasn't to ask Adele about Leila Stone's ex-husband. That was a ruse to disarm Adele. They wanted him to find out what she knew about Leila Stone, to find out if she knew anything they didn't want her to know. The Stone woman might have slipped and told Adele something she shouldn't have, or Adele might have discovered by accident something she wasn't supposed to know. Ray suspected Leila was an informant, a plant, before she was killed. Adele didn't. He was the one they should worry about.

Now, she had a wary look in her eyes. "I thought you'd want to know what she said about being scared. I'm trying to remember if there was anything else."

He nodded. "I do want to know about that, Adele. I need to ask about some other things, too." He paused and regrouped. "Suppose you tell me what happened the night Miss Stone came to your apartment. From the beginning. Everything you remember."

Adele told him what Leila had told her during the late-night visit, that Leila had run into her ex-husband accidentally and that he'd found her apartment. "She wouldn't let me call the police. She said she knew someone who could stop him, who could protect her from him."

"Did she tell you who this person was?"

"No."

"How well did you know Miss Stone?"

"The more I think about it, the more I realize I didn't know much about her, only what she wanted to tell me. She showed up to work at the library. She asked a lot of questions." Adele paused for a moment. "She was from Texas, a town south of Dallas. Harry told me the name of the town and I found it on Google. I'm going to her funeral. Perhaps I'll find out more about her—and her ex-husband—then."

Cosgrove went over with Adele everything she remembered about Leila Stone, who her other friends were, what her interests were, anyone she talked about, any place she talked about. He didn't learn much. He suspected he could find out more about Leila Stone from the Intelligence Division or from Brad Campbell.

Adele's expression was quizzical. "Didn't you get her employment records from the library?"

"Not yet." An embarrassing admission for a detective. If he were listening to himself describe his investigation, he'd think he was incompetent. Intelligence grabbed the employment records. They treated him like an errand boy.

One of their CIs gets whacked, maybe by someone she was monitoring. They don't want a light shining on their operation, so they need a quick resolution. A full-scale murder investigation brings on the press, so they keep homicide on the sidelines. The last thing they want is someone watching them when they're watching everyone else.

As he drove downtown, Cosgrove was half aware of the midday clogged streets. Usually the traffic drove him nuts; he tried to fight it. Today he wasn't in a rush. Poking along, bumper to bumper, gave him time to think.

Before he'd gotten far, a text message interrupted his reverie; it was from the Chief of Detectives Office and told him to call Brad Campbell—the last thing he needed. Not fucking likely he'd find out anything useful from Campbell, but there you go.

He made the call. "Mr. Campbell? Mike Cosgrove here." He sounded deferential, and it pissed him off. Like calling on royalty. "I got a text to call you."

"My office is at 55 Water Street. I'd like you to stop over this afternoon. Pull up in front. There's valet parking. Tell them you're there to see me."

Cosgrove bristled. "I'm not sure I can make it his afternoon, sir. I'd have to—"

"I cleared it with your chief. Within the hour, say?"

Cosgrove grumbled and put his phone down on the seat beside him. A half hour later, he navigated through the narrow canyon-like streets of lower Manhattan to pull up in front of a massive office building. Not the tallest building in the city, he understood 55 Water to be the largest office building in terms of space, spread out over four blocks, or what were blocks before the building went up back in the seventies. Bradley Campbell Security was on the thirty-ninth floor. The elevator to reach that part of the building was down a long marble hallway from the lobby he entered, so he walked down a long hallway with a security guard, whose uniform logo read Campbell Security.

"You know the boss?" Cosgrove asked as they walked.

"Sam? I know Sam." The guard was Latino, Dominican probably, with a strong accent.

"The big boss, Campbell."

The guard looked at him blankly.

It wasn't so long ago when you walked into a building, on Wall Street or anywhere else, and you ran into an elevator starter if you ran into anyone at all, and then the elevator operator. So they replaced the elevator operators with self-run elevators. That worked until every building needed security; now there was a guard at every door.

He wasn't much of a political thinker. What might be a political thing for him, no one talked about. It was private police forces, like Campbell Security. It was okay when you had night watchmen, old guys retired from the cops making a few extra bucks in retirement, stumbling half-asleep around a warehouse or an empty office building at night. Now, companies like Campbell's, with thousands of mercenaries and stashes of armaments that would be the envy of small to mid-sized countries, had their noses into everything in the city, in the country, in the world. Something was wrong with that. Private armies made him uneasy.

Campbell came out of his office when the receptionist announced Cosgrove. He wore a pinstriped suit, a white shirt, a red tie tight against his throat; tanned, athletic, not one of his brown hairs out of place, he looked like a *GQ* model. What kept him from being a pretty boy were the lines and creases in a rugged face and the hard expression in his eyes, friendly maybe, lively at any rate, no uncertainty, not a lot of sympathy, the eyes of a veteran cop. He'd watched a few people die.

"Thanks for coming over." He put his hand lightly on Cosgrove's shoulder, steering him toward his office. "I don't want you think I'm stepping on your investigation. Can I get you a coffee?" He gestured to the receptionist.

So the former chief was respectful of another cop's terrain, one tough cop to another. Bullshit. How long since the murder, a week? Now, for the first time he talks to the homicide guy who caught the case?

"We got lucky right away." Campbell sat down in a leather armchair in front of his desk and waved Cosgrove toward an equally formidable leather couch. "He was on a watch list."

"Oh?" Cosgrove was distracted by the receptionist, a pretty, dark-haired girl, wearing a business outfit that included a fairly short black skirt and high heel shoes. She smiled beatifically as she placed his cup of coffee on the glass table in front of him. "Just black," he said before she could ask about cream and sugar. She met his gaze with her pretty dark eyes. "Thanks," Cosgrove said. For some reason he winked, as if she and he had a secret from her boss.

Campbell seemed not to notice the arrival, presence, or departure of the young woman. "A Palestinian. His father was a leader in Al Fattah, a founder of the PLO. This guy's probably a member—"

"Probably?"

A flash of irritation darkened Campbell's eyes. "They don't keep membership lists. Member or not, he's got the bloodline. We're not sure what he was doing here—if there's a sleeper cell.

We don't know what Leila found on him. He got to her before she gave anything to us."

Cosgrove sipped his coffee and waited. The coffee was good, like you get in the yuppie coffee places. "So what do you want from me? I don't have anything. I don't know what they found at the murder scene. I haven't interviewed the suspect."

"You interviewed a woman at the library." Campbell's expression hardened. "You talk to the wise guy librarian, Ambler."

Cosgrove absorbed the rebuke. "The woman I interviewed, Adele Morgan, had no idea what the murdered woman was up to in the library." He met Campbell's gaze. "Ray Ambler made her, though."

Only the slightest flutter of an eyelash indicated Campbell's irritation. "Leila's body was found in his office. He seems to be pals with the suspect. He's got a radical history, you know."

Cosgrove placed his coffee cup on the glass table in front of him. "You think he had something to do with the murder?"

"He arranged a lawyer for the suspect. A Commie lawyer. I assume you wouldn't discuss the case with him." Campbell raised his eyebrows, a kind of emphasis.

Cosgrove caught himself before he exploded. He picked up his cup and tried to take a sip, but his hand was shaking so he put it down. "You brought me in here to tell me who to talk to? Tell me over the fucking phone." He tried again to hold back, couldn't. He stood. "First, I know how to do my job. Second, Ray didn't murder anyone and if he did wouldn't leave the body in his office. Finally, it doesn't make any difference if I talk to him because I don't know a fucking thing about the case."

Campbell sat with his long legs crossed smoking a cigarette.

Cosgrove braced himself, feet apart, next to the glass coffee table. "You're not a deputy chief anymore. You're not my boss. I'll talk to whoever the fuck I want." He headed toward the door. "You got a complaint take it to the Civilian Review Board."

When he got to the doorway, he stopped and turned. "Where's Paul Higgins?"

Campbell's eyes widened. He paused, the cigarette on its way to his lips. "What do you mean?" He lost his edge. Like you'd been punching at him and nothing registered; he was impervious. Then you threw a shot, and you see it. A flinch. You'd landed. He was hit, hurt.

"I can't find him, thought he might be doing something with you."

Campbell stared. "You can't find Paul? How long? You know where to look?"

Cosgrove rolled his eyes. "I guess not, since I haven't found him. If you happen to run into him, ask him to give me a call."

"Yeah. Sure." Campbell was off in his own world, no more aware of Cosgrove than he had been of the receptionist delivering coffee.

Chapter 13

Ambler visited his son at the prison in Sha-wangunk every month, often twice a month, and had since John was sentenced. Each visit was heart wrenching, arriving was bad, leaving worse. The expression in his son's eyes each time he left—a kind of helplessness and at the same time expectation—was an accusation, no attempt to relieve Ambler of the guilt he felt for his part in creating the boy's chaotic, destructive childhood.

John had earned tickets to the honor room, where visiting was less awkward than in the main room. Seated across from one another at a small cafeteria table, they talked for a few minutes about day-to-day life in prison, John flip and nonchalant, implying he could handle it, while Ambler and most people probably couldn't. And perhaps he was right.

Ambler told him what Johnny had been up to, how he did in school. "He doesn't read as much as I'd like," Ambler said.

"Neither did I." John smiled.

"He does like music." Ambler didn't want to bring up again

that the boy was desperate to see his father, so he said, "You didn't want to talk about Devon on the phone."

"The phones are bugged. What I didn't say . . ." He looked over his shoulder at the guard behind him who stood like one of the carriage horses along Central Park West; you couldn't tell if it was asleep standing up or awake and dumbly awaiting its next job. "I heard someone took out a hit on Devon."

"A hit?"

"Someone from the outside hired someone inside to kill him."

"Heard from where?"

John shook his head. "It's what I heard. No reason for anyone in here to kill Devon. He was the grand old man of the joint. Out of nowhere, this guy has a beef with him?"

"Who on the outside?"

John's eyes sparkled with amusement. "I thought you'd know. Devon told me you were going to get him out of here."

Ambler looked steadily at his son. "He said he didn't commit the murder he went to prison for. I haven't found anything that would help. And now it's too late." He told John about the murder at the library, the Paul Higgins collection, and Higgins's possible connection to Devon.

"Paul Higgins was a narc?"

"He was what they call a handler; he worked with the informers—confidential informants; they reported to him. Sometimes they infiltrated the mob, sometimes drug dealers, in some cases political groups. The woman murdered in the library was monitoring Muslims doing research. I don't know if she had ever worked with Paul Higgins. Higgins denied knowing anything about Devon. I didn't necessarily believe him."

After a moment, John said, "You think your guy Higgins killed the woman? Took out a contract on Devon?"

"I have no reason to think either of those things." He told John about Gobi Tabriz's arrest.

"You don't think he killed her?"

Ambler shrugged. "He might have. She was spying on him. So far, there's no evidence he killed her. I started looking into the killing Devon was in prison for, barely got started, and Devon is murdered. Quite a coincidence, even before you told me it was a contract killing. Tell me about the man who killed him?"

"Hector Perez." John shook his head. "He's with the Muslims."

"Perez? A Muslim?"

"A convert. It happens a lot in here. Muslims are good to be in with, protection."

Ambler let that sink in. Muslim? Could Gobi have ordered Devon killed?

"Are you still here?"

John's question startled him out of his thoughts. "Sorry. I'm trying to figure something out. Do you know how it happened, Devon's murder?"

John shook his head.

"No one saw what happened?"

John smiled. "In here, you don't see what happens, especially not a killing."

"I wish I knew for sure the order to kill Devon came from the outside."

A guard came toward them and John stood. "I'll find out more. It shouldn't have happened that way with Devon. Perez needs to watch someone doesn't take him out." John stopped and turned as the guard approached him. "Tell the kid I'm thinking of him. Tell him I want him to do good."

Chapter 14

Adele was nervous—and excited. She'd convinced Raymond she should be the one to visit Gobi. Now she wasn't sure why she did. Was she kidding herself? Was it an attraction to Gobi she didn't want to admit to feeling? He was intriguing. But this wasn't important now. It was a silly thought anyway. The important thing was to help him get out of jail.

The Metropolitan Correction Center on Park Row in lower Manhattan looked like an armed fortress—bleak and gray—drab gray walls, gray metal or plastic furniture, everything dull, dehumanizing, and depressing, no color, no comfort, everything impersonal, and hard, unfeeling, uncaring. It took longer to go through the processing than she expected. Rude, bored clerks acted like something was wrong with her if she had to visit someone in jail. Everything about the place and the process was menacing, disturbing.

When she finally got to speak with Gobi, she saw the strain of what he was going through had beaten him down. The confident, bemused, fearsome look was gone. His shoulders were slumped, head bowed, circles under his eyes. He wore an orange jump suit that seemed to take away his personality. He looked dispirited, fragile, scared.

"I'm so sorry this is happening to you." Adele said. "It's awful and unfair. Have you contacted your embassy?"

"I want to thank you and Mr. Ambler for arranging the lawyer," he said. "I dared not hope for such kindness. Mr. Levinson asked about the embassy as well. I wasn't sure. The political situation is complicated."

"Are you okay? You're not mistreated, are you?"

"I'm fine."

"Do you know what you're charged with?"

Silence and then, "Something political, I think."

"Do you need anything? Can I help in any way?"

"I appreciate your concern."

She wasn't getting through to him. His tone was reserved, polite, formal, as if he were speaking to an official. And why shouldn't he be careful? She was a stranger. Why had she thought otherwise? She should have let Raymond handle this. He knew about people in prison and what to do. What did she know?

"You don't have to answer questions." She paused. "I guess it's the lawyer's job to tell you about that." Gobi gave no indication he had anything to say, so she kept talking. "Is there anyone I can contact for you?"

"My family is in Syria. It's better for now they not know."

"Can I bring you anything? I don't know what we're allowed to bring. Do you have anything to read?"

"There are books in the library. There are Muslim prayers. The first day or two—I'm not sure how many days—were not good. I was alone, moved from place to place, interrogated. I had no idea what would happen. Now it's better. Thank you for coming. Thank you for your concern." His eyes met hers, so hard to read what she saw in them, fear, sadness, but something else. Rage?

"Raymond thinks Leila was spying on you."

He nodded.

"You think so, too?"

"The interrogators said she monitored my research. They asked many times what she found." He shrugged.

"What do they think you were doing?"

"I told them I'm a scholar." His expression was pained. "They have information from when I was a student in Syria—organizations I belonged to, activities they said were anti-American."

Adele didn't know how to respond, so she waited through a long silence.

"The political situation is complicated." He paused. "I need to tell you something. I hope you'll understand. You'll find out soon from my interrogators."

He waited for Adele to say something. She knew he waited and felt tongue-tied because she didn't know what to say. She nodded.

"My passport is Syrian. I'm Palestinian." His eyes searched hers. "I'm in the United States as a Syrian, so it's easier in this country to say I'm Syrian. Palestinians travel on different passports—Jordanian, Egyptian, Syrian. Palestine cannot issue passports. Our country is occupied."

Once again here was someone who wasn't who he seemed to be, deceiving her. "Are you here illegally?"

"No." He glanced around uneasily. "I want to ask you for something. The thing I am asking you to do might make me more suspicious in your mind. It's a great deal to ask, for you to take me into your confidence, as I have done with you."

"You can ask," Adele said. "I guess I feel that you won't mislead me." Did she really believe this? After Leila's betrayal, why wouldn't she toughen up, become more cynical, distrust until people prove themselves trustworthy? She had more reservations after Gobi made his request. She said yes because she didn't know how to say no.

The favor was to retrieve something from his apartment in Bay Ridge, a section of Brooklyn, in an Arab neighborhood east of Fifth Avenue. Adele knew Fifth Avenue as a child when it was lined with Scandinavian markets, Italian restaurants, and Irish bars. She went there that evening as Gobi requested, to do what he'd asked her to do. On her way from the subway to the address he'd given her, she walked past Halal meat markets, Mediterranean restaurants, clothing stores selling kaftans, hijabs, and head scarves; on the sidewalk, she passed women in traditional Muslim dress, men speaking what she assumed was Arabic, young girls wearing hijab and niqab.

The buzz on the street was the same as any neighborhood in the city, everyone in a hurry, bent on their own business. The street felt safe, not friendly exactly but not threatening, so she thought if she needed to she could stop someone to ask directions or advice, like which way to the subway, or is there a drug store near here, which there was.

The brick apartment building she went to off Fifth Avenue was worn but not rundown, five stories maybe, four apartments per floor, clean, not spiffy and shiny, a rental building that hadn't been updated; nothing in the neighborhood had been updated, the developers not venturing into Bay Ridge yet. She rang the bell under the mailbox and waited nervously. She should have called. What if his roommate wasn't home? It was a long trek, almost an hour, and she was leaving the next morning for Texas. The door in front of her buzzed, so she opened it.

"Who is it, please?" an accented male voice called from a couple of floors up the stairs.

"A friend of Gobi's," Adele said. She looked at the name she'd written and hoped she'd pronounce it correctly. "Are you Aquib Quadir?"

"Yes. Please come up."

"Would you like tea, please?" The man, who was young, slight, and bookish-looking down to his horn-rimmed glasses, ushered her to a seat on the couch. He pulled down a teapot and two small and ornate glass cups without handles from a cabinet. The cups were delicate, patterned in red and trimmed in gold.

"Gobi asked me to get some things of his from your apartment," Adele said. "I hope you don't mind."

Aquib busily arranged the cups and their accoutrements. "A very disturbing situation." He fussed with the cups and didn't look at her. "I don't know what to do. Gobi and I share the apartment. I don't know him well. I hope this is a misunderstanding."

He placed a small, glass cup on a small table in front of the couch she sat on, another cup at the far side of the table along with a bowl of sugar and a bowl of mint leaves. Engrossed in the ritual, he seemed to find in it peace in turbulent times. He asked if he might prepare the tea for her. She said yes, regretting it as she watched him dump a shovelful of sugar into the cups. He tasted his and seemed satisfied, so she took a small sip of hers. It tasted like sugar syrup.

She was tempted to ask him about Gobi, until she had second thoughts. Aquib was younger, more innocent seeming than Gobi, with close-cropped black hair, black eyes, a trimmed and shaped black beard. He spoke softly, carried himself gently, politely, on the border of obsequiousness. She decided to ask about him.

He was Syrian; he told her—not Palestinian, Syrian, he said when she asked—studying engineering at Brooklyn College. His family had lived in lower Manhattan and then Bay Ridge for generations.

"Gobi asked that I get some files from his room and that I

keep his laptop for him." She tried to sound confident to ward off the misgivings she expected Aquib to have about the request.

He surprised her by getting up and walking to one of the bedrooms off the living room. He opened the door. "This is his room. I don't go in. I don't know what's there. You can find what you're looking for."

Gobi's room was spare and neat, a double bed, made-up, an armchair, a desk with a laptop, a stack of file folders, some loose papers. A bookcase leaned against one wall, half-filled with books, stacks of papers on some of the shelves. Gobi told her the papers he wanted and the laptop would be on the desk.

A window overlooked the street. On the other wall was a closet. Gobi told her that in the closet she'd find a leather bag she could use to carry the papers and computer. She pushed through some sports jackets, slacks, and dress shirts on hangers.

The jackets were of a heavier material than American jackets, the cloth of the coats she associated with Europe, Eastern Europe. The one strange garment was a military jacket of some kind of thick, stiff, dark green material, brass buttons, and some insignias she didn't recognize. The closet smelled faintly of cigarette smoke and a pleasant incense.

On the floor of the closet, she found a worn, lopsided, brown leather bag, shaped like a gym bag and like the suit coats it had the flavor of Eastern Europe or old Europe, the kind of valise you saw on trains in spy movies about World War II. She took it out of the closet and opened it on the bed. Some shirts were bundled up in the bottom of the bag. She began to take the bundle out before she put the papers and computer in, thinking it incongruous that the papers and computer and the clothing be in the same bag.

She stopped when she felt something wrapped in the clothing—something heavy for its size. She unfolded everything enough to recognize the barrel of a handgun. Her heart skipped.

She crumpled the clothes into a lump, pushed them back into the bag, and stuffed the files and the computer in on top of them. Halfway finished, she whipped around to make sure Aquib hadn't seen anything, took a few deep breaths to calm down, brushed her hair back from her eyes, took a quick glance at herself in a mirror over the bureau and thought she looked a fright.

On the slow and jerky R train back to Manhattan, she tried to understand what was happening. It was surprising the FBI, the police, or whoever they were hadn't searched Gobi's apartment. Yet his arrest was so strange, it might be they didn't want to push their luck and search without a warrant.

A good citizen, she supposed, would turn over what she found, especially the gun, to the police. She was a good citizen, law-abiding and all that, wasn't she? Well, almost all the time. Pretty much, she sealed her fate when she agreed to take things from the apartment for Gobi. You'd have to think he asked her to do this to keep the police from finding something, including the gun.

Certainly, she'd taken on more than she'd bargained for. If it had been Raymond who visited Gobi, he wouldn't be smuggling papers and guns from under the nose of the police. She didn't know if she should tell him. This was her problem, not his. She hadn't asked for his advice and he hadn't given it. Still, he had more experience with situations like this.

By the time she got off the train at 57th Street, she'd decided she wouldn't do anything for the moment. She'd gathered some things of Gobi's. She'd put those things in a closet and hang onto them until she talked to him again when she got back from Texas.

Chapter 15

"What you look like," said McNulty, "is a guy crying in his beer. I usually let the guy go right ahead without butting in. Your case is different."

"Why is that?" Ambler realized he actually had been staring into his glass of beer, so he looked up at the bartender, surprised by the sadness he found looking back at him.

"Sometimes it feels like a guy needs to talk," the bartender said.

"It's been a bad couple of days since I saw you last." Ambler told him about visiting his son in prison to talk about Devon's murder.

McNulty poured them both shots of Irish whiskey. "May he find peace," he said, and slugged down his shot.

Ambler drank his shot as well. "It's not easy." He stopped, not sure how to say what he wanted to say. "Devon watched out for me when I was a kid. He was smarter than I was about the streets . . . and that's what you needed to be smart about when you were a kid. He called us partners, Butch and Sundance from the movie, never hinted he was smarter or tougher; always we were partners."

McNulty nodded once or twice. He was easy to talk to. It's what made him a good bartender, what brought him the loyal regulars.

Ambler told him what Devon had told him about his brother and the murder of Richard Wright.

McNulty emptied the remains of a coffee cup into the sink, rinsed the cup out, and after a glance over his shoulder, filled it from the beer tap. "The poor bastard. His brother was a rat?" Unasked, he took Ambler's beer mug and refilled it. He wiped the bar in front of Ambler before replacing the coaster and putting the mug on it. "This guy murdered in prison, now that he's dead, you think you owe him to find out what happened anyway. And you think the ex-cop who donated his papers and is now on the lam knows more than he let on."

"Two people are dead. As far as I know, they never met, never had anything to do with one another. What they have in common is undercover work. Devon's brother was a confidential informant years ago who, Devon said, took the rap for a murder he didn't commit, until Devon took the rap for him. Leila Stone was a confidential informant monitoring Gobi Tabrizi, and perhaps others in the library. Tabrizi, the man arrested for the murder, had more reason to kill her than anyone else we know about. Adele thinks he's innocent. I'm not so sure."

"That Arab guy was in here with you and her? Rugged. Dark. Handsome. The kind of guy women go for?"

Ambler felt himself flush, heat in his cheeks. He looked down at the beer so he wouldn't look at McNulty.

"Hoping," McNulty said.

Ambler laughed. "She was spying on him for a reason."

"So the Arab killed the woman for spying on him. Then, he would have had your friend in prison murdered . . . for what reason?"

"The prisoner who killed Devon is a Muslim. If Gobi did have a reason to have Devon killed, it wouldn't be difficult . . . through a network—"

They were silent for a few moments. McNulty took a slug of beer. "This union guy who was murdered back in the day, the truckers union? Pop would know about that. Not much happened with unions in the city in his day he didn't know about."

Ambler placed a credit card on the bar to pay his tab.

"Where you going?" McNulty asked.

"Back to the library. I have an exhibit to put together and I keep getting distracted. The Paul Higgins collection started all this trouble. It arrives at the library; Leila is murdered. I ask Higgins about Devon. Devon is murdered." He signed his credit card slip. "Ask your father. The murdered man's name was Richard Wright."

Ambler stayed until midnight sifting through the boxes of papers and memorabilia Paul Higgins thought worth handing on to posterity. Strangely, at least strangely to Ambler, Higgins held on to things he'd accumulated as a child: report cards, citations that went with trophies for playing PAL baseball. Higgins played PAL baseball in the Bronx, not so many years before he and Devon played in Brooklyn. Whatever few citations and awards Ambler won were long gone. He wondered what Devon might have left behind. He had no idea what, or even whom, Devon left behind.

Higgins kept his discharge papers from the Marines, including a letter of commendation from a commanding officer and an insignia that read U.S. Marines Military Police with the Semper Fi logo in the middle. The most interesting discovery was a packet of letters from his younger sister, Maureen, a dozen or so letters she'd written to him when he was in Vietnam.

The letters were chatty, about her teenage friends and enemies, complaints about their father and mother and the unfairness of life. Ambler sifted through them, skimming for a word or phrase that might jump out. The return address on the last few letters was from M. O'Brien in Woodside, New York, signed Love, Sis. What did it tell him? Higgins's sister married a guy named O'Brien and lived in Woodside, which was then an Irish neighborhood and still was to some degree. She might still live there some forty years later. Some people stayed in the same house their entire adult lives.

Sometimes, the simplest things are the most useful. He got a phone book off his shelf. It was a couple of years old, but he found a Michael O'Brien on 56th Street in Queens. The next afternoon, Ambler left work early, caught the Flushing Line 7 train beneath the library and climbed down from the elevated station at 61st Street and Roosevelt Avenue a half hour later. He stood for a moment at a busy intersection in front of down-to-earth diner named Stop Inn to get his bearings and then headed for 56th Street. The block the O'Briens' might still live on was lined with brick attached houses and brick steps leading to the front doors.

A woman's voice with an echoing memory of the Bronx answered his knock with a question.

"A friend of Paul's," he said.

"What's your name?"

"Ambler. Ray Ambler."

"How do you know my brother?"

While her tone wasn't combative, it did have a no-nonsense edge. He didn't know if he should lie. How would she know who her brother's friends were? It was easy to get trapped with lies, so he thought better of it. "We're working on a project together."

This probably wouldn't be enough for her; at least it was an answer.

The words were hardly out of his mouth before she asked, "Are you a cop?"

He answered without thinking. "No. I'm a librarian."

The woman answered with a hoarse chortle. "A librarian figures. Paulie spent half his life in the library when we were kids." She unbolted the door.

Maureen Higgins had the rough edges and tough veneer of a lifelong working class city woman, and made no apologies for it. In the doorway before ushering him in, she appraised Ambler, seeming to judge that he was more or less harmless.

"Sit down," she said. "Would you like a beer?"

He thought about it for a moment before saying yes. She brought him a can of Budweiser and didn't ask if he'd like a glass. For herself, she brought a can of Diet Pepsi. When he looked at it, she nodded toward the beer can. "I can't stand the stuff. It ruined my mother's life." She paused to take a sip of her Pepsi. "No problem for you to drink it. Don't get me wrong. Unless you're going to go home and beat your wife."

In the small living room, everything was in place, nothing modern, the furniture comfortable looking, not worn or frayed, but from another era, more photos than books on the bookcases, on the centerpiece wall unit the few books edged out by ceramic knickknacks, mostly owls of various shapes, sizes, and colors.

"You've lived here quite a while, I imagine," he said.

"More than forty years." Her eyes were misty but with sadness not regret. "Long enough to raise a family and bury a husband." She paused, maybe chasing down memories, maybe chasing them away. "So Paulie disappears and everyone comes to me looking for him."

Ambler felt a jolt of something that told him what would come next. "Someone else was here asking about your brother?"

"The police. Twice. One was a nice guy, a detective, journeyman cop; you could tell."

"Cosgrove?"

"Right. He said to call him Mike."

"The other one?"

"I didn't like him. Stuck up. Condescending, is that what you call it? Thinks he's better than you."

"Tall? Thin? Expensively dressed? Perhaps smoked cigarettes?"

"That's him." Her eyes bored into his. "You sure you ain't a cop? How do you know these guys, and my brother?"

Ambler took a sip of beer. "I guess you don't know where Paul is."

"He's hard to keep track of. Always was." Something in her tone, a glint in her eyes, hinted she knew more than she was saying. "Neither of the detectives said why they were looking for him. Like you, they were friends." A slight smile and her penetrating gaze made her words an indictment. When he didn't say anything, she said, "Seems to me if you were all such good friends, he would've told you where he was going."

Ambler liked Maureen O'Brien, nee Higgins, and he believed she knew where her brother was. He made an educated guess. "Things were tough when you were young and Paul looked after you, protected you, right?"

"If you know my brother, you know that's him. Stood up to the bullies, took care of the little ones. Our home life wasn't great. The old man worked at a printing plant. He came home, filthy, ink-stained, ate dinner, sat in an easy chair in the living room, and drank cans of Ballantine Ale until he was in stupor. On Friday nights, he brought home a bottle of whiskey to drink with the Ballantine Ale. On those nights, he slapped my mother around, until Paulie got big enough to stop him."

Ambler nodded, as if in approval.

"I got married and moved here to Queens when Paul was in Vietnam. The old man died not long after that and Paul got a hardship discharge to take care of my mother. When he came home, he joined the cops. My husband Michael was a cop, too. But he and Paul never got along. No fight or anything, just different people. For Michael, NYPD was a job, same as if he punched a clock in a factory. For Paulie, it was something else. Gung-ho, I guess you'd call it. He got on Michael's nerves." She stopped talking and looked at Ambler expectantly.

He told her why he was looking for her brother.

"So you're not a cop. You're the mystery novel expert on the case?" She laughed, holding up her hand to stop his protestation. "Go on with you." She stood and beckoned for him to follow to the next room, the dining room, one entire wall of which was a bookshelf, packed with books. "Mysteries," she said. "I've a bit of a collection myself; I read two or three a week now since I retired, at least on the weeks I don't have the grandkids."

She made tea and served it with ham sandwiches on white bread, along with a raisin bread she called Irish bread. "You think Paulie killed that woman?"

"I don't know." Ambler munched on his sandwich.

"He's killed men as a cop, in the war more than once." She was thoughtful, looking at a sandwich on the plate in front of her, not eating. "The war made him a hard person. He came back different—"

"Angry."

"Not angry so much as hard, untouchable, unfeeling. He was never a softie, even as a kid. After he came back, nothing moved him. Things would get other people sad he didn't feel, or if he felt, he didn't show it. I guess that made you tough as a cop, not feeling sorry for anyone. Anyone he went up against got what they had coming. My husband didn't take pleasure in other people's misfortune." She picked up her sandwich, examined it closely, put it down. "My brother had to wear the white hat. He wouldn't be a bad guy for anything. I don't see him murdering someone."

She met Ambler's gaze and held it a long time. She knew what he was after. "Uncle Dan in Boston, my father's kid brother, he's a retired cop, too, a lot like Paulie, a good few years older." The expression in her eyes was sorrowful. "He didn't ask me not to tell anyone where he was. I don't know he went there. I'm not worried. You'll find him and find out he didn't kill her."

On the train ride back to Manhattan, Ambler called Mike Cosgrove and told him Paul Higgins might be in Boston. He also told him Brad Campbell had been in Queens questioning Paul's sister.

Chapter 16

Leila's real name was Susan Brown, Adele learned from Mike Cosgrove before she left for Granbury, Texas, the small town south of Dallas where Leila's—now Susan's—funeral would be held. In the cab to LaGuardia, she wondered why she was doing this. Last night, she smuggled papers and a gun out of Gobi Tabrizi's apartment. Today, she headed to Texas to the funeral of a murder victim, where she might run into the murderer himself. Raymond had done this kind of thing for years. For her, even a couple of short years ago she could not have imagined doing anything like this.

The drive to Granbury from the Dallas/Fort Worth airport took an hour and a-half, through some of the flattest land she'd ever seen. She went straight to the funeral parlor and found there wouldn't be a viewing, only the funeral the next day. The funeral director told her where she might find Susan Brown's father.

The small, one-story house she stopped in front of was the length and breadth of a house trailer, set back from the road on a lot of weeds and clumps of untended grass. The man who opened the door to her was wizened if anyone ever was, with a tiny mop of wispy gray hair, a long, thin face, and a few discolored teeth, a walking symbol of a hardscrabble life. The saddest thing was the dull expression in his eyes, barely registering her presence when he opened the door and looked at her.

"I was a friend of your daughter, Susan. I'm so sorry for your loss."

He nodded.

She waited for him to say something. When he didn't, she asked if she could come in. He moved slowly out of the way, so she could pass, closed the door behind her, and followed her to a tiny living room with a linoleum floor, a stuffed chair, and a couch. As soon as they were seated, she began to tell him about Leila in New York but stopped because he didn't seem interested. When she asked about his daughter's life in Texas, he didn't have much to say. It was as if he didn't know her well or perhaps he wasn't used to speaking. Some men were like that. They didn't say much. He sat there waiting, waiting for her to leave probably. Still, she kept trying.

"Susan's mother? She's not here?"

"In Dallas."

Oh, so what did that mean? Shopping? Moved out years ago or yesterday? "Leila—I mean Susan—did she tell you much about her work in New York?"

"I don't know what she did."

Adele tried to smile. "Would her mother know more about her? Will she be back soon?"

He shook his head. "She left a long time ago. I raised Susan."

"By yourself? That must have been difficult. Does she have brothers or sisters?"

"No. I raised her till she graduated high school. She left for Dallas. I don't know what she did after that."

"You didn't stay in touch?"

"No."

"Did you go to her wedding?"

"Wasn't invited."

"Do you know her husband's name? Her married name?"

He shook his head.

Adele was stumped. Had she come this whole way for nothing? She wasn't going to find out anything at all about Leila's past? That wasn't possible. She'd get something out of this old fart if she had to shake it out of him. She wasn't leaving until he told her something useful or dragged her out the door.

"Do you remember when she left Dallas for New York?"

He didn't.

"She must have told you something. She never wrote to you? You don't know anything about your daughter's life over the last fifteen years? Not a Christmas card?" Something finally struck a chord. Some life came into the expression in his eyes. She watched him wrestle with his memory. "You didn't save any letters or cards she might have sent over the years?"

With some difficulty, he hoisted himself out of the chair he'd sunk into. "Some years back she left off some boxes of her things for me to keep for her. She said she'd be back for them. I put them away in her old bedroom."

"Are the boxes still there?" Adele tried to keep the eagerness out of her voice.

"I s'pose so." He walked toward the back of the house. She wasn't invited but followed anyway.

The bedroom was tiny, hardly a room at all, a quarter the size of Adele's tiny bedroom in New York. The floor was also linoleum, the walls green, faded almost to white, a tiny window was too high to see anything out of but a leafless tree limb and a piece of the sky. A child's bed was pushed against one wall. On it were three moving boxes.

"Have you opened the boxes?"

The old man had stepped into the room and stood next to the wall opposite the bed. He looked at the boxes on the bed as if he'd never seen them before. "Nope. Never looked at them since the delivery guy dropped them off."

"You don't remember when?" Adele stood in the doorway. "Could it have been when she was leaving Dallas for New York? Could she have left her husband, dropped off these things, and gone to New York to get away from her husband?" Adele asked the questions as if she were asking Leila's father. Really she was asking herself, thinking out loud. This time he answered.

"Might be. A man came looking for her not long after she left the boxes."

"Her husband? Her ex-husband?"

"Didn't say. Told him she was gone."

"Did you tell him where?"

"I didn't know where."

Once again, someone would let her look through someone else's possessions, as if she had a perfect right to do it. Like Gobi's housemate in Queens, Leila's father had no objection to her opening Leila's boxes and searching through them. It was amazing. Some people didn't know how to say no. The first box had clothes, blouses and summer dresses. Maybe they weren't appropriate for New York or she'd grown too old for them by the time she could send for them. They were girlish. The second box was the one she wanted. Notebooks, diaries, bills, and photos, some of her wedding. She didn't recognize the man in the photo. Yet her heart stood still when she looked at the tall, broad-shouldered, redheaded, cocky man standing beside Leila the bride. She put the photo aside and kept digging, pretty sure she'd find something to pin him down.

As she dug through the possessions Leila left behind, she was aware that what she searched through was not so different than what she might find in any of the boxes in the manuscripts and

archives collections. Leila wasn't a writer, so no actual manuscripts; aside from that, it wasn't so different, the things people
save and collect in their lifetimes. For others, all they possessed
got thrown out, so in a way they disappear from history, especially if they didn't have children or a family that would keep
some memory of them. For some people, shortly after they died,
it was as if they never existed.

Her hands shook when she pulled the official-looking enve-
lope out of the last pile of envelopes at the bottom of the box.
It was the marriage license: Susan Brown and Paul Higgins,
March 21, 2003.

The name rang a bell. Paul Higgins was the name of the
ex-cop who'd donated his papers to Raymond's crime fiction
collection, the guy who took him on that crazy ride through the
city, the man who disappeared right after Leila's murder. She
picked up the wedding photo. She recognized him now. She and
Leila had seen him with Raymond and Mike Cosgrove on the
stairway in the library shortly before Leila's troubles with an ex-
boyfriend or an ex-husband began.

Adele stared at the document in her hands. Had she tracked
down a killer?

"Are you sitting down?" Adele sat behind
the wheel of her rental car in front of Leila's father's house.

"Yes." Ambler said. "I'm sitting at my desk in my apartment
reading email on my laptop."

"I found Leila's, or actually Susan Brown's, ex-husband."

"Found him—" His tone was sharp.

"Found out who he is . . . someone you know."

"Who? Someone I know?"

"Paul Higgins, the—"

Raymond wasn't sitting anymore. She could picture him
pacing the floor of his small living room, his mind whirring.

"I found the marriage certificate and a wedding photo. Before I leave Texas, I'm going to talk to the woman whose name is on the certificate as a witness. Leila's father said she went to high school with Susan Brown. They were friends until Susan left Texas. I already called her. I'm meeting her in an hour."

"Did she know Paul Higgins? Have you told Mike?"

"I will right now."

She called Cosgrove's cell phone and told him what she'd found. He had no reaction. It was difficult to surprise him. Without a real pause to absorb the news, he asked if Mr. Brown would let her take the documents she found. "I can make the request through the local police department if we need to, or I can talk to the father if that would help."

"I have them. He didn't mind at all."

As she was getting ready to start the car, a black SUV pulled up behind her, ridiculously close, almost on her bumper, for no reason since there weren't any other cars at the curb anywhere near her car. Bulky men in suits got out of the front seat on either side and approached her car, one on the driver side, one on the passenger side. On instinct, she shoved the marriage license and wedding photo under the front seat.

"Good afternoon, ma'am," the man on her side of the car said.

"What do you want?" Adele locked her eyes on his. She wasn't at all surprised when the man flashed an identification card and said HOMELAND SECURITY. He flashed the ID quickly, so quickly she didn't see what was written on the face of the card. It had his picture and a seal of some sort. She was going to ask to see it again but decided not to push it. Instead, she looked him in the eye and waited.

"Did you come out of that house? Do you know who lives there?" He nodded toward Leila's father's house.

Adele glanced at the sad looking house for a moment. She

didn't know whether to cooperate or demand a lawyer. She didn't know what they were after, but it probably has something to do with Gobi. "I'd like to know what's going on. Have I done something wrong?"

"I don't know, ma'am. We'd like to know why you're in Texas and what you were doing in that house. If you haven't done anything wrong, you don't have to worry."

"Is there some reason you can't tell me what this is about?"

The man's expression hardened, his jaw tightening, his eyes narrowing. "Is there some reason you don't want to answer my question?"

Adele felt an adrenaline shot of anger. "Yes there is. It's none of your business what I'm doing here, unless you tell me why it is your business."

The man, who'd been bent at the waist talking to her through the window, straightened up and surveyed the street and neighborhood around them. It was quiet—no one on the sidewalks, no one in the yards, no cars passing on the street. The sun had dipped behind the houses, giving a kind of dullness to the waning daylight.

He bent to the window again. "Did you take anything from the house?"

Adele bent forward and started the car. Once the motor was running, she faced the man at her window. "I don't have to talk to you, do I?"

He stepped back from the car and put his hand on his hip. For a moment, she thought he might reach for a gun. "No. You don't, ma'am. You're not under arrest. You being uncooperative does suggest you have something to hide." He shook his head, his lips pursed with disapproval. "I don't understand, ma'am. Most people want to cooperate. They understand our job is to keep the country safe."

"Try your sanctimonious bullshit on someone else." Adele reacted with another surge of anger to memories of being talked down to, pushed around. She'd never taken to it, not on the streets of Brooklyn growing up, not from men bosses when she was younger. "Because I won't answer questions you've given me no reason for asking, you try to goad me into answering by implying I'm a traitor. I hope most people aren't stupid enough to fall for that."

The man's expression was impassive. "I don't suppose you're in contact with Gobi Tabrizi."

She paused, flustered for the moment, remembering her trip to Gobi's apartment. "Yesterday. You probably know that."

"You haven't been in touch today? You don't know where he is at the moment?"

"He's in jail."

"Not any longer."

Adele caught her breath. "What do you mean?"

"He was released. He's already violated the conditions of his release. He's disappeared."

She turned off the car's motor, feeling suddenly helpless. "I don't know where he is. I didn't know he was released."

The man waited a couple of beats. "I'm sure you know whose house you were in."

"I do. And if you know, why ask me?"

He was unfazed. "A formality. What were you doing there?"

"Maybe you know that, too. Were you following me?"

"We don't want you to inadvertently become an accessory to a crime. Did you take anything from the house?"

Adele started the car's motor again. "I hope you're not going to harass that poor old man when you get through with me."

She glared up at her interrogator, wondering if he was experienced enough with this sort of thing to recognize false bravado. He might want to search the car and do it anyway even if she told him no. And if he'd followed her here, he or someone like him might have followed her when she went to Gobi's apartment. She dropped the shift lever into drive. "I'm sure you know how to reach me." She slowly pulled away, cringing, expecting any second to hear a command to "Halt!" Shots fired in the air. She got to the end of the block and turned the corner before she breathed.

Susan Brown's friend, Barbara Jean Allen, the woman who signed her marriage certificate, told Adele she'd meet her at an ice-cream parlor off the town square in Granbury. Driving into the town, Adele felt she'd come upon a movie set for an old time western. The blocks of stores were one or two stories with a raised sidewalk in front of the stores, roofs overhanging the sidewalk, and iron pillars every few feet holding up the roofs.

The buildings were different colors, browns and gray and dark reds, nothing garish, and made of brick or some sort of stone. Nearly every store had its own overhanging roof, also of different colors, which were actually the floors of second-story porches. The town was as cute as a button. No one in Brooklyn would believe such a place still existed. The ice cream shop, too, was straight out of the fifties. Though still unnerved by her encounter with the men in black, she calmed herself for her talk with Susan's friend, who at least wouldn't be threatening.

Barbara Jean spotted her as soon as she walked through the door, waving and yoo-hooing from a tiny, round, marble-topped table. She had blondish hair, twinkling blue eyes, and had dabbed on some lipstick and makeup for the occasion. Slightly plump, she was pretty, mostly because she sparkled with cheerfulness, rather than glamorous. Adele felt overdressed in a black skirt and gray blouse. She'd dressed for a funeral.

Their conversation went surprisingly easily. Barbara Jean was a chatterbox and because of her friend Susan's recent death, filled with memories. At another time, the memories might have interested Adele; she did want to know about Leila's past. At this moment, she wanted to know about Susan Brown's ex-husband.

"He was a cop from New York City who came here, actually to Dallas, to train their police in what he did, which was to pretend to be a bad guy and do everything with the criminals until he got the goods on them and then arrest them all. It was dangerous what he did. He was a brave man."

The problem was Barbara Jean lacked any filters. Once she got started on a story, she went on at the length of a Russian novel, unable to distinguish what was interesting or important from what wasn't either of those things. Adele had to interrupt her stories, pulling her back from where she was heading, to get any worthwhile information. That the man Leila married was a New York City cop who worked undercover sealed the deal that the Paul Higgins who donated his papers to the library's crime fiction collection was Susan Brown's, alias Leila Stone, ex-husband.

A hot fudge sundae and a cup of coffee later, Adele had learned all she was going to from Barbara Jean. She hadn't seen or heard anything about Paul Higgins since Susan left him. She did hear from Susan every year at Christmas and at other times, few and far between. She hesitated when Adele asked when she'd heard from Susan last. She said it hadn't been so long ago; then, she said she couldn't remember when it had been.

Adele turned down an invitation to have dinner and meet Barbara Jean's family. Surprisingly, she liked her, as in a surprising way she'd come to like Leila, whom she had a hard time thinking of as Susan. Yet she was tired and couldn't take much more of Barbara Jean's chatter, as harmless as it was. And she wanted to get to a hotel room to call Raymond and tell him about her encounter with the men in black.

The funeral the next morning was somber. Along with Leila's father, Barbara Jean and her family, whom Adele got to meet after all, and a couple of older women Adele assumed were Susan's aunts, she listened to a boring preacher drone on about God's will and the unbroken circle in the sky, by and by. She turned down another invitation to visit with Barbara Jean, this time because she had a plane to catch.

On the way to the airport, Adele regretted her decision not to have dinner with Barbara Jean the night before. As chatty and forthcoming as Leila's friend seemed, it felt like she might be holding something back, not fully trusting Adele the first time she laid eyes on her. If she'd had more patience, she might have won her over and found out something more about Leila or Paul Higgins.

Chapter 17

"Pop is here," McNulty told Ambler when he delivered his mug of beer on a damp, cold evening portending snow.

"Good," said Ambler. McNulty had called him at the library before he left for Woodside to let him know the senior McNulty would be at the Library Tavern that evening.

"That's him." McNulty gestured with his head toward a man sitting alone in a booth across from the bar with a glass of white wine in front of him. "You don't need an introducer. I told him you'd be along."

Ambler took his mug of beer to the booth. The older man stood and looked him over, making no bones about sizing him up. His hair was cut short so it failed to cover a scar on his forehead. His nose was bent in a way that suggested it had been broken more than once. Battle-scarred in the same way Paul Higgins was. His eyes were clear, brown, and lively, giving the sense he enjoyed life and at the same time was ready for a good fight if one came along.

"Kevin McNulty." He held out his thick, workingman's hand. "My son thinks highly of you." His eyes sparkled. "But he's friends with half the ne'er-do-wells in the city so I don't know how much that says for you." He waited a beat or two before he laughed and cuffed Ambler on the shoulder. "I knew Devon Thomas. Knew Richard Wright."

Something changed in his expression, sadness, regret, nostalgia. Whatever it was, the pain it brought with it was visible in his eyes. "I wonder what might have been if we'd known the real story—the one you told my son—that Devon did the time in prison to protect his brother. I knew his brother, too, Trey. Scared kid, useless as tits on a bull. We thought Devon was framed. Never thought his brother was part of it."

"It looks like he was."

Kevin McNulty took a sip of wine, put the glass down carefully. "What he, Devon, told you, that his brother Trey was a snitch, I'm not surprised. All radical groups, especially black militant ones, were riddled with informers."

McNulty junior came by with a wine bottle to refill his father's glass and a mug of beer for Ambler. "Recruited him yet, Pop?" he asked.

Pop ignored the question. "I know what you did. The FBI leak and all that. And what they did to you." He held up his glass in a toast. "Took guts."

"More guts than brains, I suspect."

"The feds got you blacklisted. Happened to the best of us." He laughed, genuinely, not bitterly. "I laugh now. Ruined a lot of lives. Looks like you did okay."

Ambler chuckled. "I coulda been a contender."

The older man gazed into his eyes, seeing more there than most people did, Ambler thought. For the first time, he talked with someone who understood what had happened to him. What it took out of him. What it had cost him. Understood the uncertainty, still, after all this time, that the sacrifice had been worth it. In this wordless moment, he felt a kinship with this aging subversive.

"Richard Wright and some others in The United Truckers of America were part of a national movement to pull together all of the workers in transportation—airline, train, truck, bus, cab, anything that moved—into one union, a national transportation union. If they'd succeeded, the union would have had the power to shut the country down."

Although Kevin McNulty sat comfortably relaxed, he broadcast a tremendous energy. Not a big man, he came off as powerful, perhaps because his shoulders were broad, his neck thick, and his head large, and because of his battle-scarred face. His voice, too, was large so even as he spoke softly, you could sense that if he roared the sound would be fearsome.

"The feds called Richard Wright the most dangerous man in America. That wasn't the first attempt on his life, the one that got him. Not long before that, someone shot into a car he should have been riding in and wasn't. Not just shot at it. I mean a fusillade of bullets from a car that pulled up alongside. The official story was a rival group of black militants."

"Are you saying—?"

Kevin McNulty shook his head. "I'm not a conspiracy theorist. I don't know who killed Richard Wright. I never thought Devon Thomas did. You tell me you don't either."

After a long silence, Ambler said, "I think Devon knew, or he was about to discover who did kill Richard Wright. That's why he was murdered."

"An interesting hypothesis."

Devon Thomas had a younger sister, the elder McNulty told Ambler when he asked about Devon's family. He took a small, aged, black address book from his inside jacket pocket, thumbed through it until he found something. He took out his cell phone.

After exchanging greetings and a couple of hearty laughs with whoever was on the other end of the call, he asked about Angela Thomas and wrote something down.

"She lives in Harlem. Teaches in Harlem." He handed Ambler a phone number. "Tell her you got it from me by way of Reverend Zeke Daniels."

Chapter 18

Mike Cosgrove finished the call and disconnected. No one in Texas owned up to the Homeland Security stop Adele told him about. It could be they were watching the house. Not much reason they would be. It could be Campbell's doing. No reason for that either, unless he knew Higgins and the Stone woman had been married. Cosgrove wanted to talk to his chief anyway; now was as good a time as any. The boss for sure wasn't going to like an ex-cop as a murder suspect.

As brass went, Pat Halloran was a decent guy. He didn't bother with the small stuff if you did your job and didn't call attention to yourself or put the department in a bad light.

"There you have it," Cosgrove said when he finished his tale, including what Ray had told him about Higgins's uncle in Boston. He sat across an ancient wooden desk from his boss.

Halloran's glare was hard and unflinching. His chest heaved. His mouth tightened. He winced. "What do they have on the Arab?"

"Nothing. Circumstantial. She was monitoring him." Cosgrove took a breath. "I don't have much on Paul either. He was married to the victim. He disappeared. Paul worked for Campbell at some point. The Stone woman worked for Campbell. It's possible Campbell knew about the marriage. If he had someone watching her father's house in Texas, thinking Paul might show, it's likely he did know. A witness told me the victim came to her apartment a couple of nights before she was killed, terrified of her ex-husband. Nothing puts Paul at the scene. He's gone missing. That doesn't make him guilty."

"You're a pain in the ass, Mike." Halloran gripped the arms of the worn wooden chair he'd ridden for years, his jaw clenched so tightly you could hear his teeth grinding. "Go ahead. I'll take the heat." He looked at Cosgrove over his glasses. "Make sure you're on good terms with your union rep."

Cosgrove worked out with Halloran that he'd take a couple of days off to go to Boston. The chief would reimburse him from police foundation funds—a kick in the ass for Campbell. When he got to Boston, he'd leave word around he was looking for Paul. Cops live in their own world wherever they go; not unlike their counterparts in the criminal world, they drift toward certain neighborhoods, certain hangouts—greasy spoons for breakfast, bars, often owned by ex-cops, donut shops for coffee.

Dan Conroy, a friend since Quantico, retired from the Boston cops, met Cosgrove at Logan and took him to Mulroney's, a cop bar in Hyde Park. The eponymous owner was behind the bar; a half-dozen drinkers hunched over their draft beers in the mottled, faded light of a wasted afternoon. Gerry Mulroney, who didn't say whether he knew Paul or not, listened to what Cosgrove had to say. Cosgrove didn't want a beer. He didn't like drinking in the afternoon; it made him feel logy the rest of the day. He ordered one anyway because Dan did and Mulroney looked to have a couple under his belt already, so it seemed the thing to do.

There wasn't much to talk about. The TV was tuned to one of those stupid talk shows where a disheveled fat girl was trying to figure out which of the two dumbasses on the stage with her was the father of the unfortunate child who would be born to her, and everyone, including the audience, was screaming at everyone else.

What little talk there was beyond this was about the Bruins game the night before and some polite enquiry about the Rangers that he couldn't answer because he didn't pay attention to hockey. He didn't hang out in cop bars back home. He didn't especially like to drink and he especially didn't like being around cops when they were drunk. He didn't mind a beer with a pal now and then, and a couple of glasses of good wine with a meal, but that was enough.

The bar he sat in now was a refuge for those for whom drinking was a centerpiece of life. All he could do was wait to see if Paul wanted to talk to him. He had a second beer and, the bar's one redeeming feature, a couple of pickled hard-boiled eggs and watched the doofuses on TV argue, goaded on by the slick MC who came off as slimier than most people he arrested.

It was difficult finding anything to talk to Dan about, too. They were heartily backslapping glad to see one another at the airport, reminisced about their time at the FBI academy on the drive to the bar, complained about their respective departments, lauded the benefits of Dan's retirement. But they ran out of things to talk about pretty quick. Finally, with Dan half in the bag after a couple of shots to go with his beers, he left the bar in mid-afternoon, telling the bar owner he'd be back that evening. Mulroney told him to come back the following day. That probably meant something.

He didn't want to ride with Dan, who was undoubtedly

legally drunk. He didn't have any choice, not knowing where he was. He was staying at a hotel near the airport and persuaded Dan to drop him off at a T stop, where he could get a train back to the airport. When he got to the hotel, he took a nap, got up in evening darkness, ate dinner at the hotel, read for a while a Donald Westlake novel Ray had given him, and went to sleep again.

The next day, he took a cab from the airport to Mulroney's in the early afternoon. Gerry Mulroney's greeting was a barely perceptible nod. This time, he ordered a ginger ale. He was through trying to impress anyone. The bar owner made a major project of digging out the bottle of ginger ale from deep in the cooler, as if the out-of-the-ordinary request disrupted the normal operation of the establishment. Mulroney finally got the bottle, poured the ginger ale, and plopped the glass on the bar in front of him; then, he went to the far end of the bar to conspire with two men, one considerably older than Cosgrove, the other younger, all three of them turning now and again to look at him.

Cosgrove showed no interest, though he recognized the hard-eyed stare and jaded manner of cops. After a time, the older man walked over to stand next to him. The younger man stayed put watching him, pretending he wasn't.

"NYPD?" the man said.

"You want a badge?" Cosgrove said.

The man shook his head.

"Mike Cosgrove."

"I know."

"I'm a friend of Paul Higgins."

"So I heard." He didn't say where he'd heard and it wouldn't do any good to ask.

"I'm here on my own time. I take it he doesn't want to talk to me."

"How would I know?"

Cosgrove shrugged. "His ex-wife was murdered. I expect he knows that. I'd like to know for sure."

"Is he a suspect?"

"I was hoping to keep him from becoming one."

"If I run across Paul, I'll let him know you came by." The expression in the man's eyes was hard, if not cruel. It reflected the cold, hard knowledge that men actually do kill one another. The look might sometimes have been in his own eyes. It might be there now. "I can tell you this. He didn't kill her."

"You don't happen to know who did?"

The older man almost smiled, despite the tension. "Paul knows what he's doing. You don't need to find him. He'll find you when the time's right."

Chapter 19

Ray Ambler stood in the hallway of a Harlem middle school with a visitor's pass pasted to his coat. The antiseptic scent in the building brought memories of middle school, as did the marble hallway floors that were buffed to a shiny glow. At different junctures along the walls there were glass-enclosed bulletin boards. He felt like he was back in IS-62 where he first met Devon. The classroom he wanted was on the second floor. Walking up the stairs, he couldn't remember if he was supposed to be on the left or right, as a herd of boys cascaded down the stairs toward him.

The woman waiting in the classroom was slight, light-skinned like Devon, with his angular features. He saw the resemblance right away and wondered for a moment if he might have known her when they were kids. She didn't smile when she looked up at him, yet he saw gentleness in her eyes.

"Mr. Ambler?" She stood and held out her hand. "So you're the mysterious Ray, the white kid who played second base. I was you when he practiced turning double plays. I could show you the pivot to turn and throw to first base." She laughed, an easy, pleasant sound.

Ambler must have expected something else, hostility, a general anger at him representing the white world coming uptown to Harlem. White guilt. He didn't have it when he and Devon were kids, despite the wide gulf between them, the stability and relative prosperity of his life compared to Devon's. He knew it wasn't fair. But that was how things were. "I'm so sorry about the loss of your brother."

"My brother was the best . . . ." Her voice faltered. The whites of her eyes reddened. "I visited him every month for more than twenty years. We wrote hundreds of letters. He's why I'm a teacher, why I'm an activist."

She'd been standing in front of her desk, leaning back against it. He'd stood halfway between the doorway and her desk. When she went behind the desk to sit down, he pulled a sculpted plastic chair from behind one of the student desks and set it in front of her desk.

"I'll understand if you don't want to talk about things that are none of my business. I'll tell you why I'm here. You can decide." He told her about his visit to Devon shortly before his death, what Devon had told him about his brother Trey, and what Devon had asked him to do.

She absorbed what he told her stoically. If she was shocked by what he said about Trey, she didn't let on. She took a moment, nodded. "We lost Trey long before he died, lost him to the streets. If Devon served that time for him, he shouldn't have. I wouldn't have let him do it if I'd known, nor would my parents have."

"Before Devon went to prison, do you remember what he and Trey were doing . . . anything you remember about a truckers union?"

"I was the baby of the family. He was much older than me. Trey and I didn't ever get along, even though we were closer in age. I didn't like him, didn't like him from the moment he was born. He was never right even when we were kids, something wrong with his head. God forgive me for saying this. He was born evil. Devon tried to look after him. He was the man of the family."

"Do you remember when Richard Wright was murdered?"

She stared off toward the back wall of the classroom before she spoke. "I was young and didn't understand, except I was scared to death when Devon was arrested that they'd take him away from me. . . . And they did." She burst into tears. Ambler wanted to comfort her, to hold her or something, but he felt constrained, and instead sat uncomfortably and waited. In a moment, she stopped. She smiled very slightly but didn't apologize.

"None of us believed the stories in the papers about drugs and payoffs. I never believed it about Devon. Everything was twisted around." Her gaze traveled around her classroom; she seemed to gather some strength from the place. "I was a nerdy schoolgirl dreaming of college. I didn't know how the system operates. . . . I understood when I was older Devon was set up."

"Did you know Trey was a police informant?"

"We knew Devon was set up . . . 'railroaded' . . . whatever the term is. We didn't know Trey had anything to do with it. We knew Devon wouldn't kill someone, not the way this happened, not someone like Richard Wright, who was an upstanding man. Devon might kill or die protecting me or his family or his friends. Not like that. It was ridiculous, impossible. We were in shock, sick and in pain."

Her eyes closed. She shook her head like a child banishing demons. "Devon wouldn't talk about it. Not then. Not ever." She bit at her lower lip, her eyes reddening again. "We failed him."

Angela Thomas didn't tell him anything he didn't know. What she did do was remind him who Devon was and why he believed what Devon told him, in the face of a good amount of reason to doubt it. Finding the truth and making it known wouldn't help Devon. It would be what he'd want, though, and would be something he deserved.

Chapter 20

Adele had been back in her apartment for about fifteen minutes after her trip to Dallas when Raymond called. She'd talked to him the night before about the men who'd accosted her in front of Leila's father's house and told him what Barbara Jean had told her. It was awkward to talk about Gobi, so she hadn't mentioned him and neither did Raymond. This time, she told him about Gobi's release and that the men who accosted her in Texas told her he'd disappeared. "Would you call that lawyer and ask if he knows where Gobi is?"

Raymond said he would but sounded irritated and impatient. Something was bothering him. And, just like a man, he didn't want to admit it, so he was pouting, hoping she'd figure out something was wrong and ask him.

"What's bothering you?"

"Denise was arrested for smoking pot."

"Oh dear. She's not in jail, is she?"

"No. . . . Johnny was with her."

"That's awful. She should know better than getting Johnny

involved in something like that. Was she arrested? Did they take him in?"

"She should know better. They gave her what's called a desk appearance ticket, so they weren't hauled in. He wasn't traumatized. He's on her side, mad at the police and worried what will happen to her. With that and his father in prison, he's taken on the attitude of an outlaw; cops are the enemy. I'm worried about when his grandmother finds out. She'll tell the court I'm an unfit guardian."

They talked for a few more minutes before he hung up. Raymond wasn't convinced Paul Higgins killed Leila. He was stubborn like that, and it irritated her. Paul Higgins kept his marriage to Leila secret; he was a violent man; he'd threatened her; he disappeared right after the murder. All of that may not be ironclad proof he murdered her, but it was enough to make it pretty likely.

She was searching through the refrigerator for something to make for dinner when the phone rang again. When she heard the heavily accented voice, she knew it was Gobi. "How are you? Are you all right? Where are you?"

"Adele, I'm sorry. . . ." He seemed unable to go on.

"You shouldn't have disappeared like that. It makes you look guilty."

"I know." He sounded contrite. "Some things happened I didn't expect. I wish I could explain."

"Why can't you explain?"

He didn't answer for a moment. When he did, his tone was hesitant. "I don't want to involve you again. But I need your help."

She didn't like this. It wasn't right. "What kind of help? There are limits, you know, to what you can ask someone to do. You already—"

"I understand."

"It's not as if I share your cause, whatever it is." She scowled at her phone as if it could transmit her anger. "I helped you because we're friends." Her voice softened, a reflex, to a cooing sound. "Because I like you. You. . . ." Her voice stiffened again. "You're involved in some political crusade. You didn't tell me that part. I thought you were a scholar."

"There are things that take time to explain, time we haven't had." He lowered his voice. "It's awkward for me to speak now. Can you meet me at a place I will tell you? I need you to bring what you took from my apartment."

Her heart pounded. She spun around, looking at her apartment as if the couch or the small table or the blue walls could tell her what to do. Things like this didn't happen to her. She didn't run off into the dark streets, her heart beating wildly, to rendezvous with a fugitive. She needed to calm down. Really, she couldn't do this. Whatever foolish romantic notion she had of helping Gobi, this had to end before something terrible happened. "I don't know." It came out as a whisper. "I don't think I can."

His voice was calm, soothing. "I understand. It's too much to ask." She listened to him breathing into the phone.

"You shouldn't have run off," she said again. "You'll get everyone in trouble. You're doing this the wrong way. . . . I found out something that might mean you won't have to hide at all. When I was in Texas—"

He interrupted. "I can't talk now. Someone is giving me instructions to give to you. Tonight at 9:00 p.m., begin walking west on 53rd Street. Bring my bag with the documents. Cross Eleventh Avenue. We'll meet with you alongside the park."

She didn't know what to say. "I'm not sure I want to do that. Can't we talk now? I need to tell what I found out in Texas. It's really important."

His voice was soft, purring. "You will tell me, Adele. I want to see you. I think about you every day, how much you have become my friend."

She was taken aback. Speechless. He thought about her? She

wasn't sure she believed him. It might be a trick, manipulating her to help him. "It's nice that you think about me, flattering. I'd like to see you. I want to help you. Before I do, I need an explanation." She took a breath and calmed her voice. "You have to tell me what this is about. Why are you hiding? Who are you with?"

There was a long silence again before he spoke. "I wish you believed I didn't kill Miss Stone."

"That's what I'm trying to tell you. I found out something that will help you, that might prove someone else killed Leila—"

He interrupted again. "Someone will pick up the bag. Do as they say. No need to talk." He laughed, a genuine laugh. "Hard for you, I know."

When they disconnected, she stood for a moment staring at the phone in her hand. What on earth was going on with her? Why would she take such a risk? She should call Raymond. She knew she should. But she wasn't going to. She'd asked him to find out where Gobi was. He'd try to find out and call her back. Now, she knew more than he did, and she wasn't going to tell him.

She paced the floor. It was unlikely she read Gobi wrong, yet it was possible. She'd misread Leila, who it turned out wasn't even Leila. Gobi asked her to take a big risk taking things from his apartment, including a gun. He was asking her to take another risk now, meeting him when he was a fugitive. Why would he do that? She had to consider the possibility he was using her.

Raymond called around 5:00, before it was fully dark. "He was released. Not on bail. He wasn't charged."

"He's not a fugitive?"

"The attorney told the feds to charge him or release him, so they released him. There's some disagreement between the NYPD and the FBI. Someone thinks they don't have enough evidence yet for either charge. They'll arrest him when they're ready."

"He's not a fugitive? Why did the man in Texas say he disappeared?"

"Because he did. The lawyer doesn't know where he is either." He paused before he asked, "Do you want to have dinner?"

"I can't." She hated saying it.

"Oh," he said quickly. "Sorry. Maybe later this week when I'll have Johnny."

"Of course. That would be great." She didn't like the wheedling sound of her voice and felt awful when she hung up.

She always went to dinner when he asked. She didn't explain why this time was different, and he didn't pry. He wouldn't. He sounded so awkward, so hurt. She should have told him what she was doing. Why keep it a secret? Telling him she was meeting Gobi would hurt his feelings. That was why. And she hurt them anyway. It was all so stupid. She was like a besotted schoolgirl. Gobi was exciting. Handsome. Dangerous. She was charmed by his interest in her. Was she that gullible? She shouldn't be meeting him. She certainly shouldn't have agreed to give him back his gun. She didn't want to go. She wanted to call Raymond back and have dinner with him, have dinner with plodding old, calm, safe Raymond.

"I need you to do me a favor." Adele smiled at McNulty as he set a white wine spritzer in front of her.

"I don't do favors." McNulty didn't smile.

Adele felt her smile fade. "Oh."

"You want something, tell me. Skip the platitudes."

"You're not making this any easier."

"What could be easier than drinking your spritzer—more of a summer drink, by the way—and telling me what you want?"

She told him.

"I particularly don't like favors that have within them, 'If I don't come back.'"

"Everything will be fine. I wouldn't do this if I thought anything could happen. I need someone I can tell, who won't tell anyone . . . just in case."

McNulty was dismissive. "What you do is your business. What you tell Ray or don't tell Ray is up to you."

Her smile returned. "Oh, you're a peach."

McNulty raised his eyebrows. "I'm not a peach." He let that sink in. "People assume it's the man stepping out that I don't say anything about. You'd be surprised how often the indiscretion is at the hands, or lips, or other body parts of the female party. She has that extra drink; the next morning she realizes she'd been nuzzling at the bar the night before with Clarence from accounting. What the hell she saw in him is beyond me. I could've told her right then she'd regret it the next day, even if she didn't have a regular boyfriend who was out of town. . . . Him no prize either, if you ask me."

"I'm not stepping out. It's—" She couldn't think of exactly what to call it. But she certainly wasn't stepping out.

"You need to stop by here when you're finished. Make sure this guy knows I know where you went and I'm waiting for you."

"Okay." her voice sounded small to her, uncertain.

Later that evening, Adele headed west on 53rd Street, walking on the north side close the curb. She carried Gobi's bag in her left hand. Few cars passed. She didn't like that the traffic came from behind, cringing when the sound of a motor closed in on her. She'd gone back and forth on whether to do this herself. In the past, she wouldn't have done something like this without Raymond; she'd have loved the adventure and doing it together. She made fun of the women in Raymond's detective books who go off by themselves into empty warehouses or creaking old mansions when they could easily bring someone with them. This was different. It would be too embarrassingly like bringing one boyfriend along on a date with another one. Gobi wasn't a fugitive, even if he acted like one, and he had no reason to harm her.

She'd crossed Tenth Avenue and gotten most of the way to Eleventh when she heard a car motor getting louder as it came near and then quieting as it slowed alongside her. Gobi called her name. He sat in the passenger seat; the window was open. He smiled, but his face was drawn and the smile didn't reach his eyes.

"Are you all right?" he asked.

The car double-parked, leaving enough room for passing cars to get by. Gobi's expression was so sad and pained her heart went out to him. For a moment, they looked at each other, as if neither knew what to say. She certainly didn't; she watched his smiling sad face as he leaned on his hands in the car door window.

After a time, he said something to someone in the car with him, opened the door, and got out. He took the bag from her, handed it into the car. They were near Eleventh Avenue. He took her arm, leading her across 53rd Street to an Italian café on the corner.

"Who are you with?" she asked as he looked over the menu.

"I'm crazy about pizza since I've been in America. Do you mind?"

She couldn't not smile. He had a kind of childlike eagerness, despite the weariness about him. "Fine." She regarded him for a moment. "You're the strangest man I've ever known. I don't know why on earth I'm here with you."

His eyelashes like curtains rose to reveal his gentle gaze. "I promised to myself I'd take the bag and tell you to go. It's dangerous to be with me. Someone might be watching."

"I'm sure someone is." She told him about her encounter in front of Leila's father's house in Texas.

"America's secret police?"

The idea of secret police shocked her. "It's not secret police. . . . Not exactly, I mean. There's Congress and the courts. The government can't do anything it wants."

He smiled like a wise old uncle at a precocious but innocent niece. When the server came back, he ordered the pizza and two Cokes for them without asking her.

She wasn't sure if she liked that or not, or liked it in spite of herself. Again, she asked whom he was with. Again, he didn't answer. Deep in her consciousness, fear began to form. She'd been mistaken. He wasn't what he seemed to be, wasn't what he said he was. A heavy silence hung between them.

"The marriage license I found proves a man who had seen Leila in the library was her ex-husband, a man she was afraid of, whom she'd been hiding from, who'd threatened her. This should convince the police that he's the most likely killer, not you."

Gobi leaned across the table, with that avuncular expression, an air of superiority, even if kind, she didn't like. "I hope what you say will happen. I don't want to face your legal system again." He studied her face. "In the beginning, I didn't tell you the whole truth. I couldn't. Still, it's not right to mislead someone who trusts you. You prevent them from knowing you by your lie." He didn't look superior at all; he was ashamed. "Nothing good comes of that."

"Will you tell me the truth about what you're doing?"

The server arrived with the Cokes. When she left, Gobi took a sip from his glass. "The men I'm with are from my country. Anything I tell you would jeopardize them."

"Are they terrorists?" He wouldn't answer truthfully if they were. She asked because she wanted him to know she'd considered that possibility, that he wasn't pulling the wool over her eyes.

"One man's terrorist is another man's freedom fighter." His quick glance was a reprimand. They were silent until the pizza arrived. Gobi picked up a slice.

She waited for him to look at her again. "I'm not going to be a patsy. I helped you—" Tears gathered behind her eyes and that made her angrier. She pushed herself away from the table to stand.

He reached for her hand. "Please don't. You helped me without judging; that was kind and honorable."

She wasn't sure what he was saying. She heard the words and knew their meaning, understood the sentiment; but the context, that she didn't get. Was he praising her for seeing past his role as a terrorist to their shared humanity? Was what he said charming, heavily accented double-talk?

She sat back down. "I'm asking you questions and you're not answering them, which is the same as lying. Why do you have a gun?"

He took a bite from the slice of pizza he held, his expression the irritated embarrassment of someone caught in a lie. "That isn't important."

"It's important to me." She tried to find an opening through those dark, troubled eyes.

"We prepare for contingencies."

"What kind of contingency requires a gun . . . killing someone?"

"Killing myself is one."

She froze. Whatever stance she thought she was taking crumbled. The seriousness of the present pressed on her. Whatever he was involved in was too much for her. She didn't want anything to do with killing or dying. She wanted to take care of Johnny. She wanted peace. Gobi was a haunted man; for him, danger, or even death, lurked around the corner.

"I've made a mistake." She folded her hands in front of her. She'd neither touched the pizza nor the Coke. "Whatever your fight is, it's not mine. I can't help you anymore. I shouldn't have helped you at all. I never should have given you your gun. I need my head examined."

His expression resembled a smirk, but it wasn't; it was embarrassment. "No one will be hurt because you helped me. Like almost everyone in your country, you're blind to what the world really looks like."

She glared at him. "Stop lecturing me. I'm not an idiot. I know there's a lot wrong in the world. Even so, I'm not going to kill or die to fix it, like you. I don't believe in any movement or ideology or religion enough to kill for it. You do. That makes us different."

He picked up another slice of pizza, moving deliberately. "We're not so different. I want peace, to love, to have children, to read the texts of ancient Islam. Where I live, children dress in rags, go to bed hungry, die before their time. How do I seek only my own peace?"

She looked into his dark eyes. "I don't know Gobi. I don't know what I'd do."

They looked at each other in silence.

Her cell phone rang. It was Raymond and she smiled. He'd probably gone to the Library Tavern to pout when she wouldn't have dinner with him, and McNulty, reneging on his bartender's code of silence, told him where she was. She knew what his reaction would be, pictured him fidgeting on the barstool, shaking his cell phone to make it call faster. When he was agitated, he looked like that, jumpy, unable to sit still, beside himself, as her mother used to say.

She clicked the phone on. "Don't worry about me. I'm fine, Raymond," she said before he had time to speak.

"Where are you?"

"At a café near the river, where the car dealerships are. If you wait, I'll join you shortly."

"How do you know where I am?" She pictured his bewildered expression. When he was agitated like this, he ran his hands through his hair repeatedly until it stuck up all over the place and he looked like a mad scientist.

"Tell McNulty I'm disappointed in him." Raymond's silence told her she was right. "See you soon."

Across from her in the booth, Gobi was halfway through the second-to-last slice of pizza. She took a sip of her wine.

"You told someone you were coming to meet me." He stood and took a small packet of bills from his pocket.

She stood also and touched his hand. "I'll get the check. You'll need your money." He looked at her hand touching his. Remembering, she pulled it back.

He smiled and reached out to take her hand. "My feelings are a surprise to me." He looked at her hand in his. Feeling his intensity, she wished she could read his thoughts. "I don't know if I'll ever see you again."

"I'm afraid for you, Gobi." She looked down at their hands also. "Or I'm afraid of you. I'm not sure which." The wave of emotion from him was almost overpowering. He might take her in his arms and kiss her or he might put his hands around her throat and strangle her. She didn't know. She didn't know what she'd do either. She might succumb whatever he did.

The moment passed. He let go of her hand. "I will think of you, Adele. In the future, if you are someday lonely, you will know someone thinks of you." And then he was gone.

When she slid onto the barstool beside Raymond, her feelings were so jumbled she didn't know if she could hold up her end of a conversation. In the cab on the way over, she'd felt a kind of giddiness from the release of the dreadful tension she'd felt while she was with Gobi, the sense that any second the world might crash down around them—tension he must feel all the time. She wondered if his life would ever be normal again; or would he from now on be a fugitive, or a prisoner, depending on his luck?

McNulty approached her, squinting, examining her face. "What you need," he said, "is a stiff drink." He poured cognac into a snifter and placed it in front of her with a glass of water alongside.

She took the snifter in both hands. "Do I look like I need a drink that badly?"

"Drink it," said McNulty.

She didn't want to talk about where she'd been or what had happened. Somehow she knew neither Raymond nor McNulty would ask her to, and they didn't. At first, absorbed in her own worries, she failed to notice Raymond's glum expression or that he, who always drank beer, had a brandy snifter in front of him, too.

She took a big swallow of her cognac and asked him what was wrong. He mumbled something. It was always difficult for him to talk about what bothered him. He was so easy to talk to when something bothered her, yet when he was troubled she had to drag it out of him—he was old school enough to think it unmanly to tell someone he was hurting. She finally got out of him that his lawyer called to tell him Denise's arrest had been reported to the family court judge.

"The judge wants me in court on Monday."

"Smoking pot with a group of other kids doesn't seem such a big deal," Adele said.

"The report the judge has is from a private investigator. There might be other things. They've been following Johnny and me and everyone connected to us."

"Somebody's following everybody," Adele said.

Raymond lifted his gaze from the snifter he'd been staring at. He had amazingly expressive cobalt blue eyes, like his grandson's. When he was troubled, they became even more intensely blue. "I wish I knew what was in the report."

Chapter 21

The next day, Saturday, Ambler called Mike Cosgrove from the library to ask about Denise's arrest. He didn't want to come right out with it, so he hemmed and hawed and asked about Mike's trip to Boston looking for Paul Higgins.

Mike said he came up empty. But he was philosophical. "Over the years, I've gone on a lot of chases like that. Trips that produce nothing tangible far outnumber the trips that produce something you can put your finger on. But because a New York City homicide cop, on his own time, spoke to Paul Higgins's uncle in that last-stop-before-the-graveyard gin mill, something will turn out differently than it otherwise would have."

Ambler told him about Devon Thomas's sister. "She said her brother idolized Richard Wright and would never have killed him. She believes he was set up."

Cosgrove cleared his throat. Ambler waited for the skepticism he knew was coming. "Something bad happens . . . your son, your brother kills someone. You don't want to believe it. You can't believe it; your heart won't let you. So you look for other explanations. There's a mistake. Someone's lying." Mike spoke softly, and you could hear the undertone of sympathy. He cleared his throat again. "I'm not saying it doesn't happen, hasn't happened. . . . I know you've been through that with your son. And I know what the feds did to you. I never doubted you were set up by whoever doctored your papers."

"The FBI doctored my dissertation, so it looked like I plagiarized part of it. Payback for my releasing their files. All fair in love and war. . . . Water under the bridge." Ambler fought off a rush of anger. "So we know entrapment, false evidence, such things happen."

"Digging up bones," said Cosgrove. "Sorry." Silence hung between them until Mike said, "Right now, I gotta look at an estranged husband killing his ex-wife—a retired cop to boot. Someone I thought well of. To track that down, I need to come to an understanding with the folks in intelligence who have their own suspect, your friend the Muslim. I don't have room in my head for whatever you're adding to the list with your prison murder and the other murder the prison victim did or didn't commit a long time ago. Even if you're right about those two—and nothing I've seen or heard comes close to saying you are—how could you connect them to the Stone murder in the library?"

"There's a thread I'm following. Still loose ends. If I find something that tells me there's no connection, I'll stop." Another awkward silence, Ambler had trouble putting this next thing together. "Uh, Mike, I need to ask you . . . I don't want to pry. . . ." Uh, Johnny was with Denise—"

"I know. I know. The fucking kid. I'm really sorry about that." His voice caught for a second. "To drag the boy into it, that's unforgivable. I'm really—It's my fault. I've been easy on Denise, too easy."

"No. No." Ambler didn't want to make things worse for

Denise. "Except for this, she's been great with Johnny. It's just that I'm in this custody battle—"

"Something's come up. I'm not sure what happened. I need to talk to her. I'll get back to you when I know the score."

After talking to Mike, Ambler went back to work but was distracted, thinking too much about Adele's clandestine rendezvous with Gobi Tabrizi the night before. She didn't want to talk about it, so he hadn't asked. Yet he knew that, at least on some level, her interest in Tabrizi was romantic. He wouldn't admit to himself he was jealous, that his heart ached. Thinking about her with regret and resentment wasn't good for either of them. They'd been friends. Then the possibility of this love thing came along and complicated everything. He wished it wasn't so, that he was concerned for her as for a friend, that he didn't long for her.

At first, he was going to stay late. He had a lot to do to get ready for the exhibit. Yet as it got closer to 6:00, he changed his mind. He packed up his work and went and waited near the bottom of the main stairs and caught up with Adele at the guard stand at the Fifth Avenue door. Since they'd known one another, he and Adele had gone on walks together. Often, finding themselves leaving the library together after work, they'd start walking side by side. Most of the time, they headed uptown, more or less toward Adele's neighborhood.

This evening seemed as natural as the others. She wasn't surprised when he caught up with her; it was as if she expected him. They walked up Fifth Avenue, the sidewalk less crowded than usual because it was the weekend. Saturday, even a chilly one like this, brought shoppers and tourists, rather than crowds rushing home from work, and a slower pace. The evening grew chilly as the sun went down; a hint of dampness hung in the air.

"I don't want to pry," Ambler said.

Adele shook her head. They waited with a crowd to cross 49th Street. She reached for his arms and turned him toward her, her face colored by the cold, her eyes shimmering. "I never knew what you wanted. You wouldn't tell me."

The light changed, so they began to walk again, carried along by the crowd. He didn't look at her. "I don't know what to say."

They were quiet for a couple of blocks. So many things ran through his mind, yet he couldn't find words for any of them.

"We're friends, Raymond."

He didn't want to mention romantic love. It wasn't fair; Adele was too young and vibrant to be stuck with a recluse like him. "It's difficult for me to think of our being friends again in a way that isn't as close . . ."

He reached to take her arm as they walked, but let go when he felt her stiffen. They walked in silence until they reached Adele's block where he expected her to turn. Instead, she kept walking uptown. They walked past the Plaza Hotel, crossing 59th Street, past the carriages and horses, into the park. He watched her out of the corner of his eye.

Despite the cold, when they came to a bench, she sat, so he sat beside her. As if she read his thoughts, she said, "I can't figure myself out Raymond. There's no reason you should be able to."

He wanted to ask her about Gobi, but he didn't. He was about to suggest she have dinner with him and Johnny, something they used to do a couple of times a week and lately hadn't been doing.

Before he could, she said, "I think I was wrong about Gobi."

His heart jumped, a gush of hope, and then a question. He wasn't sure she meant what he thought she meant.

"He's not a scholar, or he's not only a scholar." She didn't face him as she spoke, which was unusual; she almost always looked him in the eye. "He's involved with something, some group that's helping him." She met Ambler's gaze. "He had a gun . . . has a gun." She described her clandestine meeting, the phone call, the cloak-and-dagger handoff of his bag, their conversation in the pizza café.

"I was afraid of him." She paused to regroup. "I don't think he'd hurt me, yet there was danger around him, danger in being with him." She closed her eyes for a moment. "I'm sure you don't want to hear this . . . my concerns about another man. I don't know why I'm telling you." She began to cry softly, so he touched her shoulder. This time she didn't stiffen but softened under his touch.

He could feel her trembling beneath his hand. "I liked him. I still like him. There's something strong, almost brutal, about him, yet there's wisdom and kindness, too."

He tried awkwardly to be comforting. "Sometimes people who suffer develop tolerance and wisdom. Other times, it goes the other way. Brutality begets more brutality."

Her shoulder stiffened again under his hand. "Gobi isn't brutal."

"I didn't say that."

"You implied it." She stood. "For him, it's life and death. There's no room for pettiness."

"Pettiness?" He stood also.

"Jealousy. Nothing's going to come of it, you know. We're not lovers, if that's what you're worried about. Is that what you think, that I want to sleep with him?" Tears gushed from her eyes.

"I'm sorry, Adele. I—"

"I don't want your pity. I'm going home. I don't know why I wanted to talk to you."

"Adele," he said, as she walked away. She didn't look back.

Chapter 22

Mike Cosgrove was about to do something he'd never imagined he could do. On the kitchen table in front of him were photographs of his daughter Denise making the sale of a plastic bag of marijuana to an informant wired for sound. Across the table from him, the evidence in front of them, Denise sat crying, terrified. His heart was shattered.

She liked to go to the city with her friends. He wasn't happy about it. But he let her go as long as she continued to do well in school. A guy she met in her travels—a cool guy, she said, not a dope dealer—told her she could buy pot from him, sell it to her friends, and that would pay for her own pot. It wasn't really selling—

Cosgrove interrupted her, bellowing, "You're a dope dealer, you fucking idiot." That's when the tears started, a torrential downpour, crying harder than she ever had, even as a child when she gashed her head open roller-skating and blood streamed out of the cut. He watched her shuddering back as she bawled into her hands. A few minutes before, she'd been talking about babysitting Ray's grandson and he'd told her she could kiss that good-bye, too.

An operative from Campbell Security, Ed Ostrowski, had pulled him aside on Monday after a meeting at One Police Plaza with the Intelligence Division on the Leila Stone murder. They went for coffee at a café on Chambers Street, where Ostrowski placed a manila envelope on the table between them and told him what was in it.

Ostrowski wasn't anything like a friend—they knew each other from a few cases over the years before Ostrowski retired. Now, he came on like an old buddy helping out a pal. When a guy's handed you evidence of your daughter's crime, you're not going to try to straighten him out on anything.

Square head, thick neck, gray hair, ruddy complexion—as Polish as a plate of pierogi—Ostrowski came across as oily when he tried for sincerity. Wearing a thin smile and pained expression of feigned sympathy that made you think of constipation, he folded his pudgy, hands in front of him on the table. "Brad says give you these."

"How'd you get this?" Cosgrove waved the envelope.

"You know what we do—protectin' people. Might be we were shadowing someone and ran across this. You know how it works."

He didn't like Ostrowski when he was on the force. He ran his precinct like a vigilante operation. It was in a tough neighborhood in Brooklyn that included the drug-infested Red Hook Houses. He made it worse—wrongful death suits; excessive-force complaints; cowboy cops shaking down drug dealers. The brass pushed him into retirement before the neighborhood revolted.

"What's in it for Campbell?" He and Ostrowski eyed each other like stray mongrels. "Do you want to answer or do I talk to Campbell?"

"Brad turned this over to me; he washed his hands." Ostrowski was a nasty man, the nastiness near enough to the surface that it flowed from his pores like the stench of body odor. His face reddened. The guy wasn't dumb. He recognized contempt. Cosgrove wasn't doing anything to hide it.

"You're the hero cop, right? You think that means something? The brass don't give a fuck about your citations. They think of me and you the same. I do it my way. You do it yours. Just do it. That's all they give a fuck. Something goes wrong, they don't know you, like they didn't know me."

Ostrowski finished his diatribe and told him what Campbell wanted, something Cosgrove began to see the outlines of once he got over the shock of what Denise had done. No reason for the police to follow her. The amount of pot was too small. The surveillance was by Campbell's operatives, who had no reason to follow Denise either. She was ancillary to a surveillance case Campbell Security was getting paid to conduct. They picked up something by accident. Now, Campbell was using it.

Cosgrove knew how it worked all right. If he kept the envelope, he'd keep his daughter out of the system. If he didn't, it would be hell for her. If he kept the envelope, Campbell would own him. Better than twenty years in, a few years from retirement, he'd be a dirty cop. He said he'd think about it. He and Ostrowski both knew the deal was done as soon as the messenger walked out the door of the coffee shop leaving the envelope behind.

"It's a crime, Denise." he'd told her. "It could mean jail."

Eyes swollen and red, face blotched, lips trembling, she looked up at him as helplessly as she had as a baby. "If you send me to jail, I'll kill myself."

He ran his hands through his hair. Right and wrong had always been easy for him. He'd known cops who'd run up against Internal Affairs for trying to help a family member—guys on track for lieutenant busted back to patrol. A cop's wife breaks up with him. The cop goes nuts—assault and battery, assault with a weapon. Time drags on. Evidence gets lost. In time, the case disappears. A traffic stop, cop is drunk. The guys take him home. No record of the stop. They call it selective enforcement. Not something everyone did, but it happened. You didn't ask for the break; you got it. Some families it was a cousin in the jewelry business, so you got a deal on a ring or watch. Here your old man's in the police business; you get a break on crime.

He'd never blown the whistle on another cop. Thank God, he'd never been put in that position. Some people shouldn't be cops. Some things, if he'd seen them—cops dealing drugs, beating up suspects—if he knew for sure, he'd have gone to the rat squad. He'd always been clean. He didn't make a big deal of it. Like most cops, he did his job and minded his own business, did the right thing. It gave him an edge, confidence whether he went up against bad guys, solid citizens, politicos, or department brass. He knew he did it right, so he stood his ground. He worked in the daylight. Now for the first time, here was something he needed the dark for. You do right until it's too hard not to. For him, it's his daughter. Who knows what it is for the next guy?

Chapter 23

Sunday morning, Ambler—who'd brooded through the night after his talk with Adele, staring at the street-light reflections on the ceiling and listening to the quiet steady breathing of Johnny in the small bed beside his—returned to the library to pour through Paul Higgins's files. When thoughts of Adele, sometimes only the echo of her voice, came, he forced himself back to work, the work now a distraction from his images of her. He searched the files the old-fashioned way—no "keyword," no search term. He browsed through the boxes, skimming reports, transcripts, news articles, photos, waiting for a word or a name or a face to jump out at him.

Higgins was an orderly guy; a sharp observer, good with details, straightforward. This made it easier to follow, through the files, what he was doing at a particular time, but it was still difficult. Higgins did a lot. At a given time, he had a dozen or more CIs reporting to him. Worse, a lot of what was in the reports was cryptic, shorthand or street slang or cop slang that Ambler didn't follow.

His heart beat faster when he found a folder of clippings from the African American press about Richard Wright, including a profile from the *Amsterdam News* when he was elected president of the United Truckers local. Wright was an impressive guy. An ex-Marine, he'd grown up in Harlem, served in Korea. Back from the war, he became a civil rights activist in the fifties. Later, he was a minister at one of the nondenominational churches scattered in storefronts along 125th Street. He was one of the Freedom Riders who rode interstate buses through the segregated South in 1961, and he worked in civil rights projects in the South through the midsixties.

In the midseventies, he became an organizer for rank-and-file reformers in the truckers union when one of his parishioners asked for his help. Over the next decade, the union activists overcame organized crime resistance; the government stepped in with a monitor; Wright was elected president of the local. Then, he was murdered. There was a sheath of articles about the murder—the result of what the tabloids described as a battle between rival gangs over drug territory. Nothing in the files indicated Higgins or any of his informants were involved with Wright's union. Still, it was curious Higgins would have material on Wright in his files.

One thing he read in the profile that did interest him was that Wright had a son. His name was Martin and he would be in his forties now. Ambler sought out Benny Barone, a research librarian in the Millstein Genealogy Division, and asked if he could track the son and his mother down.

Benny called an hour later. "The mother is deceased. You'll like this. The son is a cop."

Martin Wright worked homicide out of the 73rd precinct in the Brownsville section of Brooklyn. Ambler called the next morning and made an appointment to meet him that afternoon in the precinct's detective bureau. When he got there, he found a black man with a stocky build, a shiny dome, granny glasses, a thin mustache. Wright had an engaging smile, a kind of friendly openness. The smile threw Ambler off. He lacked the cynicism Ambler expected in cops, especially detectives who worked on homicides, especially in neighborhoods where violent death for young men was almost as common as high school graduation. Ambler told him he wanted to ask about his father's death and told him what he'd learned so far.

"I looked into it," Wright had a deeply modulated, rhythmic voice like a preacher might have. "When my father was killed, I was too young to understand what happened. When I first joined the force, I talked to cops who remembered the case. You mentioned Paul Higgins. I might have spoken to him." Wright seemed to search his memory as he spoke. "Nothing came up about an undercover operation."

Ambler wanted to ask about the drug allegations against Wright's father but he couldn't flat out ask if he thought his father was a drug dealer. "Were you satisfied with the investigation of his death?"

"You think they didn't get the right guy?"

"Devon told me his brother was involved but wasn't the killer."

"Did he know who was?" Wright's gaze was piercing.

"He said 'they.' He didn't say who 'they' were."

"Who do you think they were?"

"I don't know."

Wright's amiable manner didn't change, yet his questioning was probing and direct. "You wouldn't be here. You wouldn't be asking these questions if you didn't have some idea about who *they* were."

Ambler took a moment to gather his thoughts and Wright didn't press him. "Can I ask you something?"

He expected an argument but the amiable cop said, "Sure."

"Did you know about your father's union work?"

Wright scrutinized Ambler's face. "You think it was that? I've heard that. Union guys I talked with told me that was why he was killed. I didn't believe or not believe. Nothing to follow. No way to know." He paused and stood. Standing, he had a presence, broad shoulders, thick chest, fit. He pulled his jacket from the back of his chair. "I have an appointment. I'll walk out with you. There's a car service stand across the street."

Outside, Ambler hunched into his jacket. He'd come out by train and walked quite a distance to the precinct house, past littered vacant lots, asphalt playgrounds, forbidding high-rise projects, boarded-up apartment buildings, steel-gated liquor stores and markets. He kept his eyes on the sidewalk but felt the stares of the young and not so young men loitering on the stoops or in front of the liquor store as he walked by. He didn't belong there. This was why Wright walked out with him and put him in a cab. He didn't say anything, perhaps thinking he saved Ambler some embarrassment.

"My father wasn't corrupt. He wasn't corruptible. You'd know that if you'd known him. He had high standards for me, for himself. I got all As in school. I never got in trouble. He lived what he preached in church. No one who knew him believed he did what they said he did."

"If that's the case . . . if he was set up, the people who framed him—"

Wright stopped. "You're surprised I'm a cop, right? I'm not my father." Wright's easygoing manner didn't change, except he might have stood straighter. "After my dad's death, a police foundation helped my family, especially me, sent me to private school and college, paid for it. I wanted to give something back. Help people, like my dad did. This is my way."

He stood, smiling easily and made a small gesture with his

arm, a kind of salute, to the weary city blocks around him. The gesture and the smile suggested a comfort with himself and his place in the world. He opened the back door of a ten-year-old Buick, with at least one dent for each year of age.

As Ambler climbed into the cab, Wright touched his arm. "I'm thinking the Lord helped you track me down. I thought I might one day clear my father's name."

Denise Cosgrove had called Ambler the night before and asked him to meet her after school. She went to Hunter College High School on the Upper East Side, not far from Johnny's school. He'd be up there anyway to meet Johnny, so he said okay.

He met her at a coffee shop on Lexington Avenue, not far from the school. She wore jeans and a North Face jacket. Her face was flushed from the cold; too much mascara and eyeliner masked her cuteness and made her look tawdry. Yet, she was surprisingly cheerful as she wrestled off her overstuffed backpack and threw it ahead of her into the booth opposite him.

"I'm so so sorry about what happened, Mr. Ambler. It was so stupid. I wouldn't do anything to hurt Johnny." She spoke a mile a minute. "I really really wouldn't. It was all *sooo*—I don't know what . . . Oh never mind!"

"Are you hungry?"

She frowned. "I don't have any—"

"I'll give you an advance on your next pay—"

Her face brightened. Everything about her was so close to the surface. "I'm not fired?!" It was a statement and a question.

"You made a mistake. You've been so good—Johnny would never forgive me."

Her squeal interrupted him. She bumped and stumbled out of her side of the booth and clumsily dove into the booth on his side to wrap her arms around his neck and bop her head against his, an action he guessed was meant to be a hug. "Oh, thank you. Thank you so much. I was so afraid. . . . I'd miss Johnny so much." She settled back into her seat. The waitress came by to refill his coffee and Denise ordered a hamburger and French fries.

"Your mom might not be okay with—"

"I know. She's having a cow. She's such a fucking—" Her face froze; her hand went to her mouth.

He almost laughed. She'd gotten on a roll and forgotten she was talking to a grown-up. He made a dismissive gesture with his hand.

She offered him a sheepish shrug. "I'll let my dad tell her. She thinks I'm an international drug czar." She lowered her gaze for a moment and then looked up. The seriousness of everything etched into her face. "I'm in big trouble, though. I could get kicked out of school. I could . . ."

"No running away this time, right? If things get too bad at home, you'll let me know first." She didn't answer, so he waited. When she still didn't answer, he reached across the table and lifted her chin. "We have a pact."

Her eyes were pools of sadness. "What if they send me . . . to reform school?" Her eyes reddened and her lip trembled. She was trying not to cry, so Ambler looked away.

"We're not going to let anyone send you away." He felt a piercing flash of sadness as he pictured his son's last agonized glance as he was led out of the courtroom to prison.

Johnny was subdued as they walked from his school to the subway. He might have been angry because Ambler was late, but usually he didn't mind. Asking him what was bothering him wouldn't do any good; he'd have to wait until the boy got around to telling him. This didn't take so long.

"A man came to grandma's apartment yesterday and asked me a lot of questions."

Ambler stopped, so Johnny stopped, too. "What kind of questions?"

"About what I did when I stayed with you, about Adele and Denise."

"Did he seem okay with your answers?" Ambler tried to keep his tone casual.

"I didn't tell him anything bad. I said everything was fine. He asked if you left me alone a lot and how often I was with Denise or Adele and not with you."

"It's okay. Did your grandmother say anything?"

"She gave me a booklet about a boarding school upstate. She said it would be fun going to school in the country. There'd be a lot to do. Football and baseball and horses and stuff." He said this matter-of-factly, but Ambler could hear the worry behind the words and see it in his eyes.

He put his arm around his grandson and began walking again. "She can't send you to a boarding school unless I agree."

"You won't let her, will you?" Johnny stopped and looked up at him, his eyes full of entreaty. "I'm not a lot of trouble, am I?"

Ambler tousled the boy's hair. He'd no more send him away than cut off his arm. "I'll keep you around if you behave."

"I behave." Johnny's expression was earnest.

While they waited for the subway, Johnny asked if they would see Adele.

Things hadn't gone so well the last time he spoke with her, so he hesitated. Yet he wanted to see her, too, so he called.

When she answered the call, there was an awkward silence as if she hadn't expected to hear from him and didn't know how to react. He felt a moment of embarrassment, his cheeks burning.

She recovered quickly. "How nice." There was ripple of

laughter in her voice, and that lilting tone that was cute and flirtatious. She gave him a list of things to pick up at the corner market on Ninth Avenue and said she'd make dinner.

Poking around in the store, grabbing this and that, with Johnny at his heels asking for chips and cookies and a candy bar, talking veal cutlets with the butcher, gathering the bags of groceries, and walking out of the warmly lit store into the bracing chill and darkness of the winter evening brought back memories of going to the neighborhood grocery store with his father. A feeling of tenderness came over him, for Johnny and for Adele and the rightness of the simplicity and domesticity of what they were doing, gathering up provisions and going home to have dinner, the three of them.

Adele waited in the doorway as he and Johnny walked from the elevator. She searched his face with an expression he didn't recognize. She bent down to hug Johnny, who was excited to see her but anxious to get to her TV. When she straightened, she and Ambler looked into one another's eyes for a moment before she came forward and leaned against him while he tried as best he could to put his arms around her while hanging on to the grocery bags.

In a moment, she pushed herself loose and took the bags, putting them on the counter and pulling things out. She gave Ambler an apron and put him to work peeling and chopping butternut squash, apples, and sweet potatoes. That task done, she gave him a metal hammer to pound the veal into thin strips. They didn't speak during most of the preparations. For his part, Ambler didn't know whether to go back to where they'd left off, which felt awkward, or talk about mundane, everyday things about work, which felt forced. Adele seemed content with the silence, so he kept quiet until she spoke.

"I've been by myself too much. I'm glad you're here." She

broke an egg into a small, flat, metal pan, poured flour from a canister into another pan, and bread crumbs into a third. "Has anyone found Paul Higgins?"

Ambler said no and told her about Martin Wright and Devon's sister.

She stopped what she was doing and stood still in front of the counter. He sensed she was thinking about what he told her, wondering what it had to do with Leila's murder. If she asked, he wouldn't be able to tell her.

She went back to breading the cutlets. "Is Mike Cosgrove looking for him—for Paul Higgins? Has he given up on Gobi as a suspect?" She turned to face him, holding out her hands caked with bread crumbs.

"He may have. The Intelligence Division hasn't."

They ate dinner at the small table he'd sat at many times before. Johnny told them about a field trip to the Museum of Natural History. "We walked there lined up by twos like a bunch of dorks. Next thing, they'll have us holding hands like nursery school kids."

"Did you like the museum?"

"Most of it was lame, skeletons of dinosaurs and then skeletons of other old-time animals. Some of them were millions of years old. I guess that's pretty cool. But I don't know what we're s'posed to get from it." He glanced at each of them. "Me and some other guys got out front before they could line us up, so we walked back by ourselves. Mr. Gottfried was really pissed."

"He should be," Ambler said. "Boys your age shouldn't be on the streets by themselves."

Johnny rolled his eyes, the gesture reminding Ambler he was talking to a kid Adele found roaming the streets late at night when he was younger than he was now.

"What was that all about?" Adele asked Ambler after Johnny told her about the man who'd questioned him at his grandmother's and was back watching TV. They'd begun cleaning up in the kitchen. "Don't you go back to family court with Johnny soon?"

"Tomorrow morning. I suspect the man questioning Johnny was part of her plan to prove I don't provide a wholesome environment for a kid to grow up in. She wants primary custody. The man questioning Johnny, I'd bet, was a private investigator."

"That's ridiculous. You're doing a wonderful job with him—and you love him. He goes to a great school. I don't know what she could be thinking."

"I'm not rich. She pays for the school."

"Rich isn't everything. It's not the most important thing."

"He'd like it if he saw more of you. We both would."

Adele stopped as she wrapped a plate of leftovers for him to take home. "I'm busy, Raymond. I'm behind at work. I don't have as much time as I used to." She didn't mention Gobi. But he might as well be sitting on the table in front of them. She came closer. "Johnny's your responsibility, legally and in every way, not mine, so it's hard for me sometimes." Her voice wavered. "At one time, you led me to believe—" She abruptly turned from him and went to the small living room to sit with Johnny for a few minutes before he left.

The Manhattan Family Court is on Lafayette Street, a few blocks below Canal Street and a few blocks above City Hall, a modern-looking building that embodied an architectural style known as Brutalism, which seemed appropriate.

The court provided Johnny with his own attorney, a blunt-speaking, unfriendly, elderly woman who didn't seem to like either Johnny or him. Ambler liked his earnest, young attorney. She was proper and respectful to him and everyone else—sneaky smart, as McNulty would say, easy to underestimate because of her seriousness, her relative inexperience, and an expression of wonder she wore when someone else was speaking or some procedure took place, as if she'd never seen such a thing before. It was she who told Ambler they were in trouble.

"What do we do?"

"We ask the judge for some time so we can paint a picture of you that's a 180 degrees different from the one the private investigators presented to the court."

The picture provided by the private investigators from Campbell Security was one of neglect: a photo of the boy wearing wet sneakers walking in a half foot of snow, another of him sitting in a booth in a bar on a school night with a gigantic ice-cream concoction in front of him, Johnny and two of his friends on the street by themselves during the school day one afternoon, Johnny standing with his babysitter while she and a group of teenagers smoked pot in a pocket park near Tudor City. The judge knew about Johnny's life before he came into Ambler's world, but she didn't mention it. Ambler didn't bring it up because he didn't want to say anything negative about Johnny's mother. Whatever she'd done or not done, she was the boy's mother and she was dead. Johnny would someday need to sort through his memories of her and determine what she was to him. For now, Ambler wouldn't speak badly of her.

"You'll need character witnesses," the young lawyer said. "A minister?" She raised her gaze from her the papers on the table in front of her.

"Nope."

"Priest? Rabbi?"

He shook his head.

She regarded him with some sympathy and more disapproval.

"My supervisor at the library is an ex-priest."

She shook her head. "I don't know if that helps or hurts."

"A friend who's a police detective?"

She brightened. "A high-ranking officer?"

"Not so high ranking, he's a sergeant."

"Someone with standing in the community?"

"I don't suppose a bartender would do?"

"Absolutely not."

He thought of McNulty's friend, David Levinson. "A lawyer? An attorney?"

She brightened. "Maybe. Who?"

"His name is David Levinson. He's—"

"Oh, dear . . . Not the radical David Levinson?"

Ambler smiled wanly.

"The judges hate him."

Ambler had a thought, not something he was ready to talk about, so he told the attorney he'd come up with a character witness. His thought was Johnny's grandmother Lisa Young. The opening of *A Century-and-a-Half of Murder and Mystery in New York City* was that night. Some of the library trustees would be there, including her.

She was his adversary, yet he hadn't seen her or talked to her since the custody battle began. Everything on her side was done by her attorneys. Long before, when he first met her, before her daughter's death or either of them knew they had a grandchild, they'd seemed to have a kind of sympathy for each other. Perhaps if he spoke to her tonight. . . .

Chapter 24

"What you can do," Ostrowski said, "is work with us. Brad says you do a good job. Tell the truth, I'm surprised he'd want you along."

Cosgrove was driving Ed Ostrowski from Queens where they both lived to Brad Campbell's office in lower Manhattan. He'd been summoned to a strategy meeting now that he was back on the reservation and told to pick up Ostrowski in Rego Park.

"You're looking for the Arab? You ready to book him?"

"Why'd he disappear?"

"You would, too, if you were being railroaded."

Ostrowski glowered at him from the passenger seat, holding his hard stare as minutes ticked away. "I don't know what's with you, Cosgrove. This ain't cops and robbers. These Muslim guys don't play by no rules."

Cosgrove kept his eyes on the road.

"You weren't in combat, were you? Didn't see your buddies killed when they stopped to talk to a kid. Shot by the kid's old man hiding a gun behind the kid. That's how these gooks fight. You a fucking Boy Scout . . . you wanna fight fair? Who believes that shit?"

Cosgrove reached down and turned on the radio. He had his own memories of the war, not something he wanted to talk to Ostrowski about.

The few people at the meeting in Campbell's office—Campbell, Ostrowski, and two men Cosgrove didn't know—shared the assumption of Gobi Tabrizi's guilt. Cosgrove thought about questioning it. Then again, what was the point?

"He never went back to his apartment," one of the men said. "You'd figure—"

Campbell interrupted. "No. You don't figure. You know." He directed a scornful glance at the man who'd spoken, a well-dressed, dark-haired, swarthy man, who took the rebuke without change of expression. "Someone should have picked him up when he left the corrections center."

On Campbell's desk was a foot-high pile of intelligence reports on Muslim groups in the city. Campbell said one of the groups was protecting Gobi Tabrizi and they had enough intelligence on all of the groups so they'd find him. They knew more about this stuff than he did, Cosgrove would allow. So if they were going to find the guy, why did they need him? He kept his mouth shut and watched and waited until Campbell asked him, "What would you do?"

Cosgrove glanced around the room. Everyone was better dressed than he was—expensive suits, no mismatched sport coats and slacks, like a meeting of lawyers or bankers, except for him. He met Campbell's gaze. "I'd make sure I had the right guy."

The expression in Campbell's eyes hardened. "We have the right guy. What do you do when he skips?"

"You guys didn't just fall off the turnip truck. Why ask me?"

Ostrowski tried to drill a hole in Cosgrove's head with his glare. The other two men watched with mild interest. Campbell's face was expressionless.

"You want me to do something, tell me. You clear this with Halloran? Who I don't see here is anyone from NYPD, homicide or intelligence."

"You're from homicide," Campbell said mildly. "Two detectives from the Intelligence Division have the case. We're helping out. They're in charge. This," he gestured to include Cosgrove, the two men sitting on the couch, and Ostrowski who sat in a matching armchair to the one Cosgrove sat in, "is to bring you up to speed. They got better things to do."

"I ask you again, what do you want from me?"

"Find the Arab," said Campbell.

"What do I do when I find him?"

"Tell me."

Cosgrove shook his head. He knew he'd sold his soul to protect his daughter. "You did me a favor. I'm willing to pay it back. But you gotta ask for something I can do. For twenty years I've investigated homicides. I know how to do it. If that's not what you want, let me go somewhere else."

"That's what we're asking," Ostrowski shouted, rising from his chair.

Campbell held up his hand like a traffic cop. Ostrowski sat back down like an obedient attack dog. "The Arab's a suspect. I'm asking you to bring in a suspect. You don't have to know if he's guilty. Bring him in for questioning."

"I don't bring in suspects to private citizens."

"Who were you planning to bring Paul Higgins to?" A slight flicker in Campbell's eyes told an entire story.

If he was supposed to be shocked, too bad. "I wanted to ask him about his ex-wife."

A flash of annoyance across Campbell's face gave that round to Cosgrove.

"This is the deal." Campbell gave him the names of the intelligence detectives in charge of the case and said he could bring his suspects to them if he preferred. "No more freelancing. You got that. That's the return on the favor."

Cosgrove nodded.

Chapter 25

"I think my attorneys advised me not to speak with you," Lisa Young said when Ambler approached her.

She'd blended in perfectly with the well-dressed crowd mingling amidst the marble pillars and glass display cases in the Gottesman Exhibition Hall. As openings went, this one was low key. Though the library's president had stopped by for a few brief words, the brevity and content of his remarks made it clear the man wasn't much of a mystery fan.

"I suppose I should ask them." She laughed. "But I'm not going to. This business about my grandson has never been personal."

They spoke cordially for a few minutes, until Ambler told her he wanted to talk about their differences over Johnny outside of court. She didn't respond right away. He remembered her well enough to know she couldn't be talked into anything. When she did speak again, she invited him to her apartment. "No time like the present," she said.

He didn't want to go to her apartment. But he could because Denise was at his place with Johnny, and Adele hadn't come to the reception. He didn't know why she hadn't come but it saddened him. The reception was winding down anyway, so reluctantly he agreed to meet Lisa Young at her apartment when he finished at the library.

The building she lived in on Central Park West was distinguished enough to have a name—The Beresford. It faced the park on one side and the Museum of Natural History on another side. A doorman announced him. An elevator took him to an upper floor landing with two doors. A few seconds after he pushed the doorbell at one of the doors, a maid in a black uniform with a white starched apron ushered him into a lavishly appointed foyer and then led him to a room off the foyer, something between an office and a library with oriental rugs, floral-patterned couches, ornate armchairs, bookcase-lined walls, a library table, and a large dark wood desk.

He sat stiffly on a tapestry-covered continental armchair and waited. He was about to get up to examine the bookshelves when the door opened and Lisa Young entered. She'd changed clothes and now wore a pale blue pantsuit with a colorful silk scarf around her neck. Whatever she wore, she maintained a well-bred elegance, tall, slender, and graceful. She was attractive, in the way rich women often were, sleek and well-maintained, pleasant to look at rather than glamorous.

He stood and shook hands with her. She sat down on a couch across from him. "I've asked Juanita to bring us martinis." She didn't say who Juanita was—he assumed the maid who'd let him in—or ask if he wanted a martini.

"I think you're right. It is time we talked." She stared into the space in front of her for a moment. "I've allowed the attorneys to handle everything when I should have taken charge." He thought he'd come there to talk to her. She had other ideas. "After what he's been through, the boy needs more structure than either of us can give him."

He didn't catch on right away that she was talking about boarding school, so he nodded as she spoke until he did catch on.

Juanita arrived with the drinks, placing Lisa Young's on the table in front of her, handing the other to Ambler. Lisa Young had stopped speaking as soon as the maid entered the room, waiting until the door closed behind her before speaking again. She did this automatically, as you might wait for a car to pass before starting across the street.

"I'm sure it's been ages for you, too, since you attempted to reason with a child."

He began to say something halfway in agreement. Johnny, because of how he grew up, was more self-reliant than you'd expect a boy his age to be. Unused to rules or requirements, he had a chip on his shoulder about being told what to do. Ambler however said none of this because Lisa Young wasn't looking for confirmation or any response at all.

Perhaps the two large swallows of the martini he took while she went on about Johnny's stubbornness gave him courage. "I'm not going to send Johnny to a boarding school," he said, interrupting her. "I don't know what I'd do without him."

She considered this for a moment, frowning. "The point of this is not what's best for you, Mr. Ambler. The boy needs structure—"

"He needs his family."

She lifted her glass from the table for the first time and sipped from it. "That isn't what he has. He has two elderly people in his life who are ill-equipped to raise him." She let the words carry their own weight, no raised eyebrows, no meaningful glance.

"He's my family."

She spoke to him over the rim of her cocktail glass. "A somewhat dysfunctional family." Before he could respond, she met his gaze, her eyes reflecting a depth of pain he'd seen in the past. "I'm surely no one to talk about dysfunctional families." She smiled, the smile chiseling the look of sorrow more deeply into her face.

"He needs you, too," he said, though he hadn't planned to say this and didn't know where it came from. Something had opened up a vulnerable place in her. For a moment, he didn't know if he meant what he'd said, but picturing Johnny, hearing him complain about his grandmother in a kind of possessive way, he knew it was true. Johnny needed his grandmother, as cold and difficult and aloof as she was. She was his connection to his mother.

"Johnny doesn't want to be kept away from you," he said quietly. "I was too stubborn to hear what he was saying."

Her attitude changed. She was more subdued, conciliatory. They talked for a while longer. Defenses down, they reached an understanding. The terrain they asked Johnny to travel over would be difficult. He'd have to live in two different worlds. Ambler's modest existence, despite occasional adventure and notoriety because of his dabbling in criminal investigations, was the everyday world of the civil servant. Lisa Young lived in the rarified world of CPW mansions, ski chalets in Vail, summer cottages in Newport, society balls, hobnobbing with the power elite. You had to think at some point Johnny would have to choose one world or the other. For now, there could be peace. They agreed to meet with the judge, just the two of them, no lawyers.

Before he left, he told her about Denise's arrest and asked if she'd hired private detectives to investigate him. "Did you ever hear of Campbell Security?"

She shrugged. "Brad Campbell's company provides executive protection. He's done work for my husband for years."

Ambler followed her gaze around the room—the leather-bound books on the shelves, the ornate, gilded picture frames, oriental rugs, tapestries, mahogany library tables. She lowered her voice to a whisper. "We're not supposed to talk about security." She nodded toward the ceiling at one corner of the room, where a tiny light on a small camera blinked.

"Campbell provides security here?"

She smiled. "Wealth requires precautions in this day and age. It brings with it some danger, kidnapping and such things. My husband might have arranged protection for our grandson. He wouldn't necessarily have told me. The boy wouldn't know. It's done discretely."

He hadn't thought of that. Kidnapping. One more danger in the poor kid's life; because his grandmother was rich, he could be a target. The boarding school might not be a self-serving idea, after all.

Lisa Young watched Ambler curiously. "We know the Campbells socially. Would you like to meet him?"

The idea of chatting with Campbell over cocktails and canapés made him smile. "We've met. We didn't hit it off."

She looked at Ambler dubiously but with a smile as if she got the joke. "Did the disagreement have something to do with the recent murder at the library?"

He told her the police found the victim's body in the crime fiction reading room.

"Do you do something to draw murder to you, Mr. Ambler?"

"I hope not."

She pursed her lips, looking at him appraisingly. "You're getting your back up already. I can see why you and Brad might not hit it off. It's too bad. You're both engaging in some of the same ways."

Ambler stared at her. Was she being flirtatious?

"It would be fun to put you together at the right gathering." She put her fingers to her chin. They'd been moving toward the foyer as they talked and had reached the door. She held out one hand toward him and opened the door with the other. "I'll think of something. I'm an accomplished matchmaker."

Chapter 26

Adele almost always walked home after work, even in the darkness and chill of these winter evenings, though on the city sidewalks it was never really dark. Usually, she walked uptown with after-work, homeward-bound crowds, though she might be walking in the woods for all the attention anyone paid her.

On this January evening, she walked briskly. She'd stayed late at the library reading about Islam instead of going to Raymond's reception. She'd been reading about the religion since the last time she'd seen Gobi, not so much trying to understand Islam as trying to understand him.

One thing she discovered was that under Islamic law Muslim men could marry non-Muslim women—if they were Christians or Jews. Such women were called women of the book, a certain irony in that for her. Not only that, Islamic law said a Muslim man could marry up to four women of the book. She doubted Gobi wanted four wives but he was so inscrutable, she had no idea. He might have three already.

She giggled as she walked, picturing herself as one of four wives. Unfortunately, there was a deal breaker under the law of Islam. The woman of the book had to be a virgin when she married, a state of being Adele last held when she was sixteen. Although, given how things had gone lately, she may have reverted.

When she turned from Eighth Avenue onto her block, the street was darker than usual. Some stores near the corner that were open when she got home at her usual time were closed, their dim facades and the metal gate on one of them casting a pall on the usually cheerful street corner. The darkness was even deeper because a streetlight down the block near her building was out. The only movement on the street was two men on the opposite side of the street walking slowly in the direction she came from and talking to each other. All of the curbside parking spaces were occupied, though there was no streetlight near her building to reflect off the car windshields.

She wasn't concerned by the darkness, barely noticing it because she was distracted by her thoughts. Her neighborhood was safe. She had no qualms about being on the street anytime day or night. Yet tonight it felt ominous, perhaps the darkness, and the empty street. Surely, she'd walked down the street before when no else was on the sidewalk. It was a quiet street. Yet, strangely, tonight, the street didn't feel quiet. It felt deserted.

When she was still a good ways from her building, she heard footsteps behind her and turned to see the two men who'd been walking on the opposite side of the street coming toward her, walking faster than they had been earlier. The purposefulness of their stride, walking in lock-step, set off an alarm. She began to walk faster, turning to find them gaining on her. When she turned the next time, they'd almost caught up with her. She clutched her purse tighter and prepared to run.

"Miss Adele Morgan," the man who was now almost beside

her said. In the dark she couldn't see his features except to notice he was bulky and darkly handsome in the same way Gobi
was. This encounter, she knew, would be different than the one
in Texas. No one flashed a badge.

"Who are you?" She should scream and run, yet she didn't.
If one of them had grabbed her, she'd have screamed. Since
the man closest was talking to her, it seemed right for her to
talk, too.

"We're sent by Gobi Tabrizi. He wishes to see you." The man's
voice was heavily accented but calm. She couldn't see the expression in his eyes because of the dark and because he didn't look
directly at her.

"If he wants to talk to me, he has my phone number."

"You don't understand, Miss Morgan."

She moved two steps away from the man toward her apartment building door. She thought about opening it but was afraid
the men would follow her into the vestibule. Instead, she looked
toward Ninth Avenue, not far, where there was activity, lights,
traffic, people. "I don't want to get you into trouble. But if you
don't leave me alone, I'll scream for help."

"No need, Miss Morgan. Gobi is afraid your phone is tapped.
I can give you a note that will tell you where to find him. But
you must come tonight, if not with us, by yourself. Before the
night is over, he'll no longer be at this place."

"You'll walk away and let me get there by myself?"

"Yes, Miss, if that's what you want."

This reassured her. "Where is he? How far?"

"Quite far," the man said. "In Brooklyn."

Adele remembered her trip to Bay Ridge, an hour on the subway or forty or fifty dollars for a cab. She looked at the address
the man gave her. Sure enough, Bay Ridge.

"This couldn't wait until tomorrow?"

"No, Miss."

"I don't understand why he can't come here."

"Your place, we must think, is watched."

"Then they're watching you, now."

He shrugged.

"And they'd follow you if I went with you, wouldn't they?"

"Perhaps. Perhaps not. We would make it difficult to follow."

Something changed in his manner. He glanced around quickly, showing the first signs of impatience. He exchanged glances with the man beside him. They looked up and down the street. It was as if something clicked on; they'd received a call to action. She'd been tricked. She took a step toward Ninth Avenue. Her reaction came too late. The second man, the quiet one, moved quickly behind her, taking something out of plastic bag he took from his jacket pocket.

Before she could scream, he grabbed her from behind, one arm around her neck, the other hand stuffing a horrible smelling rag into her mouth. She gagged and choked. She tried to scream and thought she did. He told her to be quiet and not to struggle or he'd break her neck. She felt herself being dragged into the backseat of a car. Soon she was dizzy. Not long after, she felt herself passing out.

She came to, groggy, a splitting headache, half sitting, half lying across the backseat of a car. Alone. She opened her eyes and closed them again as soon as she opened them. Her head pounded so much it was difficult to think. She felt a moment of panic when she did open her eyes, realizing she was a captive in a moving car. She peered out the windows on either side. The buildings and intersections they passed blended into each other and nothing seemed familiar. She'd lived in the city her whole life. How could she not recognize anything? She didn't know if they were in Brooklyn or Manhattan—or the Bronx, Queens, or Staten Island, for that matter. She wasn't thinking straight—whatever knocked her out scrambled her brain. She didn't move. Despite the fogginess and the pain, she knew her captors expected her to be unconscious or they wouldn't have left her alone in the backseat. She kept still, closed her eyes, hoping her mind would clear.

In a few moments, she opened her eyes. Her brain started to work. They were cruising along a city street, not a highway. Because she was still half lying down, she looked up at the buildings they passed, not ahead in front of her, the way she usually saw the city. That was why she was so confused. Now, out the driver's side window, she recognized a very tall, granite building with ornate arches at the entrance, followed by a short squat building across from an intersection of three or four wide streets. She knew where they were . . . on Flatbush Avenue, passing the Williamsburgh Savings Bank Tower and the Atlantic Avenue subway station. Because it was a city street, the car slowed down and stopped at traffic lights, even though it moved at a pretty good clip between the stops.

She knew she had to get out of the car, or at least get a door open and cause a fuss. For sure, she wasn't going wherever it was they wanted to take her. She had to take a chance. If the car doors were locked in such a way that she couldn't open them, she was out of luck. But she had to take a chance, opening the door, jumping out, screaming, and running when the car stopped at a light. Things could go wrong. The door might not open. She might fall. One of the men might run after her and catch her. One of them might shoot her.

She was scared, yet it was the right thing to do. The men didn't know she was awake. It might be the only time she'd have an advantage on them. She waited for two lights past what she believed was the intersection where Flatbush, Atlantic, and Fourth Avenues came together. The third time the car stopped, she waited what she thought was long enough for the light to change back to green, felt or heard the car barely begin to move, took a deep breath and lunged for the door.

She lifted the handle and pushed with her shoulder. The door opened and she more or less rolled out, got her feet under her, screamed, and began running into the street that intersected Flatbush Avenue. She quickly gave up screaming in favor of running and ran for a full block past storefronts that were mostly restaurants, noticing the mildly surprised expressions on the people she ran past.

Only in New York does a young woman running wildly down a street in fear of her life attract nothing more than mild interest from passersby. As she crossed the first street she came to, she saw she was on Fifth Avenue. She'd escaped into trendy Park Slope. After another block she slowed and looked behind her. The two men hadn't followed her on foot.

They might have stayed in the car and might now be circling the block. The safest thing was to duck in somewhere. Stupidly, she didn't want to cause a scene and embarrass herself, so she walked another couple of blocks until she came to a pizza place, well-lit, brick-walled, not too fancy, not crowded. She sat for a moment in the first booth she came to and tried to gather her wits. In a moment, she realized she should do something so she ordered a personal pizza with buffalo mozzarella and took it to a booth at the back of the restaurant, against the wall as far from the door as possible. When she looked at the pizza on the table in front of her, an image flashed through her mind of sitting across from Gobi not so long ago while he devoured a pizza.

He couldn't be behind what happened to her. She wouldn't believe he would be part of something like this. It was hard to believe it happened at all. She should call the police, yet all she could do was sit there stunned, staring at a pizza she wasn't going to eat. She sat for a few more minutes, not seeing, remembering the first day she met Gobi, the confrontation between him and Leila, how whatever went on between them was on a level they understood and she didn't.

She pictured each time she saw him, actually only a few times. He had a presence, something that drew her to him, like a guru. Maybe he did have four wives, after all. She called Raymond on her cell phone.

When he answered, her voice broke. Tears gushed into her eyes. With sobs breaking up her voice, she told him what happened. By the time she got to where she jumped out of the car, the tears had stopped and she'd gotten her voice under control. Raymond listened calmly. Sometimes, his placidness bothered her—he didn't get angry at things that should make him mad. Now, it comforted her.

"Are you hurt?" he asked when she paused.

"I'm okay." She told him where she was. "I'll wait a little bit and get a cab back."

"I'll come get you. Those men might be looking for you. Have you called the police?"

"No. I don't want to, not yet. I need to think." She almost choked on the rage rising in her. She didn't know if she was mad at Gobi or the men who'd accosted her or, for some reason, Raymond. Really, she was mad at all men because at heart they were bullies, who, when push came to shove, relied on being bigger and stronger than you were. From wherever the anger came from, she lashed out. "What good would you do? I can get back by myself. I don't know why you think you're helping me."

"Okay." He sounded hurt. "Ask the waiter or bartender to get a cab for you and call the police." He hung up.

As soon as he was gone, she was sorry. She'd attacked him. He offered to help and she struck out at him, as if he'd done something to hurt her, when she was the one who'd hurt him. She did want him to come and get her. Now, it was too late. She couldn't bring herself to call him back.

Chapter 27

Ambler was furious with Adele for not letting him come to Brooklyn to get her. She was too stubborn for her own good. He kept himself under control because Denise and Johnny were doing homework right behind him. If he'd been alone, he might have started throwing his dishes against the wall. Adele was the only one who could do that to him. So she didn't want his help. Good. Let her get out of the mess herself. She got herself into it. Enough was enough. She could do whatever the hell she wanted.

He was surprised the kids couldn't see him smoldering. He stared out the kitchen window at a blank wall. As angry as he was, he still couldn't get rid of the feeling he was bound to her in some way. She needed him. Whatever she said or thought at the moment, she needed him. That's how it was. He punched in her number.

"Hello?" Her voice was small.

"Where are you?"

"I'm still here." He pictured her huddled in a booth, leaning against a wall, her knees up protecting her.

"I'm coming to get you. Denise is here and can stay with Johnny."

Her voice picked up some energy. "It's okay. A car service cab is on the way." With a small laugh, she said, "The two Italian guys behind the pizza counter have taken a shine to me. They called the cab and will make sure I get in it." The laugh died; her voice was small again. "I'm glad you called back. I'm sorry for what I said. I'm scared." After a long pause, "Can I come there?"

Though she surprised him, he didn't miss a beat. "Sure. Johnny will be really happy to see you. Have you eaten?"

"Pizza. But I haven't really eaten. I'll get another one and bring it for you and Johnny and Denise. Pizza from Brooklyn is the best."

Johnny had been listening. "Adele's coming?" He fought back a smile.

Ambler tousled his hair. "Yep. We need to straighten up." He turned to Denise. "You're welcome to stay. For pizza . . . from Brooklyn." He'd persuaded Mike to let Denise continue being a nanny for Johnny after school, despite her arrest. So she'd taken to staying late, hiding out from her parents, when she could.

She laughed. "You sound like my dad. Does it make a difference the pizza comes from Brooklyn?"

"Adele says it does."

Denise laughed again. She stopped and peered into his eyes. "Why are you so happy?"

He caught himself. "What? I'm the same as I always am. . . . Do you want to stay for pizza?"

"No you're not. You've got a silly smile. You're so happy. You're happy Adele is coming." She laughed and kind of danced in place.

He tried pulling his cloak of adult authority around him. "Of course, it's nice that she's coming over. Johnny—"

"Oh no, you don't." Denise laughed like a teasing child. "You're happy, a special kind of happy, she's coming over. You like her don't you?" She scrunched up her face. "I mean *like* her, don't you?"

He tried to brush her away. "Don't be silly. . . . Are you staying for pizza or not?"

She pouted. "I have to take a cab anyway. I might as well." She laughed again after her short spell of pouting. "I bet you'd rather I wasn't here, or Johnny either. I bet you wish it was just you and Adele."

His face flushed, so he turned from her and walked over to where Johnny sat at the dining room table. "Finish your homework before Adele gets here with the pizza."

"I already finished," Johnny answered in kind.

When Adele arrived, they heated up the pizza and Adele gave them a toned-down version of her adventure. Johnny and Denise were wide eyed.

"You jumped out of the car?" Denise gawked at her.

"The man you visited in prison had you kidnapped?" Johnny said. "Why would he do that?"

"I don't know," Adele said.

After they finished the pizza, Ambler walked downstairs and to the corner with Denise. She grumbled about the escort but kissed him on the cheek before getting into the cab. "I bet you and Adele can't wait until Johnny goes to bed. I saw how you looked at her." The tinkling sound of her laughter lingered as the cab pulled away.

When Johnny did finally go to bed, Ambler sat with Adele on his couch.

"Are you sure you're okay?"

She nodded, holding her glass of wine with both hands around the bowl. He wanted to put his arm around her but hesitated. They sat in silence. He took sips of his wine now and again. She didn't.

"I feel like I was in a dream, that what happened was happening to someone else."

"You don't want to call the police because of your friend Gobi."

"He's your friend, too," she said sharply.

"No. He isn't. I hardly know him."

She began to say something but stopped. When she spoke, the challenge was gone. "I'm afraid I don't know him either."

"You should call the police."

"I know. I will." She looked into his eyes. "I can't believe Gobi sent those men after me. He's not like that." She sensed Ambler's irritation and reached out to touch his arm. "Don't be angry. Thank you for helping me."

There was something fragile about her, fragile in a beautiful way like a delicately carved ivory statuette is fragile. So strong and independent in so many ways, yet so sensitive, maybe more sensitive than anyone he'd ever known, she seemed to him too beautiful for the world, so he was afraid for her. At moments like this, when he ached to touch her, when he could hardly keep his hands off her, he felt he needed to protect her from him, too. He stood and walked away from her.

She agreed that he should call Mike Cosgrove. Cosgrove, it turned out, was in Manhattan, finishing up preparation for a court case with an investigator from the DA's office. When Ambler told him what happened to Adele, he said he'd be over.

She had switched from wine to coffee and was even more subdued by the time Cosgrove arrived. She'd barely begun telling him about the two men accosting her on the street when he interrupted her.

"He gave you an address?"

Adele's eyes widened. She reached for her jacket and began rummaging through the pockets. "He gave me a piece of paper with an address on it. It was four hundred something 74th Street or 79th Street. I recognized it was Bay Ridge. I don't know what

I did with the note he gave me. He could have taken it back when I was knocked out."

"You were knocked out?" Ambler shouted. "You didn't—"

She held up her hand, once more in control of herself and the situation. She found the note and handed it to Cosgrove.

He looked at it. "This is too good to be true. You know what that means, right? Give me a couple of minutes." He headed for the door and made a call from the stairway outside Ambler's apartment. In a few minutes, he was back, wearing a wry, cynical smile.

"Well?" Ambler asked.

"No such address."

"Why would they give me the wrong address? They wanted me to go there."

"You weren't going anywhere without them. The note was so you'd drop your guard."

"Well, it worked." Adele sighed.

Ambler got Cosgrove a beer. Together, they listened to Adele's story. Cosgrove seemed perplexed as he listened.

"You'd think they'd be smarter than that," he said when she finished. "Bad guys do dumb things. Still, these guys would know better than to leave you alone in the backseat of the car. They would've known what they gave you would wear off. It's almost like they wanted you to get away—" He paused, thinking something he didn't say. "They didn't come after you when you ran?"

"No. I don't think so."

He pressed her for anything else she could remember and soon enough gave up. "We gotta look somewhere," he said as he was leaving, "might as well be Bay Ridge."

Two days later, Adele found a letter in her mailbox when she got home from work and called Raymond when she finished reading it.

"The strangest thing," she said. "A letter from Gobi. . . ."

"And?"

"He didn't say anything about the two men who abducted me. I don't think he knew about it. The letter was mailed before it happened."

"Why did he write the letter?"

She hesitated. "To tell me why he's hiding—"

Raymond interrupted. "Why?"

She didn't like his tone. It was accusatory, like Mike Cosgrove grilling a suspect. "It's complicated. He's returning to his home soon."

"Again, why is he hiding?"

"He doesn't want to be arrested again. I told him about Leila's ex-husband. He thinks they'll accuse him anyway."

"We don't know who killed Leila."

She knew he'd say that. He half hoped Gobi was guilty. She wasn't sure herself anymore. There was something else she should tell Raymond and she held back. She hadn't been able to think straight since she was snatched off the street, hardly sleeping, nightmares when she did sleep, afraid of everything. In a weird way, she'd been in a waking dream since she met Gobi. "I don't want to tell you everything that's in the letter. It's private."

"I didn't ask you to—"

It saddened her that she kept things from Raymond, knowing it must hurt his feelings, though she understood he and Gobi were rivals—rivals for her affections . . . it sounded silly. "I'm going to go," she said. She clicked off her phone and sat down to read the letter again.

My Dear Adele,

Tomorrow, next week, soon, I leave America for home. Already, an exile, I will be an exile from your country, also. To be honest, I have liked America, and many

I have met here have been honorable and welcoming and, like you, kind.

I owe you an explanation. When I was released from prison, I was met by a man I didn't know but who knew people, Palestinians, I'd known in Syria. He was part of a group—an underground organization in America. Their cause is not Palestine. They are from a sect of Islam that believes in a life and death struggle with the West, with the infidels. They accept martyrdom as part of their religion. They, in their holiest belief, would make me a martyr, too. As you might understand, I do not wish to be a martyr. I have found others who can help me to be in hiding and to leave your country under the cover of darkness.

You were kind to me. I lived too long among people for whom suffering is so much present that they do not have the room in their hearts for such sympathy as you have shown me. If it is Allah's will, I shall journey home to live among the people of the desert. Perhaps someday, when I stand in my own country, I will invite you to visit. Until then, my good friend Adele, good-bye.

He was beyond her help now. Too much about life was sad. You had to forget the suffering. You had to put out of your mind the misery of others to keep on with your own life. She'd been sitting a long time and had to shake herself out of the gloom she was sinking into. If she didn't take hold of herself, she'd spend the evening staring at the wall, thinking horrible thoughts. She needed to get up and do something.

Chapter 28

Johnny's grandmother was taking him to see *The Lion King*, so Ambler stayed late at the library and stopped to see McNulty on his way home.

"A lot of bartenders I knew in the old days were from Bay Ridge," McNulty said in answer to a question Ambler asked. "Not so many Irish anymore. Arabs. I suppose that's why you're interested."

"Our friend Mr. Tabrizi may have fallen in with bad company." Ambler told him what happened with Adele. He hadn't seen Gobi since he was arrested. If he was still in New York, as well hidden as he thought he might be, there was a good chance the police—who'd infiltrated every Muslim group in the city since September 11—would find him before he had a chance to leave. There was also the matter of the men who'd kidnapped Adele. Ambler wanted to know if Gobi knew who they were.

McNulty took a moment to glance over his shoulder, as if someone might overhear. "Pop might know someone. He's friends with a lot of Palestinians since he helped put together the Israeli-Palestinian Brooklynites for Peace, which, as I remember, is based in Bay Ridge."

"The what?"

"Pop's been involved with this stuff since the Six-Day War."

"You're kidding."

McNulty raised his eyebrows. "When do I kid? The Israeli-Palestinian thing is actually doing better lately than in the old days. I'll talk to Pop."

Early the next afternoon, he called and gave Ambler the name of a contact. He was to go that evening to a coffee shop on Fifth Avenue in Bay Ridge, and he was to go alone.

The imam, who approached Ambler when he entered the coffee shop in Bay Ridge that evening, introduced himself as Muhammed. He was stocky, stood barely over five feet tall; he wore a collarless long white shirt that reminded Ambler of a cassock, and loose-fitting cotton pants that looked like pajamas. He gestured to a booth near the front of the shop where he'd been sitting with a glass cup of tea in front of him. His voice was soft and, though he spoke with an accent, his words were clear, his diction precise.

"Because you are a friend of Kevin McNulty, I extend you every courtesy."

Ambler told him about Gobi's arrest for Leila's murder and his later release. "I think he'll be rearrested and charged with murder."

"I see. Public opinion, we must assume, weighs heavily against him because he is Muslim and studied Islam at your library."

Ambler was surprised that he took offense. "His actions since his release give some validity to the suspicions."

"And you seek this man because you believe him innocent or because you want to learn from him if he is innocent . . ." He raised his eyes from his glass cup to meet Ambler's gaze, "or guilty?"

Muhammed had the presence those in authority acquire. Some wear it better than others. He wore it well, a judiciousness in manner that required, if not deference, at least a sense that attention should be paid to what he said, his judgments respected. He carried this aura with an air of humility.

"I don't know if Gobi is innocent. I'd like to talk to him before the police get to him again."

The imam nodded. "The man you are looking for wasn't involved in political activity during his time in the United States. He is a student, a scholar. His protectors do not trust that justice will prevail for him in the legal system, so they will keep him from it. He is involved in no illegal activities—"

"There's reason to believe he has been." Ambler told the imam about Adele's abduction.

The imam shook his head. "I don't think so."

"She wouldn't make this up."

"I don't know everything that happens. I don't speak for all Arabs, certainly not all Muslims. I don't say this didn't happen. The men he was with when first released from jail, I can't speak for them."

"Can you put me in touch with Tabrizi?"

"Why?"

"I hope he can tell me something that makes it impossible for him to have killed Leila. I'd like to know also about the men he was with when he was released."

Mike Cosgrove decided the young man he'd been questioning for a half hour was an innocent. He didn't know Tabrizi well, nor much about the world around him. He'd lived at home and done what he was told until he'd enrolled in Brooklyn College and moved into this apartment that he'd shared with Tabrizi for six months or so.

"Look," Cosgrove said. Exasperation made his voice harsh and his words clipped, so he was scaring the kid. "You're not in trouble. You're a citizen. You're supposed to help the police. If your roommate didn't do anything wrong, he's not in trouble either. All I want is to talk to him. He had to have someone here in the States he visited, talked to, an uncle, a cousin, someone."

The kid shook his head. "I don't know of anyone. He kept to himself."

"Do you mind showing me his room?"

The kid stood. "You can look. The lady took his computer and a lot of his papers."

Cosgrove froze. "The lady?"

Color drained from the kid's face. "She said he sent her—"

"Relax. Tell me what she looked like, what she said. I told you. You're not in trouble. You didn't do anything wrong. Take it easy and tell me." He didn't really need the description. Adele Morgan was in this thing up to her eyeballs. No wonder someone snatched her off the street if she had Tabrizi's computer and documents.

The kid told him about a couple of hookah bars and a coffee shop on Fifth Avenue that Tabrizi would sometimes go to, so he decided to stop by one or two places before he went back to the city to have a talk with Adele.

He parked on a side street a couple of blocks from the coffee shop and approached it cautiously, keeping close to the building so he could take a look through the storefront window before anyone got a good look at him. The man facing him, sitting at the booth closest to the window, was dressed in what looked like a white cassock and wore a white skull cap, a Muslim cleric of some sort. The back of the man sitting across from him looked familiar. Given that he'd been thinking about Adele, it wasn't so strange the guy reminded him of Ray Ambler. Ray had a way of being on the same wavelength he was on during an investigation, so it might be.

He didn't have a hat to pull down over his eyes. But he could pretty much be upon Ray, if it was him, before he'd be noticed. If it was him, you'd think he'd know to sit facing the street in an unfamiliar neighborhood. Cosgrove was in the door and halfway to the booth when the older man said something. Ray turned and saw him.

"Hi Mike." Ambler stood and introduced the man he was with as Muhammed something.

"I'm looking for Gobi Tabrizi. Either of you know where he is?"

Muhammed seemed confused and waited for Ray to straighten things out.

"I'm looking for him, too," Ray said. "No dice here."

Cosgrove concentrated on Muhammed. "You know Gobi Tabrizi?"

"No." Muhammed's gaze was steady.

"Do you mind my asking what you and Ray here were talking about?"

The man turned to Ray, as if the question was directed at him.

"Muhammed is a leader in the community. I asked him to keep an eye out for Gobi."

"You're looking for him? That's my job." Before Ray could answer, Cosgrove turned on the other man. "Gobi Tabrizi is a person of interest in a murder case. I'm sure you'd want to co-operate with the police on something like this."

"Of course."

"And you have nothing to tell me?"

"Nothing." The man smiled slightly.

Cosgrove handed him his card. "If something comes to your attention, I'd appreciate you letting me know."

"Gobi Tabrizi, he's wanted by the police?"

"He's a person of interest. I'd like to talk to him."

"If you talk with him, will you arrest him?"

"You care a lot about someone you don't know."

Muhammed nodded. "I didn't say I don't know about him. Mr. Ambler explained his situation to me. He didn't say he worked with you."

"I don't work with him," Ray said.

"You don't?" He had Ray in a pickle, so it might be nice to make him squirm. "I thought, last night, we were looking for him together, you and I and Adele." Cosgrove caught himself. Nothing would be served by alienating the mullah from Ray. He'd tell him more than he'd tell the police. He turned to Muhammed. "I didn't know Ray was here. I was interviewing Tabrizi's roommate who told me about this place."

Cosgrove left Ray and the mullah looking at him blankly. He walked down the block and waited between Fourth and Fifth Avenues on the street that led to the subway. Ray left the coffee shop a short time later. He caught up with him near Fourth Avenue. "How about a lift back to the city?"

Ambler wasn't surprised Cosgrove had waited for him. "I suppose you're looking for an explanation." They walked together along the quiet street past brick row houses set a few feet back from the sidewalk on each side, the curbs lined with parked cars; every few feet undernourished trees clung to patches of bare dirt next to the curb.

"More from your friend Adele than you. Did you know she'd been to this guy's apartment?"

"Tabrizi's?" Ambler, protective of Adele, swallowed his surprise. "I thought she told you."

"She didn't."

When they reached Cosgrove's car, he opened the passenger side door.

Ambler smiled. "I don't have to sit in the backseat wearing handcuffs?"

Cosgrove didn't smile. "Not this time." When they were buckled in, before he started the car, he said, "We were on the same side. What happened?" His face was almost hidden in the semidarkness of the car, only an outline from the faint glow of the pale streetlight. He looked tired.

"You tell me. I thought Paul Higgins was a suspect. Now, all the guns are trained on Gobi Tabrizi. You've fallen in line. Why? A whole sheath of new evidence come to light?"

Cosgrove turned a few corners and took the ramp in heavy traffic onto the BQE headed for the Battery Tunnel. Plenty of time to talk; with the traffic, it would take an hour to get through the tunnel.

"I do what the people who pay me tell me to do. You don't like what the intelligence guys do. I don't like being pushed around by them either. But you know the twin towers used to be downtown ain't there anymore. As shitty as it is, this is my city. Where we just were, there are people planning to take it down." Cosgrove showed no impatience with the traffic, moving, stopping, moving again. The stop and go irritated Ambler. Or maybe it was Cosgrove irritating him.

Ambler chose his words carefully. "That man I was talking to, he's an enemy?"

"I didn't say that." Cosgrove kept his eyes on the road. "For damn sure, he knows a lot going on in that community he keeps to himself."

"He's harboring terrorists?"

"It's not just him or this neighborhood. You're outsiders, a different culture, so you're close-knit. You depend on one another. Everybody's somebody's cousin or knows somebody's cousin. The cops are intruders to you; that's who we are. These people, the Arabs, it's more pronounced. Where they come from, governments are dangerous to them, so they don't trust governments, including ours. Look, if this mullah is in touch with Tabrizi, we'll find out."

"What?"

"Never mind."

"You'll put him under surveillance?"

"I'm not going into that. You understand, I hope, we need to know what's going on out here."

"So you didn't need to talk to Muhammed."

"Let's put it this way. We're protecting you. We're protecting them, too, the ones that aren't out to do something criminal."

Ambler watched Cosgrove, who didn't take his eyes off the road. "You buy into protecting rogue cops?"

Cosgrove stiffened. His knuckles went white on the steering wheel. "What you're talking about with intelligence—if that's what you're getting at—is guys bending the rules for the good of the community, to protect the city."

He and Mike disagreed on this. They'd disagreed before. You might say they argued. They did so without anger. Mike made a case for finding and questioning Gobi. Yet Ambler sensed, even if Mike believed what he said, his heart wasn't in the argument he was making.

He tried again. "If your friends in intelligence don't want a full investigation of Lelia Stone's murder because it would blow the cover off a covert operation, so they hang a murder on an innocent man simply because he's an Arab, you'll go along with that?"

Cosgrove stared straight ahead. After a moment Ambler did also, staring into a sea of brake lights, flashing brighter every few seconds against the deepening darkness as the cars in front slowed, growing dimmer as the cars crept forward again.

After a long silence, Mike spoke so softly he could barely hear him. "I hope it wouldn't get to that." A tremor in his voice alerted Ambler. "I hope I'd put a stop to it if it came to that." The expression on Mike's face when he turned toward him was ghastly, as if he'd at that moment heard news so terrible it couldn't be absorbed, like the death of a child.

Through many more stops and gos, Mike told him how a New York City homicide detective became a twenty-first century Doctor Faustus. Once he started, the story poured out. The pain was there in the tone of his voice, but the story he told was straightforward. He didn't describe the difficulty in making the choices he made or try to justify his decision or blame Denise, Campbell, his wife, or the Fates.

"Does Denise know?" Ambler asked.

"She doesn't know." Mike laughed, like a sigh of relief. "I'm letting her squirm. She feels bad . . . not bad enough yet." The change in his expression was remarkable, the clouds parted and the sun came out. "You're the only one who knows . . . outside of my new partners. When the time comes, I'll tell Denise she's not going to jail. I won't tell her about the bargain with the devil." He banged both hands against the steering wheel and faced Ambler. "There you go. You got something on me now, just like them."

They drove in silence that was not uncomfortable until Cosgrove squeezed his bulky Ford into the tunnel and they began moving at a reasonable speed.

"Is Campbell protecting Paul Higgins?"

Cosgrove took some time to answer. "You'd think he would. Higgins was his guy. That might be a reason to hang the murder on the Arab." After another pause, he said, "Until I can find my way out of this trap, I'm not looking for Paul."

Ambler waited a moment before he spoke. "Any reason you can't tell me what you found so far?"

Cosgrove again didn't answer right away. After a moment, he said, "I don't see why not." He told Ambler about his talk, such as it was, with Paul Higgins's uncle in Boston. "The uncle said Paul didn't kill the Stone woman. What would he say? He either told the truth or lied. I have no way of knowing. My contact in Boston tells me Paul left town."

"Does he know where he went?"

"My bet would be back here, the Bronx where he grew up, or Queens, where he has family. For some reason, if you're a guy hiding out, you know you shouldn't, yet you tend to go back to places you're familiar with. He doesn't think we're looking for him, so he might not be so hard to find."

As they were approaching the 23rd Street exit on the FDR, Ambler said, "Drop me at the Library Tavern. I want to go over all this with McNulty. He thinks about crime differently than most people. More or less, he thinks like the bad guy; often he's on the bad guy's side. He may have been the bad guy at times."

Cosgrove sighed. "I could use an oracle myself."

Neither spoke again until Mike dropped him off in front of the Library Tavern.

Chapter 29

"You've been in Bay Ridge, I perceive," McNulty said when he put Ambler's stein of beer in front of him.

"How could you know that?"

"I didn't know that. It was a Sherlock Holmes joke."

"I see," said Ambler somewhat ruffled. "I guess your dad told you I was going out there." He sipped his beer. "I told Mike Cosgrove you draw different inferences than other people from what you see and hear about crimes."

McNulty put both hands on the bar and leaned toward Ambler, a customary pose of his. "In this line of work, especially here in Fun City—more in the old days than these days—one made inferences, as you call them, about criminal behavior because it was all around you. Figuring out who might have done what was a way to make sure you didn't do wrong to the kind of person who would do a crime on you."

"I see." He told McNulty about talking to Muhammed the imam in Bay Ridge, and Paul Higgins possibly having left Boston for Queens.

"That's a whole different world, the Arabs in Bay Ridge. Years ago, there were great Arab restaurants along Atlantic Avenue. I lived in Brooklyn Heights—at the time, a normal person could afford to live there—and tended bar at a place called Capulets on Montague Street. The restaurants on Atlantic Avenue were cheap, the food very good. Some of the cooks and waiters came to Capulets after work. We were friends—café-life friends, went to the ball game, the track—I moved and lost track of everyone, like you do in this business. Those newer Arab guys in Bay Ridge, I hear, don't drink."

This was a point of emphasis for McNulty, holding more meaning for him than it would for most people.

"What do you know about Queens?"

"Where?"

"Woodside."

"Woodside, Sunnyside, used to be Irish. The Irish have moved on to Maspeth."

"Higgins is Irish."

"Not off the boat."

"His father was."

"As was my mother."

"Is that important?"

"It used to be a section of the Bronx, Bainbridge, was Irish. Not anymore. Some years back, amidst unfortunate circumstances, I made a foray into that neighborhood. It's surprising what a man could find out nosing about with the pedigree of a mother from Cavan."

"Are you saying you might find out something about Paul Higgins if you went to Queens?"

"I might take a look." McNulty squinted. "What do I tell him if I run across him? I'm not going to turn him over to the cops."

"The cops aren't looking for him at the moment."

McNulty took some time to digest this, drawing a beer for

himself into his coffee cup and taking a long swallow. "I'll let you know what I find out."

"I'm not getting anywhere," Ambler told Adele. They were sharing double-cooked pork belly and shredded beef, at Szechuan Gourmet, more or less around the corner from the library on 39th Street. He'd told her about his conversation in Bay Ridge with the imam and that Paul Higgins might be in Queens.

"We should search those restricted files."

"The police—"

She stabbed at the pork belly with her chopstick. "What could they do to us? We're library staff. So we begin sorting and cataloging. We're doing our jobs. If we find something interesting, well . . ." She laughed. Lately, she hadn't done that so often.

Back at the library, she led him, not actually by the hand, though it felt that way, down into the stacks, to an area near the carpentry shop where the wood workers repaired the library's oak desks and tables and chairs. The file boxes holding the Paul Higgins collection were in a steel cage like section of the stacks without bookshelves that looked more like the dusty cement floor of a long-abandoned jail cell. Across the tops of the boxes, the police had stuck bright red labels: EVIDENCE! Warning!! Police Seal! Do Not Remove!

"We'll be hard pressed to say we didn't notice the seals."

"We'll think of something." Adele headed straight for the boxes, picked one up and carried it to one of two forlorn, dust-covered desks across from the cage holding the file boxes. She found a switch and turned on a panel of overhead fluorescent lights.

They'd done this hundreds of times, gone through for the first time a box of papers and photographs hastily gathered together by someone, sometimes by the author; other times, the executor or closest living relative of the deceased author. The deceased having made no provision for the passing along of their work, you never knew what you'd find in the file. It wasn't up to the cataloger to decide the worth of what was in the collection, only to catalog it as best they could, so some interested party—scholar or biographer—could dig through it some years later.

"How do we know where to start? We don't know what we're looking for."

"The early eighties, a truckers union and a man named Richard Wright. I'd like to find out if the police infiltrated the union."

"You can't do any better than that?"

He stopped sifting through the papers on the desk in front of him. "It was your idea to search these files."

"You didn't object."

Pretty much since they'd known each other, she'd thought of herself as in the driver's seat in terms of what went on between them. Now, it was his doing that they were searching through files that were not only restricted by the person who donated them, but had been impounded by the police. "Looped in the loops of her hair," he said to himself.

They worked in silence for how long he didn't know. Time disappeared when you didn't have much of a connection to daylight. Outside, when he took a break and went to the deli for coffee, early winter darkness was descending on a gray, damp, chilly, late afternoon. For reasons he didn't understand, late winter afternoons, when the gray of evening became the darkness of night, made him lonely and because of the loneliness, sad.

When he returned with containers of coffee, Adele told him she'd found something. "The term 'Project Red Light' came up three or four times beginning in March 1982. I didn't pay attention the first time, so I don't remember what it referred to. This time, it's in notes Mr. Higgins kept for himself, like progress notes a doctor might make." She read Ambler the note: "'Almost two years of work gone. Project Red Light gets written out of history.' What do you suppose that means?"

"I imagine, what it says. Things disappear from history. Most things aren't written down. What happened is passed along by word of mouth, like family histories; if no one passes it along, it ends." Ambler paused to let a thought catch up with him. "You know, I've been an idiot."

Adele smiled, her eyes sparkling. "It's good you've come to terms with it."

He hadn't seen her smile like that in such a long time he wanted to kiss her. Besotted, he studied her face. When her expression became quizzical, he caught himself. "One of Higgins's books has a title something like that. Operation Something or other. He told me once his books are loosely based on the cases he worked on. Do you see what I'm getting at?"

"I guess. You're the crime fiction curator. Do we have his books?"

Ambler went back upstairs to browse through the online catalog and found two books by Higgins with the word Operation in the title. They were on the shelves at the Mid-Manhattan branch of the library across the street. He went over and checked them out.

"I'll read them tonight," he told Adele when he returned to the stacks.

"Do you want to read one and I'll read the other?"

"You don't have to."

She took one of the books and examined the cover. "It would be fun. Is Johnny with you tonight?"

Ambler nodded.

"We could get take-out and read while he does his homework."

Ambler beamed. "Johnny will be happy."

They poured through the files for an hour or so longer. Every now and again, Ambler looked up from the binders he searched through to look at the back of Adele's head as she bent over the files she read through. Her hair was thin, wispy, blonde tending toward brown, her neck long and graceful. Intent on her work, she probably didn't notice he watched her, yet he wondered if she might feel his connection to her.

They walked to Ambler's apartment together. Since her reprieve, Denise met Johnny after school on the three or four days he spent with Ambler. On most afternoons, Johnny stayed for after-school activities, as did Denise, so they arrived at the apartment shortly before Ambler got home from work. Since he and Lisa Young were on better terms and Denise was on her good behavior, she now took Johnny to his grandmother's after school on the days he went there. Ambler had become more conscious of security himself since Lisa Young brought up the possibility of kidnapping.

When he and Adele arrived at his apartment, Denise was ready to leave. Before she did, she managed to get behind Adele once or twice to wrap her arms around herself, make kissy faces, and smirk. As soon as she left, he had a few minutes worth of battle with Johnny to keep the TV off during dinner and until homework was done.

With Adele curled up at the opposite end of the couch and Johnny working on his homework at the dining room table, Ambler began reading. As he had during the afternoon at the library, he stopped to watch Adele. Her face was relaxed, her eyebrows kneaded in concentration; this time there was an added distraction of her skirt riding up her thigh as she curled her legs under her.

After a while, she lowered the book she was reading to her lap. "This might be what you're looking for. There's a character here, an African American union boss, in charge of this comically corrupt union of bus drivers. He's intolerably vain and totally ruthless. I think he was modeled on Idi Amin. The bus union is a front for drug dealing. So far his henchmen have killed off a rival drug kingpin and a couple of the bus drivers. The good guy is a white bus driver, an undercover cop. He's enlisted a couple of black bus drivers as allies to take on the corrupt union leader and the drug dealers."

"That sounds like a good story," Johnny said. He'd finished his homework and was listening. "Can I read it when you're done?"

"When you're older," Ambler said. He reached for the book. "Richard Wright was the head of a trucker's union."

Ambler read for a few minutes, skimming and skipping ahead. He put the book down and stared into space. "No telling what actually happened or what's made up. But this is close enough for me to believe it's based on Richard Wright's union. If it is, Higgins had to know Wright and if he knew Wright, he lied to me about knowing Devon."

Chapter 30

McNulty had a friend, an Irish guy who drove a livery cab based in Woodside. Years before when he drove a fleet cab in Manhattan, the driver, whose name was Finnegan, had been a steady customer at a bar McNulty worked in at the time. Finnegan, who might have had a first name but if he did, no one had heard it, knew everything one needed to know about the Irish parts of Queens, who everyone was, and where everyone went.

McNulty asked Finnegan to put the word out that he, Brian McNulty, was looking for a retired cop whose name—that he might or might not be using—was Paul Higgins, and who would have recently arrived from Boston. There were three or four cop bars in the area, two in Maspeth, a holdover from the Irish old days in Woodside, and one in Sunnyside. The Irish, a clannish people, tended to patronize their own, so that when a guy more or less fitting Higgins's description arrived at LaGuardia, the car service guy picking him up was Irish, and being Irish knew Finnegan.

"He picked him up last week of a Thursday and dropped him off at O'Brien's Harp and Shamrock." Finnegan told McNulty as they drove from his apartment on the Upper West Side to Queens. "It's not your everyday place, Brian. They call me when they need a cab. I pick up but don't often go in. It's not a welcoming place.

"O'Brien himself is a bitter man from the old country, came out of the troubles with a price on his head. Should have been killed a half-dozen times—and the world would be a kinder place if he had been. One night, I watched him bash in the skull of a harmless old drunk who'd peed himself at the bar. Women don't go there. No foreigner, and that's anyone not Irish, dare go there. God help the poor black fellow who wanders in by mistake."

"I don't suppose—"

Finnegan shook his head. "I'm Irish, I live in the neighborhood. I keep my mouth shut. I go in, no one bothers me. You could go in and have a drink with me. It might quiet a conversation or two, wouldn't be a lot of smiling. But you'd be okay. Someone found out you're on a mission, I wouldn't say you'd make it out in one piece."

"Let's get a drink and see what happens."

Finnegan shrugged. "You haven't changed a bit, Brian. I thought by now you'd have gotten some sense. What's your plan?"

McNulty shook his head. "I don't have one."

"As well you shouldn't. Nothing like a plan to get you in trouble."

The stale-beer smell hit them as soon as they opened the door. The music wasn't loud, Nashville canned top-40 country music. The few men nursing beers at the bar turned to the door in unison, as if the move had been choreographed. Their faces likewise in unison registered no interest, and they turned as one back to the hockey game they'd been watching in a desultory way on the TV above the bar.

"This is a friend of mine, McNulty; he's a bartender."

The tall, thin guy behind the bar cocked an ear in their direction.

Finnegan ordered two bottles of Becks. "The beer lines," he said under his breath, shaking his head, as the bartender bent to get them.

They drank the beers. When they finished, Finnegan paid the tab. McNulty placed a twenty under his empty bottle. "I understand a man named Paul Higgins stops in now and again. Would you tell him Brian McNulty, from a bar near the 42nd Street Library would like a word with him? Ill stop in tomorrow evening around 9:00. Perhaps he can leave a message with you."

The bartender looked blankly in McNulty's direction. Seeing that McNulty was finished, he picked up the twenty, folded it, leaned across the bar, and stuffed it in McNulty's shirt pocket. "Never heard of him."

"Credit to the trade," McNulty said to Finnegan as they left. "We'll stop back tomorrow evening. See what turns up."

The next evening not long after 9:00, halfway through their second round of Becks, the door behind them opened, so McNulty and Finnegan turned with the rest of the barflies. This time, there was interest.

"Hey, Paul," someone said. A chorus of greetings followed, such that it might have been the scene from *The Iceman Cometh* when Hickey finally arrives, but the name they called out was Paul.

He carried himself with assurance, though he moved slowly, almost clumsily, carrying a lot of aches and pains. He gestured with his arm, a kind of small wave, including everyone in it, acknowledging he was the main event for the night. Nothing hostile in his manner, not truculent, but something challenging and unforgiving in his face.

Higgins sauntered over to where McNulty and Finnegan sat watching him. "You're looking for me?" His gaze was even, his voice calm, his manner unhurried. When McNulty didn't respond, he signaled the bartender for a beer and gestured with his head toward McNulty. "He's buying." There was a slight smile in his eyes.

"I was hoping to run into you," McNulty said. "I heard you were in Queens."

"You didn't find me. I found you." The menace was less in his tone than in a slight shifting of his stance. "I'm guessing Ambler, the librarian who thinks he's a detective, sent you." He took a deliberate swallow of beer and walked to a booth without looking back.

McNulty picked up his beer and followed. He sat across from Higgins. "He'd like a word with you. What he wants from you, I don't know."

Higgins pointed his beer bottle at McNulty. "I can tell you. He found out the woman who was murdered in the library was my ex-wife, so he figures I killed her."

McNulty went to the bar for another beer. Higgins nursed his. He was one of those men who could spend the night in a bar, seem to be drinking the whole time, and not be drunk at the end of the night. It didn't have to do with how well they held their liquor; it was a misdirection trick they had of seeming to drink a lot without doing so, keeping their wits about them, as Higgins did.

"So here we are. What now?"

"That's it. I gave you Ray's message."

Higgins half closed his eyes as if he could see better into McNulty that way. After a moment, he said, "He thinks he knows what's going on. He don't. You got a cell phone? Call him and let me talk to him."

"Oh?" McNulty hadn't expected this. Maybe he'd had a plan after all and this disrupted it. Still, he couldn't see the problem, so he took out his phone.

"McNulty here, Ray." He raised his eyebrows, looking at Higgins as he waited for Ray to adjust to his having called.

"I'm fine. It's not an emergency. Why would I call *you* if it was an emergency? I have someone here who wishes to speak to you. Take a deep breath; you'll have to get flummoxed all over again." He handed the phone to Higgins.

McNulty got only one side of the conversation, which told him plainly enough that what Higgins wanted was to know why Ambler thought the Arab hadn't killed his ex-wife. He interrupted Ray's answer with a few probing questions. At first, Higgins was impatient; later, he was dismissive. The one time he got his back up, he said, "That was a long time ago. You don't know what you're talking about."

He also, it seemed, had his own agenda. "I was going to look you up anyway. I need to see some of the files I gave you." He listened. "Right, the box I sealed. . . . I know it was opened." He listened again. "I don't want to see anyone." A pause. "Especially not him. . . . Mike's all right. Not on this." This time, when he paused, he looked at McNulty. They shared an uneasy glance. His face twisted into an expression Ambler would find threatening if he could see it. "I don't care what the rules are. It's mine; I want it."

He listened again, storm clouds rising in his eyes. "Okay. Okay. I get it. Let me think for a minute." He lowered the phone and stared off in McNulty's direction, not seeing him. After a moment he lifted the phone again. He tried to persuade Ray to meet him at the library that evening. It was clear Ray didn't want to do this. It was equally clear Higgins wasn't going to let up. Like a bulldog, he hung on. When Higgins's arguments became repetitious—stubbornness against stubbornness—McNulty stopped paying attention.

After some time, he seemed to have reached an agreement. "That's okay." His voice softened. "I ain't got anything against you or Mike." When he finished the call, he tilted his head back and stared at the ceiling. McNulty couldn't see his expression until he turned and said, "We'll do it tomorrow morning."

McNulty nodded and made to stand.

Higgins stood also. "I'll buy you and your pal dinner." He gestured toward Finnegan. "He can come back and take me into the city in the morning." He didn't smile, but in a strange way, he was gregarious, not about to clap one of them on the back but his threatening manner was gone. "There's a spaghetti place down the street. You okay with that?"

McNulty thought about saying no. He didn't know what the guy wanted. Still, he should probably see how things played out. Besides he was hungry.

Ambler clicked off his phone and stared out the window at the building across the street before he turned to look at Johnny who was watching TV. He'd gotten himself into a mess and didn't know how to get out, not sure he should have agreed to meet Higgins in the morning and let him look through the restricted files. He was a dangerous guy who might have murdered his ex-wife. Johnny shouldn't be in his path, even if the danger was remote. He called Adele and asked her if Johnny could stay with her until Sunday.

She caught on right away. "What's wrong, Raymond?"

"Something's come up. I need to work late tonight."

"You're not at work and you're not telling me the truth."

"If I can bring Johnny over, I'll tell you when I get there. I don't want to talk about it on the phone."

When he finished the call, he went over and stood over Johnny. "How would you like to spend a couple of nights at Adele's?"

Johnny face, when he looked up, was wrinkled with worry. "What's wrong?"

"Nothing's wrong."

"Then why did you have that weird conversation on the phone and call Adele and tell her there's nothing wrong but can I stay at her place, and you'll tell her when you get there?"

Ambler tousled his hair. "You're too smart for your own good. What do you know of what's been happening?"

Johnny turned his body toward Ambler and folded his hands in front of his chest. He pursed his lips and for a brief moment became a picture of what he might look like when he grew up. "A lady was killed at the library and you're looking for the killer, even though you're supposed to be a librarian, not a detective. Someone else was killed in the prison where my dad is. Adele knows an Arab guy—she went to see him in jail—who the cops think is the killer. You think someone else is the killer." He scrutinized Ambler's face. "You were probably talking to him on the phone just now, and you want me to go to Adele's so he doesn't come over here and kill me when he's killing you."

Ambler blinked a few times, watching his grandson. He hadn't meant to, never thought it possible that he might, put Johnny in danger because of his penchant for looking into murders. "Are you worried someone might come in here?"

Johnny turned back to the TV, answering over his shoulder. "Nah! But I'll go to Adele's anyway. There's nothin' to eat here."

It was easy anytime to get Johnny to go to Adele's. He was crazy about her. It was probably an unnecessary precaution, and he might not be safer there than if he stayed where he was what with Gobi and his friends chasing after Adele. Arabs after Adele, Paul Higgins threatening him, and kidnappers possibly lurking around his grandmother's, the poor kid didn't have a safe haven in the world.

"So . . ." Adele said when she opened the door. She bent down and hugged Johnny. "Go in my room and watch TV. Did you bring everything you need for school tomorrow?"

Johnny answered yes, politely, and went to the back of the apartment to the bedroom. The boy would challenge, argue, or go sullen with Ambler sometimes now. With Adele, he responded like she was the general and he was the private, 'yes, ma'am,' with a big smile, everything but the snappy salute.

Still standing, Adele waited, her gaze boring into Ambler, expecting, he imagined, the obedience from him she got from Johnny.

He told her about the call from Higgins.

"Call Mike Cosgrove. You've done their work for them. They can come to the library and haul him in."

"I told him I wouldn't. The police aren't after him anyway."

"Mike Cosgrove is. He went to Boston looking for him."

Ambler dropped his gaze, looking away from her at the far wall. "He's not at the moment. He's after Gobi."

As usual, she caught on. "Why? Did he find out something that exonerates Paul Higgins? . . . I doubt it. What happened, Raymond?"

He met her gaze again. "It's not his fault, but I can't tell you why."

"You won't tell me?"

"It's not me. It's Mike. He told me something in confidence."

She puffed herself up. Color rose in her cheeks. "Okay. You stay here. I'll go after Paul Higgins myself. Maybe if I find him at the library and he kills me, someone will pay attention."

He smiled. She really did act like a wet hen when she was mad. If he told her how fetching she was right now—her cheeks flushed, her eyes flashing, her jaw jutting—she'd hit him over the head with a frying pan.

"What are you smirking about, you dimwit. I swear, Raymond, there's something wrong with your head."

Something changed in her expression then, a flash of understanding and affection in her eyes. He stepped toward her; she stepped toward him. In a moment, she was in his arms. Something like happiness glistened in her eyes. Their lips met; her mouth opened and softened against his. They kissed, parted, kissed again, looked into each other's eyes and kissed again. When they stopped, he held her in his arms, her face inches from his. "You're really good at that," he said.

She stepped back and looked at him starry-eyed. "What happened?"

He stopped for a moment, not sure what she meant. Did she regret what they'd done? But no, she didn't.

"Actually, that was a lot of fun. Wanna do it again?" So they did. When they stopped, she took his hands in hers and put them on her breasts. They kissed again.

"Now what?" she said, breathlessly, her face flushed, blinking her eyes. "We have to stop. Johnny's here."

"I have to go to the library," Ambler said, rearranging the front of his pants where they bulged.

The library, with its marble hallways, cavernous ceilings, and echoing silence felt like a cathedral in the late-night emptiness. Ambler felt like an intruder, a burglar, though he was authorized to work in the library after hours. That this permission didn't include working in restricted files and breaking NYPD evidence seals he tried to push to the back of his mind. He wanted to take a look at the files before he met with Higgins in the morning, hoping he might discover what Higgins was looking for before he did.

He'd finished reading the Higgins's thriller he believed was inspired by the Richard Wright events. One thing that stuck with him, that might be authentic, was the relationship between the hero-undercover cop and his superior. The undercover cop, something of a maverick, didn't cotton to supervision. For him, the NYPD brass was as much of a hindrance as the obstacles put up by the bad guys he was after. Every few chapters, he was called on the carpet for some violation of department policy. The chief would reprimand him with a wink and a nod and tell him to make sure there was no record of his misdeeds. This reinforced for Ambler that, in the world of infiltration and undercover work, the rules we like to think police follow don't apply.

The file boxes were where he and Adele left them, so Ambler waded in. As he shuffled through the files, reading a sentence or two at the top of a page, skimming the rest, he felt frustrated because he didn't know what was in the file that Higgins would want. It took a few moments of staring into space for him to realize he wasn't going to find what Higgins was looking for because Higgins wasn't looking for what was in the file, he wanted to know what was no longer in the file.

Chapter 31

Mike Cosgrove was sure Muhammed, the mullah in Bay Ridge, knew more about Gobi Tabrizi than he told either him or Ray. He'd have to call Ostrowski to find out if this particular Muhammed was under surveillance. He didn't want to talk to the asshole, but he'd have to. He'd already had to go through him once to get a tail put on Adele Morgan—not something Ray would be pleased about if he found out.

He parked a couple of blocks from his house. Finding parking spots was harder than ever with the snow piled up. It had to melt soon but wasn't in much of a hurry. He turned off the ignition but stayed in the car and punched in Ostrowski's number.

"You find something?" Ostrowski asked.

Cosgrove told him about the mullah and asked if he was under surveillance.

"How would I know?"

"I don't know how you'd know, Ed," Cosgrove said wearily. "Maybe a little bird told you. If there isn't a tail on him, maybe you want to put one on. If there is, you want to make sure who's doing it knows to look for Tabrizi."

"What did you find out?" There was eagerness in his voice.

Cosgrove told him about Tabrizi's roommate and his encounter with the mullah in the coffee shop. He left Ray out of the story.

"We talked to the guy. He didn't tell us that." Ostrowski sounded aggrieved.

Cosgrove rolled his eyes, though there was no one to see. "It may be nothing. Up to you."

"Right," said Ostrowski. "I don't report to you."

"Nope. I report to you, and I just did."

"What about your librarian friends . . . you keeping tabs on them?"

"You're keeping tabs on her, Ed."

"Okay, Mike." He sounded friendly. Seemed like no matter who we are or what we we're up to, we have this underlying belief that others, if we explain, will understand and be on our side. Cosgrove, for his part, had no such illusion. But he let Ostrowski end the call thinking himself understood. What the hell did he care?

"Okay, Ed," he said and disconnected.

For a few moments, he sat in his car and thought about going home. He'd told Ray he'd talk to this cop in Brooklyn, the son of the murdered union leader Ray was interested in. He was tired, yet he was stalling, thinking about heading to Brooklyn. Maybe he felt guilty for putting Adele under surveillance. Or maybe he didn't want to go home after all.

Life at home had become a standoff. Denise and her mother avoided one another. Denise stayed in her room or went out with her friends. After school, she stayed in Manhattan, working as a nanny for Ray's grandson. That was the best thing that happened. The responsibility was good for her. She'd taken it on and now was working for Johnny's grandmother, too. The sad thing was he didn't see her much anymore either. Hardly ever home and she hid out in her room when she was home. He wasn't much better, hiding from his wife as best he could, too.

He started the car and headed toward the Interboro Parkway and the bowels of Brooklyn. His father once told him that the priests used to preach from the pulpit that it was a sin to drive on the Interboro Parkway. Whether it was because of the terrible lighting, the death defying hairpin curves with no median divider, or the fact that the builders of the parkway uprooted a number of Catholic graves cutting through cemeteries, his father didn't say.

He called ahead and arranged to meet Martin Wright at a Dunkin' Donuts on Eastern Parkway, not far from the precinct. Despite the plainclothes, he recognized him sitting at the counter along the window facing the street. He had two containers of coffee and a couple of donuts in front of him, and slid one of the containers and a doughnut toward Cosgrove as he sat down. Cosgrove took the coffee and picked up a doughnut.

"I haven't had one of these in years." Cosgrove examined the doughnut.

"Neither have I," Wright said.

They laughed. Wright had an easygoing manner, no chip on his shoulder. Still, he had to be a tough guy to work in this god-forsaken neighborhood. He never took his eyes off the street even as he joked with Cosgrove

"I remember him," Wright said when Cosgrove told him about Ambler and why he was there. "He reminded me of that cartoon guy who couldn't see so well and went bumbling around bumping into things."

Cosgrove laughed. "He does bumble around. Did he tell you

he was a librarian, an expert on detective novels, and because of those detective novels he's become a kind of amateur crime solver, especially murder?"

"To tell you the truth, the guy took me by surprise, asking about my dad's murder." He studied Cosgrove's face. "You're a cop. You want to talk to me; I don't ask why. You here about the same thing?"

"Yes."

"The other guy, he asked you to talk to me? Maybe I'd tell you something I wouldn't tell him?"

Cosgrove nodded. "We caught a homicide at the library, maybe a month ago. Not long after that, Ray's friend—Ray's the guy you talked to—his friend, the guy in prison for your dad's murder, was murdered himself. Looks like a prison killing. Ray doesn't think so, thinks it was a contract killing. He sees a connection to your father's murder."

Wright watched the street, once or twice glancing at Cosgrove. He didn't say anything.

Cosgrove knew his thinking anyway. "So there you go."

"What's your take?"

Cosgrove finished his doughnut that now sat like a soggy lump of clay in his stomach. "I told Ray I'd talk to you. Anything's possible." Cosgrove searched the other man's face in profile. You wouldn't know what he thought from looking at him. If he'd misjudged Wright, it could cause him a lot of trouble. Not that he wasn't far enough out on a limb already. "Sometimes in the past, Ray put things together that homicide guys, including me, missed. That doesn't mean I buy what he's thinking on this. I'm running down a couple of things on the library homicide. I haven't come across anything to link that one to the prison murder or your father's murder. The fact is it's an open case, so I'll look at anything. I'll tell him what you tell me."

Wright was silent, his eyes trained on the street. Cosgrove

followed his gaze and saw that it wasn't without purpose. A streetwise kid, who couldn't have been more than twelve, was walking in the street next to the parked cars, looking in the driver's side window as he walked. Wright sensed Cosgrove's attention. He made a gesture for Cosgrove to stay put and moved swiftly off his seat and through the door and out into the street, collaring the kid before he had a chance to look up.

For a few minutes, Wright and the kid had an animated conversation, the kid holding up his end. You'd think he'd be terrified of a big cop who had barreled down on him and grabbed him by the collar. But the kid wasn't; his expression stayed sullen; he never once looked at Wright.

When Wright came back in, he and Cosgrove exchanged glances but didn't talk about what happened. That the kid was black and Wright was black and he was white flashed through Cosgrove's thoughts. Did Wright see the kid differently than he would, or was a perp a perp? For one thing, he wouldn't have done what Wright did, stopped the kid before he did what both he and Wright knew he would do. Cosgrove would have watched until the kid broke a window and collared him then if he could. That was a difference. Wright was protective, saving the kid from himself, at least for the moment.

"There's a couple of things I didn't tell your friend. He didn't say it this way, but I got that he thought a CI killed my father and the department covered it up."

Cosgrove waited. They both knew this was possible. What you did was trust the judgment of the handler. If a handler did that, let a CI walk on something as serious as murder, you believed he had a reason. You weren't there. You didn't know, so you take it he did the right thing.

"There's a register where you log in information about your CI. You know about those?"

Cosgrove nodded.

"A few years ago, I checked. A guy named Higgins—your friend asked about him—had an informant in an investigation about racketeering in the garment trucking industry. Organized crime controlled the trucks and ran the union—until my father got elected president."

Wright paused. "Want another cup of coffee? This is a kind of long story. It's long because I don't know what it means."

Cosgrove stood. He looked out the window. It was beginning to snow. "Another coffee's good. I got it."

While he waited at the counter for the coffee refills, the snow began to fall heavily and accumulate on the sidewalk, on some of the parked cars, and in the vacant lot across the street. In Queens where he lived, there was open space between the blocks of row houses, you had lawns sometimes, and there were trees, and sometimes shrubs, so the snow falling had some connection to snow falling in fields or barnyards, something peaceful and serene. Here, the snow seemed angry, out to do harm. It would make lives already difficult more difficult—no place to park if you were lucky enough to have a car, longer waits for the bus if it came at all, trouble walking to the store and lugging the stuff home because your wheeled cart wouldn't work in the snow. The only bright spot was the snow and cold tended to keep the punks off the street and crime down.

"The funny thing," Martin Wright said when Cosgrove handed him a coffee. "My dad was kind of undercover himself. Some of the truckers belonged to his church and asked him for help. He was a civil rights activist going back to the sixties. He was friends with Martin Luther King." He paused again to scrutinize Cosgrove's face. "That's who I'm named after, Martin Luther King, Jr.

"He got a job as a trucker to help guys from the job—men who came to his church—get rid of the gangsters and clean up the union." Wright paused. He and Cosgrove watched the snow falling, heavier, no longer drifting down but driven, like rain or sleet.

"They worked on it for years. Then, a state senator Dad knew from the civil rights days held hearings. The government came in to oversee the election for the union leadership. Dad won." Wright discovered this history from newspaper accounts, most of it from African American and labor publications and obscure left-wing publications he found. "My dad was a hero to the left—to the Commies. Nothing associating him with drugs came up until he was murdered."

Cosgrove took a moment before he spoke. "So you have a take on this, too."

Wright stood and reached for his coat. "I'm telling you how it was. He fought the gangsters. They could have had him killed. They took over the union again after his death. I don't believe my father had anything to do with drugs. I have questions."

"No one knows anything about the undercover operation?"

"No one I've talked to. The CI signed a form. It's in the file with the guy's photo and a background report. What should be there are reports from the CI and reports on him the handler filed. None of that is there."

"That's it?"

"Pretty much. The union went to hell after my dad was murdered. The guy who took over got caught taking bribes from the trucking companies. The left-wing papers called my dad's death an assassination. They said he discovered the government infiltrated the truckers union all over the country and was going to expose them, so they stopped him."

"You believe that?"

Wright shrugged. "Those stories I read didn't have anything to back them up, just the charges. I don't believe what they wrote or not believe it. I know my dad never had anything to do with selling drugs."

"One more thing," Cosgrove said as he dropped Wright off at the precinct. "Ray said some foundation paid for your college. Not something set up by the union, it was a police foundation?"

Wright nodded. "Tell your friend I'll talk to him."

"Maybe the three of us will have a beer."

Wright waved, sunk into his trench coat and headed toward the precinct door, not before scanning the street and sidewalks around him.

Cosgrove headed toward the Interboro—now the Jackie Robinson Parkway; he kept forgetting. Snow fell all across Brooklyn and Queens. The traffic crawled.

Chapter 32

Ambler was groggy from lack of sleep when Cosgrove called first thing in the morning. Despite his epiphany about why Higgins wanted to look through the files, he'd stayed at the library long past midnight. What held his interest was a report of hearings a state senator held on organized crime in garment industry trucking. It was likely the exposure of the mob in those hearings led to the government-run union election in which Wright was elected president of the local.

From what Ambler could gather, the loss of control of the union when Wright became president was a temporary setback for the mob. They continued to control the trucking companies and were back in power in the union soon after Wright's murder. That the mob might have killed Wright to regain power was a grim possibility. Not long ago, Ambler read that a couple of garbage haulers who'd cooperated with an anticrime task force on Long Island were found murdered for doing their civic duty.

After Mike told him about his conversation with Richard Wright's son in Brownsville, Ambler felt Operation Red Light, the investigation Higgins was told to expunge from his files, was key to understanding Wright's murder.

Cosgrove wasn't so sure. "Let's say you're right. Something blew up in the investigation. A CI about to be exposed panicked and killed Richard Wright. His handler, say it was Paul Higgins, protected him. They needed the CI for another investigation, or exposing him would put an officer in danger; any number of reasons the handler might protect his informant. It's not in the rule book, but it happens. That's number one.

"Number two, hanging the Richard Wright murder rap on Higgins, making him complicit for what his CI did, doesn't put him in the library killing his ex-wife. Show me something her murder has to do with the Wright killing in 1983, or with your friend killed in prison. Higgins wanted to kill his ex-wife, he could do it anywhere, why the library?"

Ambler, who'd managed to make a cup of coffee while they talked, sipped it and began to wake up. "That's the point. Why the library? Leila was killed in the library because it couldn't be anywhere else. It could only be the library. Why?"

He could picture Cosgrove's irritated grimace. "Something was in the library."

"Something was in Paul Higgins's file. It's not there anymore."

"Maybe. You don't know."

"You're right; I don't . . . yet." He told Cosgrove that Mc-Nulty found Higgins in Queens and Higgins wanted to see his files. "The restricted ones. He'll know what's missing."

Cosgrove didn't ask where Higgins was or anything about him. "That doesn't mean you'll know."

"Higgins is in this up to his neck but I can't prove anything."

Cosgrove hesitated. "Higgins's CI's photo is in the CI log that Martin Wright found."

"I bet I know who it is."

Cosgrove didn't say anything.

"If it's not Trey Thomas, I'll buy you dinner."

When he finished talking with Cosgrove, Ambler went to the library to meet Paul Higgins. He found him in the Astor Hall lobby inside the Fifth Avenue door.

"The file boxes are in the stacks. I can't bring you down there. You'll have to tell me what you want, and I'll bring them to you in the crime fiction reading room."

"I told you, the ones that were sealed."

"The boxes are taped shut as evidence. It would be better if I brought you file folders rather than the boxes with police evidence tapes."

Higgins took a step back. His expression hardened. "Evidence of what?"

Ambler raised his eyebrows. "You'd know better than I would. Why are you hiding?"

"Who says I'm hiding?"

On the way up the stairs to the crime fiction reading room, Ambler said, "The police impounded your files because they'd been broken into. As far as I know, no one from the police looked at them."

Higgins seemed distracted, more concerned about who was around him than what Ambler said. Once they were in the crime fiction reading room and the door closed, he seemed to relax, not before he'd examined every nook and cranny and corner of the room. "No cameras?"

"Not as far as I know," Ambler said. "I never thought to look."

Higgins sat down behind Ambler's desk. "The files are in order by date. I need everything from the spring of 1981 through all of 1983. It won't be that much. Then, I need to be left alone to look at them."

"Maybe if you told me what you were looking for, you wouldn't have to—"

Higgins picked up a catalog that was lying on Ambler's desk, leaned back in the chair and put his feet up on the desk. "I didn't come here to chat, Mr. Librarian. Suppose you get those files for me and then disappear for a couple of hours."

"This is my office."

Higgins put down the catalog and looked Ambler in the eye. His gaze was both penetrating and vaguely threatening. "I know you're a curious guy and you think you're going to find out who killed Susan. I'm fine with you thinking you can do that and not get yourself killed in the process. For myself, I have something to take care of that you don't know about and that I'm not going to tell you about. Please get me the files." He turned his attention back to the catalog.

When Ambler returned with an arm load of accordion file folders, he said, "I imagine the files you're looking for are those from Operation Red Light."

Higgins removed his feet from the desk and got his legs under him. Something like a curtain came down over his eyes as he examined Ambler's face with a kind of shrewdness through the slits his lowered eyelids created. He folded his hands in front of his chin. "Did it ever occur to you that not knowing isn't the worst thing, that knowing too much sometimes is?"

"Is that a threat?"

"Do you think I killed Susan?"

"She was afraid of you; terrified when you discovered her here in the library the day we first met."

"Someone told you that. She didn't. She wasn't afraid of me. She—"

"You told me you didn't know Devon Thomas—"

"I didn't."

"You knew his brother Trey."

Higgins dropped his gaze.

"What if I ask about Operation Red Light?"

Higgins had a lot of confidence. You might say he was cocky in a way Ambler didn't expect. "You could ask. I wouldn't answer. I wanted my files sealed for a reason."

"How does what's in the files help you?"

Higgins ignored the question and began taking files out of an accordion folder.

"Maybe it's what's not in the files but—"

Higgins looked up, met Ambler's gaze. "You were going to be somewhere else while I was doing this."

Before Ambler got to the door, Higgins stopped him with a question. "I asked you before. How do you know the Arab guy didn't kill her?"

"I don't. She might have found something he didn't want her to know about. But there's no evidence he killed her. No witness, no physical evidence."

"So?"

"Why did you hide your connection to Leila . . . Susan? Why deny knowing Devon Thomas? Why did you disappear after Leila was murdered?"

Higgins shuffled a couple of files and put them down on the desk. "The first, it was none of your business; the second, I didn't remember the name. The third," he shifted his gaze slightly. "I had my reasons."

Ambler went to the third floor, to the maze of work modules behind the main information desk in the catalog room, where he found Adele at her desk.

"Johnny got off to school okay this morning?"

Adele's expression was dreamy. "He was so sweet. He told me it would be fine for him to walk if I was going to be late for work, which I was."

Ambler froze. "You didn't let him walk by himself?"

"Of course not!"

"He's a devious little devil when he wants something."

"I took him in a cab."

Still uncertain about kissing the night before, they were shy with each other.

"So what happened with Paul Higgins?"

"He's in the crime fiction room looking through his files."

Adele looked thunderstruck. After a moment of practically hyperventilating, she said, "I'm going to go talk to him."

"Wait—" Ambler said, but realized she wasn't going to. He nodded.

Chapter 33

Higgins glanced up when she entered the room. His face craggy, florid, a thatch of rust-colored hair, he had that Irish look she grew up around; you'd expect him to be a priest or a cop. His eyes were a nice color blue, clear and striking. He'd have been handsome when he was young, and he had a cockiness now that he would have had then. She wouldn't have liked him because of it.

"I'm Adele."

"I'm Paul." Something like a twinkle in his eyes, almost flirtatious.

"I know who you are. I was a friend of Leila . . . Susan . . . your ex-wife. I wanted to say I was sorry for your loss."

His expression changed, a sudden look of sorrow. He nodded, longer than you might expect, as if he were remembering. After a moment, his eyes met hers again. "You were her friend?" She heard the question he didn't ask. 'Did she talk about me?' 'Did she mention my name?' It was sad, the longing in his expression.

She sat down across from him.

"Sometimes you care about someone you should have left alone. I brought Susan into the kind of work I did. I shouldn't have. She thought she was tough. She wasn't. She was too sensitive. That made it easy to love her. Easy to hurt her, too; hurt her because you were thick and hard and too rough for her."

Adele was sure he felt sympathy from her because, in spite of herself, she did sympathize. She didn't know why she felt sorry for him; she hadn't expected to. "You were doing undercover work. Is that what you shouldn't have gotten her involved in?"

She should have kept quiet. He'd been in a kind of reverie. He had to focus on her face for a moment before he answered.

"Nothing wrong with it. Someone has to do it. But it kills off something inside. After a while you're not good with other people. . . . I'd made a connection with her stepfather, a dirty cop in Dallas. Fortunately for me, she hated him." He paused. Another memory caught up with him. He must have a lot of them. "The cop, the stepfather, was married to her mother and she hated her, too. She'd left Susan when she was a child—deserted her."

The cockiness was back; he was laughing as if there were a joke she didn't get. "There's no crime here, so this won't help you guys. She entrapped him. I set it up. She did what I told her. This was Texas. She didn't think about him getting the death penalty.

"By the time that came about, we were together, married. She'd gotten the bug, the adrenaline rush from the setup and the bust. She liked undercover work. She became a CI working for the outfit I was on loan to.

"Near the time of her stepfather's execution, something went off in her head. She wanted to recant. Her mother had been on her." He paused, drifting away into another memory, and then shook his head as if to drive it away. "We couldn't let her do that.

I mean she could have done it but she would have lost me and lost her job with the agency. So she didn't, and he got the injection.

"Her mother told her she murdered him. So she turned on me. I tricked her into killing her stepfather, she said. She went into a shell. She did her work, was good at it. She took everything out on me." He stopped and stared at the file folders in front of him. He sat for a long time. Adele didn't know what to say, so she didn't say anything. When she thought for sure he was finished talking, he looked up at her again.

"You're easy to talk to. I'm not used to someone like you." He might have smiled. "I knew from when my old man died, people can grieve for someone who wronged them as much as for those who were good to them. Susan's mother cut her off again. That hurt her bad, even though her mother was a rat.

"When she left me, I wanted to make her come back—I shouldn't tell you this. Maybe you're wired."

The way he looked at her, his mouth twisted, his eyes squinting, was scary. "I'm not wired," she said, quietly.

"I'm a hard guy, and it came out when she wouldn't do what I wanted her to do, when she didn't believe being with me was best for her. And it was. No one would love her like I did. It killed me she wouldn't understand. So I ended up driving her away."

"She never said she hated you," Adele said. "I think she was afraid of you."

"She didn't hate me. She loved me."

"Is that what you thought when you saw her in the library, that she loved you?"

He shook his head. "I knew she was on a job. She wouldn't act like she did if she wasn't. I wouldn't do anything to blow her cover. It could get her killed."

Adele was confused, not sure why he'd told her what he did, not sure what it meant. "What will you do now?"

"That's the best question of the day. Like everyone, I'll be trying to keep body and soul together, trying to stay alive." He smiled, a kind of knowing sad smile.

She found Raymond sitting at her desk. He looked at her questioningly. "Are you okay?"

"It was the strangest conversation. . . . Not a conversation. I listened. It must be what Harry felt like when he heard confession. Mr. Higgins told me about Leila or as he called her, Susan. He loved her."

"People kill people they love."

"I don't know. Everything he said, everything about him, was unexpected." She sat down and tried to absorb Raymond's placidness; she took comfort from the way he seemed to wrap her in some kind of warmth when he looked into her eyes. "He's a terrible man, isn't he? He as much as told me he killed people. He tricked Leila into having her stepfather executed. . . . He killed people, didn't he?"

Raymond nodded and then he stood.

"Where are you going?"

"Back to the crime fiction room . . . now that you've gotten him warmed up."

Higgins seemed less on edge than when he'd arrived.

"Find what you're looking for?"

Higgins didn't respond.

"If you're finished, I'd like to get back to work." He waited a moment. "I read one of your books."

"Oh?"

It was amazing, the spark of interest. "Which one?"

Ambler told him the title.

His expression changed. He knew what was up.

"What was it based on?"

"It's fiction. I made it up." A flicker of amusement in his eyes.

"On what happened to Richard Wright?"

Higgins's eyebrows went up. "Oh? What happened with him?"

Ambler told him. "The police said he was killed in a turf war with rival drug dealers."

"Lots of drugs around in those days." Higgins shuffled the files in front of him and began returning them to the folder they came out of. Finished, he met Ambler's gaze. "You think something different happened? Someday the truth will out. That's why this stuff is in the archives. Right? So in the future someone can put together what really happened in the past?"

"The truth is pretty slippery, even when you're looking at the past."

Higgins waved his hands over the files in front of him. "I'm not saying it's your fault. . . . That's what I was trying to do with donating my papers. Look at the mess we're in. You told me they'd be safe." He held up his hands to stop Ambler's protestations. "I said I don't blame you. You didn't know how dangerous this stuff was."

"The night we brought your collection to the library you thought someone was following you."

A shroud fell across Higgins eyes that had been alert and probing. "Yeah."

"You knew who it was."

"Yeah?"

"Is that who killed Leila?"

Higgins took his time, his expression hard to read. You had to wonder if he needed the time to form a persuasive lie. "I thought you said I killed her."

Ambler shook his head. "I didn't say that."

"Maybe not. Let's say I'm your suspect."

"You might be if I knew why you'd kill her in the library. The only reason I can think of is you needed something from the files you donated, so you cajoled or forced her to help you get them, and killed her when she didn't do what you wanted her to do."

Higgins eyes were open and alert again. "You can think anything you want."

"Who followed us that night?"

Higgins's startlingly blue eyes were lively again. "Remember what I said, 'If I told you, I'd have to kill you.'"

Ambler didn't smile. "I think I know. I need to put a few pieces together to be sure." He spoke more confidently than he felt. He was missing more than a few pieces and had no idea how they went together.

"So, I'm in the clear?"

"No. If you didn't kill her, you know who did. And two other murders aren't accounted for."

The curtains closed over Higgins's eyes. He stood. "You're good with ideas that don't have the facts they need to fly. I asked you before. What tells you the Arab didn't kill her?"

"You're supposed to prove someone guilty, not prove someone innocent."

"Why's he hiding?"

"Why were you hiding?"

"Who says I was hiding?"

"Mike Cosgrove."

This stopped him for a moment. "Is he looking for me?"

"He's looking for Gobi Tabrizi." In response to Higgins's uncertain look, he said, "The Arab."

Higgins considered this. "He must have a reason." His gaze locked on Ambler again. "I need to know if the Arab killed her."

Ambler couldn't get a handle on Higgins. In a strange way, he liked him. He did a good job, without saying so, of making you believe he was tracking down his ex-wife's murderer rather than trying to cover his tracks.

Chapter 34

Mike Cosgrove had a practice of going over the notes on the interviews he did multiple times. He didn't always take notes during an interview though often he did. Whether he took notes or not, soon after the interview, he wrote a recap. This way, he recorded things that impressed him more than other things that were said. Sometimes, it wasn't until the second or third time reading over his notes that he found what was important.

He did this more with suspects or persons of interest, but often with witnesses. He did this the morning after his interview with Martin Wright after he'd finished shoveling the walk in front of his house. Deep in thought, he'd shoveled nearly half the block as he went over everything he knew about the Leila Stone murder.

He'd been dismissive of Ray's idea that her murder was connected to other murders. But he never totally dismissed anything that was plausible, and Ray's theories usually were somewhere near plausible. That Martin Wright questioned the findings in the investigation of his father's death gave him more reason to rethink what Ray had laid out.

After finishing his notes on the interview, he called Wright and asked if he'd get him the name of the CI on the form he'd mentioned, and, if he could, find out if Brad Campbell was Paul's supervisor at the time of his father's murder. Before he hung up, he gave Wright Ed Ostrowski's name to see if it came up anywhere.

When he finished the call, he sat for a while thinking about Denise, about his career, and about his deal with Campbell. When he agreed to cooperate with Campbell's investigation in exchange for suppressing evidence against Denise, he'd assumed what seemed to be happening was what actually was happening, that everyone said what he meant and meant what he said. This wasn't how he usually looked at things.

The guys in juvenile told him Denise would most likely get probation, and the family court wouldn't reopen her case unless she screwed up, no matter what new information came out. If his cover-up came to light, the worst thing—and it was a worst thing—was he'd be disciplined for what he'd done. He'd be embarrassed—some of his former supervisors and a few of his fellow officers would like that—probably demoted, and possibly fired.

What happened that changed his mind about cooperating with Campbell was he'd gotten a scent in the Leila Stone case and—like the bloodhounds he must be descended from—was straining at the leash to get on it. Now that he knew Denise wouldn't get time, he'd asked that the family court fact-finding hearing be moved up to early next week. There wasn't an argument about the facts. She wasn't an uncontrollable child. Everyone wanted the best for her and more or less knew what that was. So the sooner things were solidified and agreed to, the sooner she could start her probation and he could get this foot off his neck. If things went well, in another week he'd be a cop again.

Chapter 35

The call from Lisa Young was along the lines of a summons. She invited Ambler to a cocktail party at her apartment Sunday evening. She was sorry for the short notice, but had to call him because, along with a few people from the library Board of Trustees and Ambler's boss Harry Larkin, Brad Campbell would be there. She was dying to have them meet under her auspices.

"You said you'd go?" Adele asked. "Of course, I'll watch Johnny. Why would you go?"

"I want to talk to Brad Campbell," said Ambler.

"Oh God, you're going to ask him about the Richard Wright murder in the middle of Johnny's grandmother's party." She laughed. "I wish I could be there."

Because he wore a suit, he took a cab. If you wore a suit and were going to an address on Central Park West, it seemed fitting you should take a cab. Snow covered the grassy areas in the park, so in the twilight, with the last streaks of the sun setting behind the Museum of Natural History, the scene was bucolic. The doorman announced him and told him the floor. The maid, Juanita, he'd met on his previous visit, opened the door and seemed neither glad nor sorry to see him. She took his coat.

The cocktail party was to begin at 5:30 p.m. and end at 7:30 p.m. according to the embossed note card that followed Lisa Young's phone call. Ambler arrived closer to 6:00. A scattering of people, the men wearing suits, drifted through the hallway and the library where he'd sat and talked with Lisa Young the last time he was there.

A young man and a young woman in tuxedos passed trays of canapés and glasses of wine. It wasn't really a cocktail party, McNulty would say; there were no cocktails. He saw Harry, a glass of wine in one hand and a canapé in the other, talking to a man and woman, both of whom were slim, expensively dressed, and enthusiastically interested in the conversation. If Harry saw him, he didn't let on.

Brad Campbell held a glass of what looked like sparkling water with a lemon wedge in it, and lounged against a wall, letting the game come to him. When one person or couple finished whatever small talk they'd engaged in with him, another person or couple took their place. Campbell seemed relaxed and amiable, accustomed to being a celebrity of sorts.

Ambler stood by the entrance, taking a glass of red wine when the wine tray came by and a canapé each time a different variety came by. He waited until Lisa Young noticed him. When she did, she approached him smiling and kissed his cheek, which surprised him.

"I'm so glad you could make it."

He'd stuffed a bacon-wrapped scallop into his mouth as she approached, so he had difficulty mumbling a reply.

"Come with me, I want to introduce you to Brad."

Out of the corner of his eye, he noticed Harry's eyebrows go up, as she steered him by the arm toward Campbell.

The introduction went smoothly enough. Campbell acknowledging Ambler with the same easy grace he acknowledged everyone else he spoke with. When the hostess headed off to greet someone in the entryway, Ambler stayed put.

"Nice gathering," he said.

Campbell met his gaze, drilling into it like a light that was too bright. His manner relaxed, his bearing languid, he nonetheless dominated the room by his haughtiness, the aura he gave of being above rather than part of what went on around him. He dismissed Ambler's pleasantry without saying anything. Ambler sipped his wine. Campbell didn't seem to care whether they talked or not.

"I understand you're watching over my grandson."

Campbell took a sip of his sparkling water. "I don't know what you mean."

"Your agency, I mean."

"It's a big agency."

Ambler sipped his wine. "I spoke with Paul Higgins the other day."

This sparked an involuntary response from Campbell, a shifting of his stance, a quick slip in his air of superiority. Ambler sensed cunning. "When did you talk to Paul?" He tried to sound casual but didn't.

"Why do you want to know?"

"No reason. It's not important. I haven't seen Paul since his ex-wife's death."

"Do you think he killed her?"

Campbell regained his air of superiority, now a rebuke. Ambler had overstepped his bounds, embarrassed himself, and needed to be put in his place. "Paul's a retired police officer, a hero many time over. What are you talking about?"

"I don't necessarily think he did. I don't think Gobi Tabrizi did either."

Campbell's reserve was now a shell of ice around him. "I actually don't care what you think. This is a social gathering. I don't have anything to discuss with you. You made yourself clear the last time we spoke." He turned away.

"Right," said Ambler. "By the way, do you remember Richard Wright, a union leader who was murdered in the early 1980s?"

Campbell, who had taken a step away from Ambler, turned. He didn't speak but couldn't hide his surprise.

"I'll refresh your memory."

A flicker of irritation crossed Campbell's eyes.

He told Campbell what he knew—or guessed—about the police surveillance of Richard Wright. He didn't mention Martin Wright or Paul Higgins's book. "I discovered something called Operation Red Light. Was that yours?"

Campbell returned to leaning against the wall. "I headed the department's Intelligence Division for many years. We conducted secret investigations of criminal activity. The operative word here is 'secret.' Do you understand? Secret. What we did was secret for a reason."

"What I'm describing happened a long time ago, why should it be a secret now?"

Campbell was dismissive. "The thing about secrets that makes them secrets is you don't tell them. A lot goes on in life you don't know about. And you're better off not knowing. No one likes a cop until they need one."

Ambler didn't like being lectured to. "Most people don't appreciate librarians as much as they should, either."

Campbell glared at him with pure hatred, but quickly got himself under control. His face was like granite. "What you ridicule is what allows you to be as flippant as you are."

"That was a joke," Ambler said.

"Humor may not be your strong suit." Campbell pulled himself from the wall. "Neither might be investigative work. It's over the line for you to besmirch Paul Higgins's name. He's one of the good ones."

Before he'd taken two steps away from Ambler, he was approached by the couple Harry had been speaking with. As they fawned over him, Ambler looked for the wine tray and found Harry Larkin bearing down on him.

"Good to see you've made amends with Mrs. Young. You should meet a few of the other board members. They like to talk to the staff." He gestured with his eyes toward the couple speaking with Campbell.

"I've done enough chitchat." Ambler grabbed a glass of wine from a passing tray.

"You were talking to Mr. Campbell. Did you settle your differences with him also?"

"Maybe not."

"Don't misjudge him, Ray. For an important police official, he's a compassionate man. He's done much good he doesn't take credit for."

"What's that?"

"His foundation works with crime victims. Not something you hear about. Nothing he takes credit for."

Ambler finished his glass of wine. Some people had already left. He went for his coat. Before leaving, as he searched the room for Lisa Young, he met Brad Campbell's gaze. Campbell bowed slightly, an acknowledgment, not quite a smile, but something like no hard feelings. Did Ambler look at him in a different way after talking to Harry? He caught Lisa Young's attention, waved, and left.

Chapter 36

Monday evening when she got home from work, Adele knew something was wrong as soon as she opened the door of her apartment. Drawers in the hallway credenza were open. Papers and odds and ends from the drawers were scattered on top of the credenza and on the floor. She blocked the door to the hallway and ran down the stairs to get the super. He called the police and went with her to check the apartment. Drawers in the bureaus in the bedroom were open, clothes strewn across the floor and on the bed, makeup and such scattered on top of the bureau, clothes torn out of the closet on the floor or the bed.

At first, she thought robbery. Her TV was on its stand in the corner; the little jewelry she had was still in the small box on top of the bureau, so it wasn't robbery. Someone had searched the apartment.

A squad car arrived. As soon as the uniformed officers learned no one was in the apartment, they called off their reinforcements, made a cursory check of the stairwell, the roof, and the basement, and left, telling her someone from the robbery team would get to her in a couple of days.

She called Raymond. "My apartment's been broken into," she said as soon as he answered. "It wasn't a burglary. Someone broke in to search for something."

"What?"

"How would I know? Johnny's coming here soon. I don't think he should."

Ambler didn't respond right away, and while she was impatient with him, she couldn't rush him. Raymond was a lot of things; quick to answer wasn't one of them. Finally, he said, "I'll see if he can go to his grandmother's. Do you want me to come over?"

"You may have to come get Johnny."

After the call with Raymond, she went through the apartment again. It didn't take long. She didn't have much in the apartment. Her notebooks and folders of poems had been rifled through but nothing was missing. The main thing she felt was an uneasiness bordering on fear, and a sense of violation. She flashed back to the men who'd abducted her, saw them again in her apartment, ripping apart her things, going through her poems and journals, her bureau, her underwear for God's sake.

She didn't know it was them. She'd told Paul Higgins Leila had been in her apartment. He might have come looking for something he thought she left in the apartment. She had the wild thought Raymond broke into her apartment to see what was in the letter Gobi had written to her. The idea was ridiculous.

She went back through the folders in the credenza. She didn't remember where she'd put Gobi's letter. Then she remembered it was in the drawer of the small table near her bed. She rushed over and pulled open the drawer. It was there, inside an Eric Ambler book she'd been reading, *A Coffin for Dimitrios*; funny, she'd never thought to ask Raymond if they were related. It was an unusual name. But wouldn't he have told her if he was? She sat down on the bed, the letter in her hands. Why in God's name was she thinking about that now?

She reread the letter. It signified the end of something. She'd come to think this was how it should be. Things would never have worked out between them. Their backgrounds and beliefs were different. She was attracted to him. That didn't mean she loved him. The buzzing phone interrupted her reverie. Hearing Raymond's familiar voice was calming. He'd arranged for Denise to take Johnny to his grandmother's.

"I can't understand why someone broke into my apartment. I don't know what they could have been looking for."

"I have the glimmering of an idea," Raymond said. "But I'll hold onto it for now."

Adele took a deep breath. "You're not going to like this but please hear me out." He didn't say anything. He wouldn't; and he probably knew what she was going to say; he was clairvoyant about her sometimes. She wanted to say it in a way that didn't hurt him. She'd done enough of that. She told him she wanted him to help her find Gobi, with the help of the imam he talked to.

"It's not what you think, though I guess I don't know what you think. Gobi might know who's behind what's happened to me. He might be hiding from the men who abducted me and they might be who broke into my apartment."

"If you're wrong, it could be dangerous."

"But you'll be there if it is."

"I will?" What a strange sound to his voice, surprise, and a kind of delight.

"I want you to come with me. Gobi knows he has nothing to fear from either of us." Her voice softened. ". . . and he won't get the wrong idea."

"The wrong idea?"

She didn't answer. She was shaken by what happened and she thought about asking if she could stay at his place, deciding against it because being with him would be too complicated. He might get the wrong idea, too. Or maybe it would be the right idea. She didn't know anymore.

It was a good thing she'd thought this through because he called back a little bit later and asked her that very thing. She told him she wanted to stay put and tough it out, while part of her wished he wouldn't take no for an answer.

She slept better than she thought she would. In the morning, Mike Cosgrove called and wanted to meet her at the library at lunchtime. Raymond had told him about the break-in.

Sometimes work is a relief. For that morning, she was filling in on the reference desk in the catalog room. It was busy, a waiting line the entire morning, so she didn't have time to think about anything other than the research questions she was answering. Near noon, Mike Cosgrove joined the end of the line, so she took her break, and they went to her module to talk.

He wanted to know about the break-in, and she got the feeling he had some idea what it was about. "You forgot to tell me a couple of things about Gobi Tabrizi," he said, after she described the break-in. "For one, that you removed some things from his apartment." Cosgrove seemed weary, as usual, as if the questions he asked were tiresome to him, or more likely he was weary of people lying to him whenever he asked a question.

She decided to come clean and told him what she'd taken from Gobi's apartment, including the gun, and how she met him at a restaurant and returned everything to him. The detective's expression was blank as he listened, no surprise, taking in what she said seemingly without judgment.

"There was nothing left in your apartment from the things you took from his apartment?"

She shook her head.

"You know handguns are illegal in New York?"

She looked at him blankly. She may have known that. She should have known. At the time, she didn't think about it since she was so freaked out about the gun anyway, legal or illegal.

He seemed not to mind her nonanswer. "When you were abducted, did those men ask about what you took from Tabrizi's apartment?"

"No. Do you think that's what happened? The break-in, they were looking for something of Gobi's?"

"Is there anything else of his in your apartment?"

This time, there was a hint of judgment, of disapproval. She blushed. He didn't say anything about Raymond. But it was there. She felt like a harlot and couldn't even acknowledge the implication that was so obviously there, couldn't do anything except feel mortified and blush. She told him about the letter.

"They didn't take it? Did they see it?"

"I don't know. It's nothing important, nothing political, nothing about Lelia or anything."

"Can I see it?"

She was horrified. "No. it's personal. You don't need to see it. I told you what was in it."

His voice was flat. "No. You told me a couple of things that weren't in it, not anything that was."

She remembered Gobi wrote in the letter that he was going to escape the country and that was certainly something Mike Cosgrove would want to know. She didn't care; she was entitled to her privacy. "I'm not going to let you read the letter. I'll burn it first."

Cosgrove closed his eyes and massaged his temples. When he opened his eyes, she saw sadness, and weariness again, and possibly sympathy, not accusation.

"He didn't kill Leila. If I thought he did, I'd tell you every-thing."

This time she struck a nerve. Irritation flashed in his eyes, and then quieted down but still smoldered. "Oh, so who did kill her? I'm having a hell of time figuring that out."

She shook her head.

"I'm not going to get a warrant to search your apartment . . . yet. Your life's been upended enough." His expression softened and he looked at her with what might be amusement. "Not that you didn't bring it on yourself. You don't have to burn your let-ter. We'll cross that bridge when we come to it."

"I talked to Paul Higgins," Adele said.

This sparked some interest. "Did he ask you to hide anything of his?"

"No. But he might think I had something of Leila's. I told him she came to my apartment. He might have thought she left something that implicated him in her murder."

Cosgrove's eyebrows went up. "Thanks for the tip. Do you know what that might be?"

"No."

Ambler had asked Mike Cosgrove to stop by the crime fiction reading room when he finished interviewing Adele. He wanted to talk about Brad Campbell.

"He's a legend." Cosgrove said, "Born of old money, to a family that may actually have come over on the *Mayflower*. When he graduated from college, he got a commission in the army, saw combat in Vietnam, decorated. He joined the department when he got out.

"A guy who could have been sitting in a Wall Street office, he drove a squad car out of Fort Apache in the South Bronx, worked vice in Manhattan, youngest guy in history to pass the captain's exam, became an assistant chief and head of the Intelligence Division—ran it until he retired a few years ago. People thought he'd be commissioner. Instead, he opened a private security company."

"He acts like he still runs the Intelligence Division."

"It's a shadowy operation, always was. They do what they do. No one asks. After 9/11, the feds came in. Homeland Security. If you weren't connected to the Joint Terrorism Task Force, you're an ordinary cop, detective or not, you might as well be driving a bus for all you knew of what they did." He looked Ambler in the eye. "I do my job. They do what they do. I'm good with that. Until they won't let me do my job. I ain't so good with that."

For a moment, silence hung between them. "I got Denise's family court hearing pushed up," Mike said. "'Expedited,' I guess is the word. This coming Friday. If it works out, I should be a free man. I won't owe Campbell. One deal I don't mind reneging on." He smiled. "It lets me try another line of thinking on the Leila Stone murder. Meanwhile, I'm getting my ducks corralled."

"I don't think you corral ducks. I think you line them up. Get your ducks lined up."

"You corral them first."

"I don't think so, Mike."

"Well, I do. I corral my ducks before I line them up." He glared at Ambler. After a moment, by way of a peace offering, he said, "Martin Wright will talk to you again if you want. Did I tell you that? He thinks what he thinks. That doesn't mean a cover-up, by the way."

"I'm talking about more than a cover-up."

When Mike left, Ambler forced himself back to work. Not long after, his phone rang. It was Adele. "The strangest thing," she said.

"Among many strange things," said Ambler.

"Mr. Campbell of Campbell Security wants to meet with me. What should I do? He said he understood I was a close friend of Leila's, that I knew Gobi Tabrizi and Paul Higgins. . . . He said he was asking my help."

"My guess is he has a reason for talking to you he didn't mention."

"I arranged to meet him at the Library Tavern, so McNulty can keep an eye on me. Will you have Johnny tonight?"

"Yep. Come over when you're finished. We're going to see his father this weekend. I need all the help I can get preparing him."

Chapter 37

Adele had only seen Brad Campbell from a distance, and from a distance he seemed aloof and forbidding. Up close, he made an effort to connect with her but what must be a vacant place inside him made connecting impossible. He was gracious and said things in a way that was almost charming, yet she felt the distance. Raymond was like that when he worked on something, distant, but you could snap him out of it, and while he wasn't so gracious and charming, he connected with you. You connected with him, too; at least she did.

"A beer would be fine," she said. "McNulty will know." They sat across from one another at a booth. Campbell ordered the beer for her and coffee for himself. She was surprised how slim he was, almost too thin. She was surprised, too, he didn't order a drink. It was that time of day. His hands, which he placed on the table in front of him, were nicotine stained; she hadn't seen that in years.

"I know Leila is as much a loss to you as she is to me." He sipped his coffee, made a face, and looked her in the eye over the lip of the cup. "She worked for me for a long time, more like family than an employee."

"What was she doing in the library?"

"She conducted surveillance. It was—"

"On Gobi Tabrizi. Anyone else? Why Gobi?"

His eyelids were like a window shade. "That's not something I can talk about."

"Why do you want to talk with me?"

"I understand you saw Leila shortly before she died. She came to your apartment."

She wondered how he knew that, probably from Mike Cosgrove. "She was afraid. Her ex-husband discovered where she was and she was afraid of him. Paul Higgins."

"That's what she told you?" He sounded skeptical.

She looked at him incredulously.

"Did she ever talk to you about her work?" He was poking around, trying to get her to tell him something without letting on to her what that something was.

"We talked about our work at the library. She didn't tell me about the devious part of her life. I didn't know she was spying on us until after her death."

The window shades went up. "You weren't spied on."

"How do I know that? Why should I believe you?"

He seemed taken aback, which pleased her. "I won't tell you the nature of her surveillance work. I can't. I can say she didn't spy on you."

"She was spying on Gobi Tabrizi."

He accepted this without acknowledging it. "I understand you're angry about being misled."

"What if Gobi isn't guilty?"

The man's attempt at sincerity might have succeeded if she hadn't already decided she didn't trust him. "If he's not guilty, he has nothing to worry about."

"Do you have evidence that he's guilty? You're supposed to have evidence before you decide someone's guilty, right? Why aren't you investigating Paul Higgins?"

He looked down at his coffee, which from where she sat didn't look like such great coffee, more like it was brewed that morning and sat around since lunch. It was a bar after all, not somewhere to have coffee in the late afternoon.

She could tell when people were exasperated with her—it happened when someone tried to push her around—and he was exasperated. "I'm not investigating anyone. That's up to the police. I can't tell you about evidence or the case against someone. I—"

"You run a private security company. Who says you can't tell me something?" He was less sure of himself than when he started, which was fine with her. If he thought he'd sit her down and bombard her with questions with no explanation, he had another think coming. "You want me to tell you something about Leila. Stop beating around the bush and tell me what."

"I don't know what you know that would be helpful. Perhaps you don't either. Did she at any point before she was killed give you anything to keep for her? Did she tell you where she might have put something for safekeeping?"

That one set off an alarm. "Put what for safekeeping?"

He shook his head. "She might have gathered something in her surveillance work that would tell us more about why she was killed."

"Wouldn't she give it to you?"

"She might not have had time."

"She didn't give me anything to hide."

"What did you talk to Paul Higgins about?"

"When?"

"In the library."

"How do you know that? Was someone spying on me?"

He couldn't control his face muscles as his exasperation shot up a few levels. Scowling, he glanced around the bar, anywhere but at her. "No one was spying on you. Why was he there?"

"He donated his papers to the library. He wanted to look at some of them."

"Did he find what he was looking for?"

She shrugged. "You'd have to ask him."

Campbell looked at his coffee twice as if he'd finally tasted it; then he looked at the service station by the bar and at McNulty as if he thought someone tried to poison him. When he turned back to Adele, he said, "Are you protecting someone?"

Adele met his gaze. "I've told you the truth. I'm not hiding anything from you. You're probably not used to that."

His bold stare right into her eyes told as clearly as if he had spoken that he didn't believe her. "Why did you go to her father's home in Texas?"

"I went to her funeral. If she was so important to you, why didn't you?"

He sighed and called for the check.

Chapter 38

Adele called Ambler as soon as Campbell left and told him about his questioning. "I wonder why he asked me about Leila's father in Texas?"

"Do you know how to get in touch with her father?"

"I have his phone number."

He asked her to call and find out if Leila's father's house was searched after she visited him. She said she would and meet him at his apartment after work. He went back to Higgins's files, hoping Higgins overlooked something about Richard Wright's murder when he was expunging Operation Red Light from his files, a long shot but possible.

A little before six, having found nothing of interest, Ambler closed up shop and walked home. When Adele arrived, he made her tea while she told him about the phone call to Leila's father. "Men in suits, driving a big black SUV, probably the same men who stopped me, told him they had a warrant and searched his house soon after I left."

"Does he know what they found?"

"He's not the most forthcoming man in the world, but he didn't think they found what they were looking for." Adele fiddled with her tea, waiting for something. How she knew he had something to say at this moment was beyond him. But she did and didn't have to ask, only look at him in that certain way.

"I'm beginning to realize—and should have thought of this before—the person who was with Leila, her murderer, may not have gotten the files he or she wanted. Perhaps what they were looking for was already gone. The killer believed Leila either took them or knew where they were. When she wouldn't say where the files were, she was murdered."

Adele smiled slightly. "That would put Gobi in the clear. He didn't have any interest in Paul Higgins's files."

"We don't know that if we don't know what was in the files."

Adele wore a pale brown sweater that was soft to the touch like cashmere. It had a V-neck and her breasts poked against it on either side of the V. He remembered touching her breasts the other night and how her shiny black pants fit snugly against her thighs, and fetchingly against her rear. Thinking about how unconsciously desirable she was made him sad.

They didn't speak for a moment, sipping tea in silence. After another few minutes, she stood. "If Leila took those documents from the file before she was killed, could she have hidden them somewhere in the library?"

Ambler put down his teacup. "She could have stuffed them in a file box of some obscure writer, and it might be fifty years before anyone looks in it, the next generation of librarians."

"Could whatever she took be in her apartment?"

"Her apartment would be too obvious."

After a few moments, he realized Adele was staring in front of her, sitting like that for some time before he'd noticed. "I have another idea." She told him about Barbara Jean Allen, Leila's—or Susan's—childhood friend in Texas. "The way Barbara Jean acted when I asked about the last time she heard from Susan didn't ring true. I felt like she wanted to tell me something, but wasn't sure she should. At the time, I let it go, Now, I wonder."

It was a possibility, one of many. The files hidden in the library where only Leila could find them was a more likely and a more disturbing possibility. "Calling her friend, this Barbara Jean in Texas, out of the blue wouldn't work. Why would she tell you over the phone if she didn't tell you when you talked to her?"

"She invited me to dinner. I should have gone."

Before they'd finished their tea, Denise arrived with Johnny. She'd played basketball after school, and he let Johnny stay to watch. The two of them had come to be like a big sister and little brother, each an only child, with discord in their lives. These last few days they'd been whispering and conspiring, as Johnny was going to see his father in prison for the first time and Denise had a court date that might send her to reform school.

This evening, Denise, surprisingly to Ambler, asked Adele to walk down to the street with her to get a cab to go home. When Adele returned, and Johnny was watching TV, she told him Denise wanted her to intercede with him. Johnny was afraid Ambler would get in the way between him and his dad but didn't know how to say this to his grandfather.

Adele got the idea across to Ambler, despite his not grasping what she was saying right away. She seemed to understand better than he did what would be happening in the prison visiting room, how emotionally fraught it was for everyone. "It will be awkward for both of them. You have to step out of the way and let them work through their awkwardness. Don't help."

Ambler had made stew a few days earlier, which they ate for dinner. During dinner, out of nowhere, Johnny asked Ambler what his father was like when he was Johnny's age, so Ambler told him about a quiet boy who loved baseball and music, who taught himself to play the guitar and the piano.

"Maybe I'm musical," Johnny said. "My music teacher said I am."

He hadn't thought of that, getting the boy a guitar or piano lessons. "We can look into that," he said. "Maybe get you a guitar."

"My dad will know what the best kind to get is. I can ask him." He said this with such certainty and joy that it almost broke Ambler's heart. He looked to Adele for help and saw tears in her eyes.

"He had a dog then, too. A stray dog followed him home from a baseball game one afternoon. The dog ended up staying. John named him Duke and kept him for a long time. You might ask him about the dog."

"Maybe I could get a dog." Johnny's excitement was palpable. Ambler looked again to Adele. She laughed.

When Johnny finally went off to bed, he and Adele talked quietly in the kitchen for some time. Murder forgotten for the moment, Ambler talked about John's childhood and his regrets. Later, he walked Adele to the corner to get a cab. They hugged when the cab stopped and kissed ever so lightly.

Chapter 39

Denise's family court hearing went much the way Mike Cosgrove hoped it would go, except for the embarrassment. He hadn't expected that. He was mortified; every dumb thing he'd ever done as parent flashed through his mind. Everyone knew terrible parenting was the cause of teenagers'—like his daughter—problems.

Denise was an angel in the courtroom, respectful and polite in speaking to the judge. She accepted responsibility for what she did, not passing blame onto her mother or father. The judge, a middle-aged black woman, was stern but seemed to like Denise, certainly more than she liked him or Sarah.

The judge did ask about family life. Denise tried to answer without criticizing her parents. It was difficult, so she stumbled trying. Cosgrove stepped up to rescue her. He told the judge about difficulties between her parents, so things weren't entirely Denise's fault, though he was proud of her for taking responsibility for her mistakes. He spoke carefully, taking a lot of the blame that he thought rightly belonged to Sarah. Sarah wisely kept her mouth shut. Denise was given probation and a mighty admonition to stay out of trouble. If she came back before the judge, she was told, she faced incarceration.

When they walked out of the Queens courthouse, Cosgrove felt like he'd been released from prison. He breathed in the fresh air and smiled at the world like a free man. He took Sarah and Denise to lunch at an Italian restaurant with white tablecloths not far from the courthouse and made sure neither he nor Sarah had any alcohol. Denise was happy and chatty, talking about getting better grades in school and going to college to become a lawyer and perhaps someday a judge, like the one she appeared before. He dropped them at home and headed for the city. He had a couple of things to check on before he told Pat Halloran, his boss at homicide, about Campbell, Ostrowski, and the withheld evidence in Denise's arrest.

"I wish you hadn't told me, Mike." Halloran looked aggrieved. "Why couldn't you keep it to yourself?"

"I can't have Campbell holding anything over my head."

"You said Ostrowski."

"Carrying water for Campbell."

Halloran gripped both arms of his chair and pulled himself forward, his eyes bulging. "Tell me you're not going to get both of us fired before I can collect my pension. Tell me you're not going after Campbell."

Cosgrove held his ground. "He's been in the way since we found the woman's body in the library. She was one of his. That's okay. He should care, want to help. Not take it over, which is what he did. Not squash the investigation."

Halloran pushed himself back in his chair and stared at the ceiling for a moment before he spoke. "It's not just him, Mike.

Intelligence took it out of our hands. That came from upstairs. You wanna talk to the commissioner about this? I don't."

Cosgrove grimaced. "It's a bigger mess than you think."

The pain in Halloran's eyes gave Cosgrove pause. It was as if he knew what was coming.

"He may be trying to frame the Arab guy. That's different than clogging up the investigation. There's a long shot possibility the murder might be over something in the files Paul Higgins donated to the library."

Halloran slumped in his seat. "Okay, tell me what you think you're after. Get it all out. Get it off your chest—every detail. Because I doubt this story, once you tell me, is ever going to leave this room."

Cosgrove's heart sank. Halloran was a stand-up guy—a pain in the ass when you wanted to stick with a case he wanted you to let go of—but he did the right thing. Now, he sounded like he knew what Cosgrove would tell him and would kill the investigation before it got going. You could say it was his call. This one wasn't going to be.

The first thing he told Halloran about was something he'd confirmed a half hour before he came to his office. "Hector Perez, the inmate who killed Devon Thomas, was Ed Ostrowski's CI when he was on the street. No telling how many scrapes Ed got him out of."

"You talk to Ed?"

"To find out what? The truth. Would you?"

Halloran laughed.

"The word was the Devon Thomas killing was a hit. Now I find out the hitman belonged to Ostrowski. That's what I got. Not something I'd take to court. Not something I'd want to ask Ostrowski about . . . not yet."

"Do you have Ed for the library murder, too?"

"I don't know."

Halloran didn't press.

"Paul Higgins is possible. The murdered woman was his ex-wife."

"Any other suspects?"

Cosgrove met his boss's gaze. Their eyes locked and held.

Chapter 40

Johnny's visit at the prison went well, or as well as introducing inhumanity to a child can go. When Ambler looked at his grandson's face as they went through the entry procedures, he couldn't imagine how all of this—bored, perfunctory guards, agitated and angry visitors, mostly women and children, mostly black and Hispanic, almost all wearing the unmistakable weariness of poverty—would be seen through a child's eyes, processed through a child's mind.

Johnny stayed close to him. Too old to hold his hand, he made sure they were touching or almost touching through the processing, his expression full of wonder as he looked around him at sights Ambler was sure the boy would remember all his life.

Fortunately, John was still on good behavior, so they met in the honors visiting room, with tables and chairs not unlike a school cafeteria. Ambler was as nervous as Johnny; he couldn't imagine how John felt; his expression, a mix of embarrassment, joy, caring, astonishment, was indescribable.

It took Johnny a while to look at his father. For the first few minutes, he stared at the table they sat at and answered his questions in monosyllables. Ambler stayed out of the way, going to the vending machines to get snacks and sodas, sitting a little distance from Johnny, watching the other goings on in the busy room, pretending he didn't listen or couldn't hear their conversation. He pretended not to but he did listen. It pleased him that John was patient with his son, accepting his mumbled responses. After a while, Johnny did look up.

"Do you like it in here?" he asked his dad.

John caught himself beginning to laugh and smiled instead. He shook his head. "Nobody likes it in here."

Johnny was embarrassed but persistent. "I mean is it okay?"

John caught that also. Ambler was surprised at how easily he intuited what his son was trying to get across. "I get along. It's not a good place. A lot of stupid rules. But you follow them, even when you don't want to, you get by okay." He regarded his son for a moment. "Like school in some ways, lots of rules, only here, more rules. You gotta do this. You gotta do that."

"So the guards are like teachers." He watched his dad for confirmation.

"Something like that, like some teachers are okay; some teachers are mean and you can tell they don't like you. Like I said. I'm okay. I mind my business and stay out other people's business—"

"Me, too. That's what I do at school, mind my own business."

"Good." John paused, looking out over Johnny's head. "The other kids at school know I'm in here, your old man in jail?"

Johnny looked troubled. "I don't think anyone knows." For a second, he looked worried, the look a kid gets when he may have done something wrong without knowing he had. He searched his father's face for help.

"Right," John said. "None of their business."

Pretty soon, they got around to baseball and after that music. At one point, Johnny called Ambler from his pretend disinterest to tell him the brands of guitars his dad suggested. Ambler was hoping they wouldn't get around to dogs, but they did.

By the time he and Johnny were ready to leave, the awkwardness was gone. A bond that had grown between father and son glowed around them. John reached to hug his son. The boy lunged for his dad's middle, wrapping his arms around him. Ambler was afraid he'd have to pry the boy off and drag him kicking and screaming out of the visiting room. But he let go. John said a couple of words to Johnny about staying out of trouble. Johnny asked when he could come back.

"Ask your grandfather," John said.

"Soon," Ambler said.

"The guitars I told him about," John said. "They don't cost a lot. You might pick one up at a pawn shop."

Right before they left, John pulled Ambler aside. "Something's going on with Perez. I'm not sure what."

"How do you know?"

"I've been getting to know him a little."

Ambler felt his heart quicken. "That's dangerous, John. I'm not so sure—"

John patted his shoulder. "I got it, Pop."

On the train back to the city, Johnny was quiet until Ambler asked what he was thinking about.

"What did you talk about when you were whispering?" His tone suggested Ambler wasn't allowed to have secrets with his dad. "Was it about me?"

"No."

"Is my dad going to get out of prison soon? Is that—?"

He put his arm around the boy. "That wasn't what we talked about. We'll do everything we can to get him out as soon as we can. Now we need to make a plan to get you a guitar."

"And a dog."

"A dog," Ambler said, turning to watch the Hudson slide by outside the window.

"How did your trip with your grandson to see his dad work out?" Cosgrove asked when he got him on the phone the next day.

"Except that I have to buy a guitar and may have to get a dog, pretty good. How'd you do?"

"I think we're okay." Mike told him in general terms about his confession to his boss.

"I guess he didn't take it well."

"How could he? He can't tell anyone above him what I told him. Campbell would know in five minutes."

The mention of Campbell was a surprise. It might have been a slip, or it might be Mike wanted him to know without telling him in so many words. He didn't press. Instead, he said, "I don't think Higgins found what he was looking for in his files. I think something was missing."

"I thought that too after the break-in at Adele's, that whatever the Stone woman's killer was looking for wasn't in the file. The Stone woman's apartment was tossed the night or morning after her murder. We held that back."

Ambler told him about Leila's friend in Texas.

Cosgrove was silent for a moment. "That's a long way to go on not much of anything. If we knew the Stone woman took the file, that would be one thing. We don't even know for sure something is missing."

"The only one who knows is Paul Higgins."

"A lot of times, a person snatches something, doesn't have much time, hides it close by. If the murdered woman took the missing files, she might have stashed them somewhere near your office, or in your office."

"She could have hidden them anywhere."

Cosgrove told him under normal circumstances he'd get the manpower to search every file box in the library but not for this one. "I'll add the woman in Texas to my list. Despite the travel, she's easier than searching the library. What's her name?"

Ambler was surprised again. "You're doing the investigation now?"

"Halloran understood my dilemma. He suspended me while he looked into my withholding-evidence arrangement with Campbell. If I do my own investigation of the Stone murder, he doesn't have to know."

Ambler laughed. "Only in New York. What exactly is your status now?"

"How about the Lone Ranger?" said Cosgrove.

Chapter 41

Adele liked to walk and think. Her apartment wasn't far from Central Park, over to Eighth Avenue, a few blocks up through Columbus Circle, and she was in the park. She'd gotten a text message from Paul Higgins and wanted to think about it. There wasn't anything suspicious, except that it came from him, and how did he get her cell number and why would he want to talk to her again? She didn't trust him, but she wasn't afraid of him anymore. She thought about him differently after they'd talked and was no longer sure he killed Leila.

Raymond said Johnny's visit with his father in the prison went well. She'd thought all along it would. Johnny was a wonderful kid; how could anyone help but love him? She wondered what John would think of her or think of her and Raymond . . . if there was anything to think about her and Raymond. She was closer in age to his son than to Raymond. She crossed over through Columbus Circle, walked a little way into the park, and called him.

"I got a text message from Paul Higgins asking me to meet him tonight at the Library Tavern."

"Why?"

"He didn't say. . . . I tried to call him back and couldn't reach him. I got a voice mail, one of those automated ones."

"That's not unusual."

"And how does he know about The Library Tavern?"

"McNulty's the one who found him. They had dinner together. Maybe they've become pals. You told Higgins you'd meet him. I'm not sure you should have done that. What are you asking me to do?"

Usually, Raymond was protective; now, because she did something on her own, he was petulant, which in some ways was endearing but also kind of controlling. "Maybe you could happen by."

He hesitated. His tone was friendlier. "I'll happen by."

Everything happened in a blur that evening. Adele planned to meet Paul Higgins at 5:00. It was Sunday near dusk, cold enough, in the twenties heading for the teens, to keep most people inside and the few people on Madison Avenue bundled up and hurrying. Because the street was nearly empty and he was arriving at about the time Higgins was expected, Ambler watched carefully around him to make sure Higgins didn't see him.

When a cab pulled up in front of the Library Tavern a couple of blocks in front of him, he slowed his pace, thinking it would be Higgins. A woman walking toward the bar from the opposite direction, about a block away, was most likely Adele. He was about to cross the street to make sure he wasn't seen when a black SUV pulled out from the curb, close enough to almost brush him. He stepped back and glared at the man in the passenger seat who glared back

The SUV sped up Madison, and slammed on its brakes in the spot the cab had vacated seconds before. The man who'd gotten out of the cab and taken in his surroundings turned at the sound of the SUV braking. Next was a quick succession of loud popping sounds. The man's hands went up in a kind discordant wave, his body jerked violently. He staggered a few steps in a small circle and crumbled to the ground.

Frozen for a few seconds, Ambler watched the SUV start up from the curb, slow again while more shots were fired. They were shooting at Adele. He ran for her, sprinting past the man on the sidewalk. She'd fallen but was already getting to her feet. Beyond her, the SUV turned right a couple of blocks north.

"I'm all right," Adele said. "I'm not shot." She ran her hands over her coat to make sure. Ambler did so, too, turning her around running his hands along the long camel hair coat she wore. As he did this, she stared down the street at the body lying on the sidewalk. Someone was bent over it. A man and a woman stood back watching. In a moment, the man watching took out his cell phone.

"Is that Paul Higgins?" Adele's voice shook. She moved slowly toward the group in front of the Library Tavern. McNulty had come out and said something to the person bent over the body who stood then. Ambler and Adele joined the group looking at the man on the ground. It was Paul Higgins.

"I'm shaking," Adele said. "I can't stop shaking." Ambler who shivered also put his arm around her and pulled her closer to him. Her body stiffened. He thought she was resisting but realized she was trying to stop shaking. She nestled against him.

A police car, lights flashing, came up Madison. Less than a moment later, sirens wailed from all directions. In no time, the block filled with police cars and ambulances. Ambler, holding Adele with one arm, extricated his cell phone from his coat pocket and called Mike Cosgrove. When he finished with the call, he tried to steer Adele toward the entrance to the Library Tavern. A police officer stopped them.

They watched as the EMS medics went through their work with Paul Higgins's body. A couple of uniformed cops worked their way through the small crowd, less than a dozen people, with notebooks in their hands.

When one of them approached Ambler and Adele, Ambler told the cop what he remembered, including that he had looked into the eyes of the man in the passenger seat. The officer took his information. "You'll need to talk to the detectives," he said.

When Adele's turn came, she told the officer what she saw, that the SUV had slowed and the man in passenger seat shot at her. "It was one of the men who abducted me," she said quietly.

The officer stopped writing. His eyes opened wider. "Stay here." He walked away quickly. A minute later, he was back leading a middle-aged man with a sour expression. "Tell him what you told me," the officer said to Adele.

She did. When she finished, the detective said, "You can identify them. That's good. What else can you tell me? You knew the man they shot. Why did they shoot him?"

"I don't know," Adele said.

"Let me put it another way. What did you, the man who was killed, and the killers have to do with one another?"

Adele shook her head. "I don't know. Nothing."

"Why were you meeting the man who was killed?"

"He texted me to meet him here. His ex-wife was murdered in the library not long ago and—"

The detective threw up his hands. "Hold it. Hold it. Wait here." He turned and strode off.

"I'm freezing. I'm shaking," Adele said. "I don't want to go over all of this again. Can we go inside?"

"Sure," Ambler said. "They'll find us in there when they want us." This time no one stopped them.

Before they were seated, McNulty had brandy snifters in front of them. Ambler noticed he had one of his own.

McNulty looked at Adele "They shot at you?"

"I don't know. I guess. I saw the gun barrel stick out the window. It jerked; smoked. The man holding the gun, the man who abducted me, was looking past me. I thought he was shooting at someone behind me."

"You've been kidnapped, your apartment broken into, and now shot at. You thought about looking for a less dangerous job than being a librarian?"

Adele laughed and whatever had been holding her up let go. She turned to Ambler, her lip trembling, the whites of her eyes reddening, and then she was crying. He lumbered off his barstool so he could get closer to her and hold her while she sobbed against his chest.

The detective with the sour expression found them after a few minutes. While he was away, he'd obviously been updated on Leila's Stone's murder and briefed on the investigation.

"You said the victim texted you?"

Adele said yes.

"He didn't have a cell phone on him. Can you give me the phone number the text came from?"

She looked at her phone and gave him the number.

He asked a few more questions about the shooting, asked for a description of the SUV and the men in the SUV. Adele answered his questions and told him about her abduction.

"You're sure it was the same men?"

"I'm sure one of them was."

"Had you seen them before?"

"Before they kidnapped me? No."

"Was one of them Gobi Tabrizi?"

"No." Her brow wrinkled, her eyes narrowed.

"You said you only saw one of the men."

"I didn't see Gobi Tabrizi."

"The other man could have been Tabrizi."

She sat up straight and spoke louder than she needed to. "The other man could have been you, for all I know. I didn't see him."

The detective was unfazed. "Ever see the man you recognized in the company of Gobi Tabrizi?"

"No."

"You're sure of that?" The tone of his voice made clear he meant, 'I don't believe you.'"

Adele stood. "I don't want to talk to you anymore. I'm going to the ladies room. I hope you're gone when I get back."

Ambler glanced out the window and wasn't surprised to see a grim-faced Brad Campbell near the Library Tavern doorway, conferring with a couple of men in trench coats and someone wearing the spiffy uniform of NYPD brass. Campbell wore a black overcoat and no hat. Every now and again, as he talked, he looked down at Paul Higgins's shrouded body and back up at the Library Tavern. Ambler expected him to come in. But he didn't. The detective waited until Adele returned from the ladies room. He handed her his card, told her to contact him if she remembered anything else, and that he'd be in touch.

Ambler didn't usually watch TV news; he read the newspaper, the *Times* more often than not, the *Daily News* during baseball season. That night, because of the murder, Adele wanted to watch the TV news, so they did at his apartment. What they got to see was a report on Paul Higgins's murder that included an interview with the former head of the NYPD Intelligence Division, Brad Campbell. He called Paul Higgins an American hero who'd helped to break up a number of dangerous plots the general public never knew about.

"That's how it should, be," Campbell said. "The work of our

counterterrorist forces goes on behind blank walls. It couldn't be done otherwise. The brave men and women who work in counterterrorism don't look for glory. Paul Higgins was one of the best of them."

The reporter asked Campbell if Higgins's murder was an assassination. Campbell said the investigation was already underway, and the NYPD would track down the killer. It wasn't his place to comment on the investigation. He said this in such a way that anyone listening would conclude his answer was 'yes.'

"How do you like that?" Adele glared at the television. She sat on the couch, holding a glass of red wine, her legs folded beneath her. Her hair had come loose from the band that held it and strands fluttered around her face, which she blew away as she spoke. With this her second glass of wine, after a couple of solid belts of cognac at the Library Tavern, she was tipsy. "He thinks Gobi did it." She took a sip of her wine, put the glass down, and stretched out on the couch. From her prone position, she squinted at Ambler. "Do you think Johnny is asleep yet?"

"He's asleep." They hadn't told him about Higgins's murder.

She beckoned with her finger. "Come sit with me." It was a request, a demand, an invitation. He sat beside her and stroked her hair. "I want you to kiss me . . . in a minute. First, I want to close my eyes for just one second."

Ambler stroked her hair and then touched her lips with his finger. With her eyes closed, she nibbled. He took the wineglass from her hand. In a few seconds, she was asleep.

Chapter 42

Ten minutes after he learned of Paul Higgins's murder, Mike Cosgrove booked a night flight for Dallas. He told Denise and Sarah he'd be gone overnight, popped a TV dinner in the microwave, and packed an overnight bag. At six-thirty, he left for the airport, parking in the short-term lot, and was through security and at the gate an hour before the flight left at 8:30.

He saw on his cell phone he had a call from an NYPD phone number. He'd wait until he got to Dallas to return the call. He'd called the number Ray had given him for Barbara Jean Allen—the childhood friend of the woman she knew as Susan Brown and Ray and Adele knew as Leila Stone—before he got on the plane so he wouldn't call too late. He sounded as official as possible, so the woman would think she was in big trouble if she didn't talk to him. Turned out she was friendly and chatty and would be delighted to see him.

At DFW, he rented a car and drove to a hotel not far from the airport. He didn't know who would pay for this trip; probably he'd end up with the tab. Even so, he picked a full service hotel, where he might get a decent glass of wine tonight and a good breakfast in the morning. He hoped he wasn't too wound up to sleep.

The next morning, Barbara Jean Allen was as chipper and friendly in person as she was on the phone. With washed out blonde hair, gray eyes, and little makeup, she wasn't glamorous, but with her cheerfulness, her smile, and her dimples, she was appealing. As soon as they'd exchanged greetings, he knew he'd like her. She cheered him up.

She offered him coffee and placed a coffee cake with white icing like an Entenmann's in front of him, apologizing for setting their meeting for 11:00, rather than earlier as he suggested. She needed to get the kids off to school and tidy up some before he got there.

He let her chatter on. He wanted her to get comfortable with him, to strengthen their rapport, before he got serious. She wanted to know about her friend Susan's death, so he told her what he knew. When he told her about Paul Higgins's murder, she was shocked into a moment of silence.

"Paul was a strange man," she said after the pause. "Scary because he seemed so capable of violence. Yet for someone from the north, from New York, he had a good bit of southern charm about him. We thought him 'exotic,' if that's the right word, a super cop, undercover, living among drug dealers and mobsters." He let her talk on about Paul and then about Paul and Susan together.

He was on his second cup of coffee after two earlier cups at the hotel, wired enough to be jittery, and he had to pee, and then he had to pee again. He had a long drive back to the airport and hated having to rush for a plane, yet he didn't want to interrupt her. She was getting comfortable with him. He listened and smiled and waited for his chance when what he really wanted was to tell her to shut up. Finally, she caught on that he might have a purpose in being there.

"I do prattle on, don't I? You're so polite to listen. People say about New Yorkers they're always in a hurry and they're not polite and actually rude—"

"Oh, Jesus, she's off again," he said to himself.

After a minute, she caught herself, or maybe she caught the look of terror on his face as he came to believe she might never stop talking. In any event, she stopped.

"So, what can I do for you besides tell you all of poor Susan's secrets? I knew she shouldn't have married Paul, as gentlemanly as he seemed. His world was too violent for her. She was a gentle soul."

"Right," said Cosgrove, loud enough to be heard next door. He for goddamn sure wasn't going to let her get started again. "We have reason to believe Leila . . . or Susan . . . sent you a package or an envelope for safekeeping."

Her eyes clouded with suspicion. He had to move carefully; one wrong move and she'd take off like one of those Texas hares he'd sent scampering across the prairie on the drive from the airport.

"She'd have told you not to tell anyone and that she'd come and get it from you, and to wait, no matter how long."

Barbara Jean seemed to pull an invisible cloak around her, becoming as wily as her open and honest disposition would allow. With folks like her, basically honest and good people, their instinct was to tell the truth, unless you gave them reason not to.

"Susan didn't expect to die. She had no idea her life would be snuffed out in her prime." He had to pee again; it was making him squirm but he couldn't let up now. With difficulty, he waited, giving Barbara Jean time to absorb what he'd said. "I know her memory is important to you. You were the only one she had, really, and her father, who, well, isn't the sort of man who could get close to a daughter. You're the person who keeps Susan's memory, who cares the most that there be closure for her." He let this sink in while he went to pee.

When he returned, they sat across from one another in silence.

"Would you like more coffee?" she said.

He probably should ask for another cup so he wasn't just sitting there. He just couldn't; he'd explode. He said no thank you and waited.

"I didn't know what to do. She never said what was in the package. It might be personal, and I wouldn't want to show what was personal to her to anyone."

Cosgrove started to speak but caught himself; she wasn't finished.

"She said if anything happened to her I should send the envelope to Paul. She gave me his phone number. After she died, I called and called and could never reach him. And now he's dead. I don't know what to do. It could be mementos from their marriage." She paused.

Cosgrove let her drift in her memories.

"They really did love one another. It's sad. . . . I didn't know what I should do when I couldn't reach Paul. I didn't want to go through her things. I'm not like that. I care about a person's privacy. Because she really really didn't want anyone to see what she sent, except Paul, I thought it might be best to destroy it."

Cosgrove's heart sank. "It wasn't personal," he said glumly, like he might say, "That train has left the station."

"How would you know?"

"I know what's in the package." He didn't know, like he

hadn't known there was a package. He'd bet his career Paul's files were in the envelope, but he didn't know. He felt a glimmer of hope. "There should be files. Open the package and look. If you don't find police files, close it up, burn it, do whatever you want. If you find police files, you might have found Susan's killer."

Chapter 43

That same morning at his apartment in New York, Ambler watched Adele open her eyes and gaze about the room before sitting up. He was across the room at what served as his dining room table, drinking a cup of coffee, watching her until her eyes met his.

"Was I awful last night? It's a blur. I think I'm going crazy."

"You were fine. You had to recover from a terrible shock. You did, and you crashed. Everything's fine."

"Thanks for helping me." She smiled as she got herself upright and then onto her feet. "I'm going home to take a shower. I'll see you at work."

Late in the morning, when she came to get him for lunch, he told her he'd heard back from the imam she'd asked him to contact about Gobi. "The message is to go this evening to the coffee shop in Bay Ridge where I first met the imam. He'll arrange for you to talk to Gobi." He examined her face, the circles under her eyes, the lines of worry at the corners of her mouth. "You've been through a lot. You don't have to do this."

She wanted to go, as he knew she would. She was sure Gobi didn't kill anyone, that the men who killed Paul Higgins and abducted her were the men Gobi had escaped from when he first got out of jail. She was sure he'd help, that he'd know enough about the men to get himself off the hook and get them arrested. Ambler didn't think problems as large as this one got solved so easily.

After work, they took the train from Times Square to Bay Ridge. The trip took almost an hour, the subway cars overcrowded, everyone grumpy and dispirited because it was Monday after work on a gray day in late winter. Ambler was plain weary and Adele, he was sure, felt worse. Every now and again, their eyes met and she'd smile. At one point, when the train lurched and she leaned against him, she put her arm around his waist and leaned her head against his chest, her eyes closed. He pressed his lips gently against her hair.

The imam was sitting at the same table, wearing the same sort of outfit, this one light blue rather than white. He stood when they entered and motioned for them to follow him. The room he took them to, in the back of the restaurant, wasn't plush and ornate like the front; it was a private, no-frills function room. Gobi sat at one of the three or four wooden booths against the far wall. He was alone.

The mixture of joy and pain on his face when he saw Adele caused Ambler's heart to sink. He was glad he was behind Adele, afraid of what her expression might say. He waited for her to take the lead.

"Hello Gobi," she said.

As Gobi raised his eyes to look beyond them, his expression changed from borderline ecstasy to a look of horror. Ambler half turned before he was brought to the ground by an arm around his neck and under his chin from the back. The last he saw was

Gobi half stand and then sit back down, a look of defeat on his face.

The room exploded into a loud commotion, men running, shouting; someone grabbed Adele, pushing her into a booth across from where Gobi sat. Ambler was on the floor, two large, black automatic rifles pointed at him by two burly men in flak jackets who looked prepared to pull the trigger. Not a time for questions or explanations, he put his head down on the floor and waited.

After some minutes, someone yanked him to his feet and patted him down. The same person took him by the arm, led him to a booth, and told him to sit. Gobi knelt on the floor across from him, his hands cuffed behind his back. Adele sat in her booth weeping. He expected to see Brad Campbell lording over the proceedings. But he wasn't there. Adele tried to say something to Gobi as the cops led him away, but they wouldn't let her out of her booth. As Gobi walked past, he glanced pitifully at Ambler. Expecting accusation, Ambler felt worse than if he'd been accused of betrayal.

"I'll call David Levinson. Don't talk to anyone."

A man in a trench coat with a badge crookedly pinned to it stepped in front of Ambler, glowering at him as if he barely restrained himself from smashing him in the face. "Shut up if you don't want to go with him."

Ambler forced himself to look the man in the eye. It was difficult because he felt helpless in front of all the firepower.

The police left the imam behind. He was philosophical about the arrest; glad it wasn't him, Ambler guessed, not seeming to accuse him or Adele of anything either. They hadn't lead the police to Gobi on purpose. Ambler was angry at himself. He should have known either he or Adele was being shadowed. Why wouldn't they spy on him?

He talked with the imam for a minute or two, after he called and left a message for David Levinson, Gobi's lawyer. The imam said he would talk to the community board and their city councilman, taking in stride that the police would come and snatch someone from his flock. He made clear to Ambler and Adele, who stood beside him red-eyed, not saying a word, although probably not consciously, that this trouble that befell his world had not much to do with the naïve couple who'd unwittingly brought the trouble with them.

The restaurant called a car service for them. On the way back to Manhattan, Adele was subdued. She hadn't said a word since the police hauled Gobi away. "We did that, didn't we?" she said, a rebuke not a question. The anger in her voice brought back unpleasant memories of the self-accusations, the self-flagellations of Liz, his ex-wife. He didn't want Adele to take this out on herself. He'd rather she took it out on him.

"It was my fault. I should've known we were being followed."

"Who were they following, me or you?"

It was probably her but he didn't want to say so. "I don't know. It doesn't make any difference."

"It was me, wasn't it? I'm such a goddamn idiot." She raised her arm to strike herself in the face. He recognized the movement and grabbed her wrist before she could do it.

He held both her wrists for a moment looking into her reddened eyes. "We're not finished yet. Neither Gobi nor the radical Muslims had a reason to kill Paul Higgins."

Adele moved her wrists from under his grasp and grabbed his hands with both of hers. He could feel her energy, her rising excitement. "What do you mean?" Her eyes lit up.

"Paul Higgins's killing was an assassination. In the papers he donated to the library was the story of a murder. He wasn't going to reveal what he knew about it. The files with the story were embargoed. He told someone what he did, or was going to do, someone with a lot more to lose if the story was discovered. The night we delivered the files to the library that someone followed us. He couldn't get the files that night, so he enlisted Leila's help to get them. Why would she help him? She had to; he was her boss. But she was loyal to Paul Higgins and took the files before her boss could get to them. When she wouldn't tell him where they were, he killed her."

Adele slumped back against the seat of the cab. "She died to protect her ex-husband? Brad Campbell killed her? But the men who killed Paul Higgins, who were they?"

"They work for Campbell. Your abduction was a ruse to implicate Gobi, as was the phone call that brought you to the Library Tavern to witness Campbell's thugs murder Paul Higgins, again to implicate Gobi."

Adele sat up straight. Her eyes shone. "Paul knew Brad Campbell killed Leila? He must have known. He knew what Campbell needed to hide and that those records were in the library where Leila was murdered."

Ambler leaned toward Adele and put his hands on her shoulders, his face close to hers. "Paul was determined to kill the killer of the woman he loved. Campbell knew that. Paul wasn't absolutely sure it was Campbell, so he wanted to eliminate Gobi as a suspect. Paul, whatever else he might have been, had enough honest cop left to need proof before he acted. And so do I need proof."

The car service dropped Adele off at her apartment. Ambler had himself dropped off at the Library Tavern; he needed to think. He tried not to look for bloodstains on the sidewalk as he went in. He drank a beer and told McNulty what happened in Bay Ridge and that he was waiting for a call from David Levinson.

"I found the guy and he dies on my doorstep." McNulty's expression was hard, unforgiving. "That's on me. I owed him a dinner."

Ambler felt guilt also. He'd been wrong about Paul Higgins. Prejudice he didn't like to admit to clouded his thinking. He should know better than to be quick to judge. "It's not your fault." He looked at McNulty squarely. "I should have known he'd be killed. I didn't put things together fast enough because I guessed. The problem is I'm still guessing."

"Pop called me. He had something for you on that guy—"

Ambler's phone rang. McNulty didn't allow cell phone conversations at the bar, so he took it outside, expecting a call from David Levinson. Instead, it was his son, John.

"The guy you're interested in? He copped to the hit."

"The contract?"

"Yes."

"He told you about the contract on Devon? Why would he?"

"Who knows? Bragging. Making himself a big deal, so he's more important than the rest of us sad sacks in here. He was a snitch for a cop when he was on the street, a higher-up cop, who got him out of jams." John paused. "So you can call me as a witness. Do I get anything out of it?"

Ambler felt a moment of panic. "I don't want you to be a witness. Even with evidence we might not convict the man we're going after. And we don't have any evidence. You'll still be in there, a sitting duck."

"I'll take the chance to get some time lopped off." There was a different tenor in John's voice, stronger, more confident, than before. "I want to get out of here while my kid's still a kid."

"Levinson?" McNulty asked when he came back in.

"My son."

McNulty looked at him with that soulful gaze. One reason for the loyalty of his bar patrons was he offered you sympathy without requiring you to explain what hurt.

"You were telling me about something from your father."

"Pop said to tell you all of the papers from the Party—that's the Communist Party—are collected down in the Village at this library at NYU. He wants you to meet him there tomorrow morning. He found something on Richard Wright."

Chapter 44

Cosgrove knew, after a quick glance through the documents in the files Barbara Jean showed him, that he'd found what he came for. He'd go through Paul's files thoroughly on the plane and take them to the DA's office when he got back. They were volatile enough he wouldn't even go home first. Nor would he log in the evidence at headquarters. He'd never skipped that step before. He didn't want to admit to himself he didn't trust his own department with the evidence. He wouldn't let himself think it.

Once the stuff was under lock and key in the DA's office, he'd tell Halloran what he had, and run for cover. On the plane, he thought about going to the press first, not sure Campbell's tentacles didn't stretch into the DA's office. He decided instead to make copies and have them ready to send to the press if something went wrong with the DA's office.

He called Dan Collins, a longtime ADA in the Trial Division, when he landed and asked to meet at a coffee shop on Church Street near the DA's office. Collins, with whom he'd worked on

more than a few trials over the years, had stood up to the pow-
ers more than once and was one of the few lawyers Cosgrove
trusted. They met. He gave Collins the files and told him what
was in them.

Collins's eyes widened. "I've got to take this to the boss,
Mike. It's a bombshell." He seemed both excited and nervous.
"I'm not sure I'm happy you brought this one to me. Are you sure
it's enough for a guilty verdict?"

"I'm not done."

"You're afraid to log in your evidence. Don't tell me you're
not worried, too."

Cosgrove left the files with Collins. Halloran was still in his
office when he called, so he walked over and told him he'd found
the missing Higgins files.

"Where are they?"

He told him.

"Why?"

He told him.

Halloran stared at him for a full minute. "You wanna get
yourself some good shoes for when you're walking a beat in
Staten Island."

"I've got copies."

"Log in the copies as evidence. When that's done, give them
to me. I'm going to talk to the chief, and we'll probably talk to the
commissioner. Be where you can get here on a minute's notice.
Needless to say, you don't talk to anyone on this."

"Only one person I need—"

"No one. Not a fucking soul!"

The morning after the disastrous trip to Bay
Ridge, Ambler dropped Johnny off at his school and headed
downtown to the Tamiment Library at NYU. McNulty's Pop
had found a transcript of an oral history interview with a man,

Walter Scott, a Communist informant for the FBI in the sixties and seventies who lost heart in what he was doing and rejoined the party. The transcript was an account of his undercover work with the FBI on a number of projects, one of them a federal investigation of trucking in the garment industry.

Ambler called Mike Cosgrove as soon as he left McNulty's father and told him what he'd learned.

"That will help. All hell's about to break loose."

"Oh?"

"I can't tell you."

"Are you back on the force?"

"Yes and no. I got a situation where I have to keep something to myself. It won't be long."

"Are you going to talk to Hector Perez?"

"I hope I won't need to."

Cosgrove bent a lot of rules and took liberties other homicide detectives wouldn't take in dealing with Ambler. Still, Mike remembered he wore a badge. "I want to tell you something about Perez I don't want you to use."

"From your son?" He didn't wait for an answer. "I told you he needed to be careful." Cosgrove paused. Ambler didn't mind the silence. He trusted Mike as much as anyone he knew. "Okay. I think I know what he told you. Here's how it works."

Cosgrove laid out a plan only someone with a couple of decades behind a homicide desk could devise. Like a good chess player, he thought out his moves a number of steps ahead of the move he was making now. "If you're as smart as you think you are, you'll figure out where I've been and what I found."

"I see you've come from Dallas," Ambler said.

Mike Cosgrove had what he needed. Ambler's information from his son—that Ed Ostrowski paid Perez to kill Devon Thomas—was more useful as a tool than it would be in court. A prisoner testifying to what another prisoner told him in jail would be challenged by a good lawyer and often not believed by a jury. Fortunately, the information had other uses. He called Ed Ostrowski and arranged to meet him at a bar on Bell Boulevard in Bayside that night.

His proposition was simple. "Brad Campbell's going down. You can go down with him or you can help me out."

"You're crazy; you can't take Brad down." Ostrowski's tone was challenging; but mean and tough as he was, fear was in his eyes.

"I've found where the bodies are buried, Ed. You did me a favor. (This one almost choked him.) Now I'm doing you one. We got you for the Devon Thomas killing. Hector Perez was yours. Should've used a stranger. I've got the CI log. Perez will testify to save his ass. I want Brad. You flip on the murders Brad did personally and get a pass on Devon Thomas." Cosgrove paused to calm himself down. He was so tightly wound, he was creaking. He needed to relax or he'd scare Ostrowski off. "I've got Paul's files. You think Brad won't turn on you? He had Paul killed, Paul who was like a brother to him. You think you won't end up like Paul someday when you cross him? Which you will, Ed, it's your nature."

Ostrowski sunk into his jowls. His eyes glowed with cunning. "Brad's connected everywhere. He talks to the president if he wants."

Cosgrove was almost finished. Ostrowski would check all of the angles. He wasn't a dumb guy; corruption had eaten away at him for so long he had nothing left to guide him to a right decision except self-interest and greed.

"Tomorrow you'll see your boss doing the perp walk, wearing bracelets. You're icing on the cake, Ed. The evidence from Paul's files is on the commissioner's desk."

Ostrowski didn't say anything. The terror in his eyes answered.

"Brad Campbell pulled the trigger. It was your precinct. You did the investigation and set up the Thomas kid." Cosgrove paused. His voice took on a different timbre. "Paul kept good notes."

Finished, Cosgrove stood, his beer untouched. He looked at Ostrowski who clung to his empty glass. "Take your time but not too long. You don't want the brass to talk to Brad and give him a chance to hang all of this on you."

"I'm not worried." A tremor in his voice betrayed him.

"I'll see you in court."

Cosgrove talked braver than he felt. He needed Ostrowski to flip to back up Paul's notes on the Wright murder case. More important, he couldn't nail Campbell on the Leila Stone murder without him. If Ostrowski didn't flip, he'd get him for the prison murder of Devon Thomas. But for that he'd need the testimony of Ray's son and Perez himself. It would be a shallow victory and not so good for Ambler's son.

Walter Scott lived in the Amalgamated Housing Cooperative in the Bronx, across from Van Cortland Park. The front door of the garden-style apartment opened directly into a small living room with wall-to-wall carpeting and modern Ikea-like furniture, a couple of easy chairs and a couch. The television was on, tuned to some daytime talk show, and, strangely to Ambler, Walter Scott made no move to turn it off. He didn't pay any attention to it either, as if he'd forgotten it was there. Ambler told him what he knew about Operation Red Light and what Devon told him about Richard Wright's murder.

"I said to my wife after you called, 'It's about time.' Thirty years ago, I reported it. My handler said, 'Hang on. We'll get back to you.' That's the last I heard until you called."

"What did you report?"

Scott stopped. He had the build of a man, muscular in his younger days, who'd gone soft in retirement, unassuming but okay with himself at the same time. You'd recognize him as someone who'd carried a lunch box all his life.

"At the time, you were an informer for the FBI?"

A shadow moved across his eyes. "I was young and believed a lot of foolishness. Richard, the man who was supposed to be the enemy, opened my eyes." He laughed and then became serious. "Richard was killed because of what he knew. I knew it, too."

Ambler waited.

"You know what happened, right? This state senator Richard knew from the civil rights movement held hearings. The hearings found the corruption but not everything. The government appointed a trustee to run the local and tossed the gangster union leaders out. Richard was elected the head of the union in a government supervised election.

"The NYPD Red Squad didn't want that. The union boss had been a snitch for the NYPD informing on Richard and the radicals. I was reporting on Richard for the FBI. The state legislature hearings gummed up the works. The NYPD Red Squad, the FBI, they didn't want no black militants getting union power. When Richard got up into the union office, he found out about the arrangement between the gangsters and the Red Squad guy."

"The Red Squad?"

Scott looked at him quizzically. "NYPD Intelligence. That's what we called it, The Red Squad. The union boss reported to the head of NYPD Intelligence."

"Brad Campbell?"

"He couldn't let it get out that he was in bed with the gangsters. When they offed Richard, I got the picture. I kept quiet. I didn't want to follow him into the grave."

"What did Richard find in the union office?"

"Stuff he showed me was phone numbers, notes from the Intelligence guy." Scott stood. "I'm going to get you something." He came back with a folder. "My stuff from back in the day." He held up a yellowed, typewritten form. "These are CI contracts. Mine is with the FBI. Richard found the gangster union guy's contract with the NYPD."

Chapter 45

Mike Cosgrove's worries were short-lived. Ray called the next day to tell him Brad Campbell's motive for the murder of Richard Wright. Walter Scott gave Ambler his FBI file and the name of his FBI handler who had the Operation Red Light files.

"I'll talk to Mr. Scott," Cosgrove said. "I can tell you now what you know already. I found Paul's file in Texas. Leila Stone took a bullet for protecting her ex-husband's files. Love is strange. Too bad Campbell got him anyway."

"The Arab killers?"

"They work for Brad. It might take a while to find them. I'll have the department's resources now, so it's a matter of time. They'll be on one of his payrolls. We're charging Campbell with the Wright murder for now. It's not out yet. But it's coming. Waiting to see what turns up on the other two."

"The other two?"

Leila Stone and Paul. I'm waiting on a phone call to see what we do with your friend's murder."

"The phone calls from Ostrowski?"

"I think he'll flip. Easier if he does; difficult if he doesn't."
He paused for a long time. "The thing is, Ray, if he flips, he'll
walk on the contract killing of Devon Thomas. We give him that
for his testimony. He's a sleazeball. Campbell's more than that.
Like that guy in the movies, a license to kill? That's what he
thought he had."

Ray interrupted him. "Devon's death matters, too, Mike.
We wouldn't have Campbell if it weren't for him. Devon spent
his life in jail and he never killed anybody. He deserves—"

"I know. I know. That's the choice, Ray. I'm sorry. That's
the way it is. You want us to charge Ostrowski, involve your son,
and let Brad Campbell walk—"

Cosgrove listened and then looked at his phone. Dead air.
Ray had hung up on him. Sure. It was a lot to swallow. Like
everyone else, Ray wanted a nice neat ending, everything tied
up with a bow, justice done. They both knew better than that.

A week later, Ambler walked down Third
Avenue, arm in arm with Adele. Johnny walked a bit in front with
a mongrel pup tugging at the leash. They were on their way to
the dog run at Madison Square Park, walking down Third Avenue rather than down Madison because Ambler didn't want to
remind Adele of Paul Higgins's body bleeding out on the sidewalk in front of the Library Tavern.

"You saw Gobi Tabrizi off at the airport?"

"He left a free man." Adele said. "Amazing he doesn't hate
us. He was sad to leave America, he said, especially the pizza."
She laughed.

"And you."

She stopped, so he did also. "I know I hurt you, Raymond—"

He tried to stop her. "You don't owe me an explanation.
We're not . . . I don't know how to say it. We're not anything—"

"Wait. I liked Gobi. I was intrigued by him." She gazed off into the depths of the city, as if trying to catch up with something. "He was dashing, mysterious, an attractive man. So I was interested." Her eyes met Ambler's. "There was never anything between us, except a slight attraction."

Ambler felt a rush of warmth. There might have been more between her and Gobi than that. But this was okay. "One thing that came out of our adventure with Gobi is David Levinson said there might be something wrong about John's trial. He said he'd look into the appeal."

They began walking again. Ambler watched a small flock of birds pecking at a patch of grass inside the entrance to the park. "Robins," he said. "A sign of spring."

Adele took his arm. "How's Mike Cosgrove? He took a beating in the press for arresting Brad Campbell."

"He's a pariah since he's been back on the force. He had to threaten to sue the union to get them to file his grievance. Everyone thinks he's a traitor."

"Because he arrested Brad Campbell?"

"Campbell bent the rules to protect the country."

"Murdering people?"

"Ostrowski will testify. When the story gets out, Campbell may not be such a hero."

They'd reached the dog run. Johnny let the so-far-nameless dog loose with the other dogs and went inside the enclosure. Ambler and Adele leaned on the fence watching him encourage the shy dog to play.

Adele put her arm through Ambler's again and leaned against him. "You know," she said. "What you said isn't true. We are something."